The Demon Comes

Too fast. They were running too fast for any mortal to intercept, like lines of fire, shrieking fire upon the maze, too rapid to follow. The kids were almost at the entrance to the maze, and the woman was standing there, not seeing what was coming. . . .

He could not think in words what it was. Fang, his eyes said. Fang, maw, eat. Red. Horror. Tangled, his eyes said. All tangled in a squirming mass. Dripping. Full of eyes. Coming out, his eyes said. It's been trapped in there, and now it's getting out. Making the kids lead it out. She shouldn't have unlocked those gates. . . .

BLOOD HERITAGE

Also by Sheri S. Tepper

THE TRUE GAME
THE CHRONICLES OF MAVIN MANYSHAPED
THE REVENANTS

and published by Corgi Books

BLOOD HERITAGE

Sheri S. Tepper

CORGI BOOKS

BLOOD HERITAGE

A CORGI BOOK   0 552 13193 8

First publication in Great Britain

PRINTING HISTORY
Corgi edition published 1987

Copyright © 1986 by Sheri S. Tepper

This book is set in 10/11 pt Baskerville

Corgi Books are published by Transworld Publishers Ltd.,
61–63 Uxbridge Road, Ealing, London W5 5SA,
in Australia by Transworld Publishers (Aust.) Pty. Ltd.,
15–23 Helles Avenue, Moorebank, NSW 2170, and in New
Zealand by Transworld Publishers (N.Z.) Ltd., Cnr. Moselle
and Waipareira Avenues, Henderson, Auckland.

Reproduced, printed and bound in Great Britain by
Hazell Watson & Viney Limited,
Member of the BPCC Group,
Aylesbury, Bucks

Prologue

They told him Carolyn and Robby were dead.

He refused to listen, refused to hear. It was some kind of grisly joke. An overturned boat didn't mean people had drowned; not Carolyn, who swam like a fish; not Robby, who was always tightly tied into his life jacket.

He kept expecting Carolyn to appear, kept expecting the phone to ring. She would be there, he kept assuring himself, telling him what a mess it had all been, what a weird happening, angry that anyone had assumed she was gone for good, wrinkling her nose in distaste at the untidiness of it, whatever it was, that had happened to her. And Robby. Robby, whooping with glee as he tried to tell the story of it – it, whatever it was.

He did not believe they were dead. After eleven months, however, he had to accept that they were gone.

1

When Badger came into his apartment, running a little late as usual because that was safest, he went to the mirror, hands working at the knot of his tie, turning his face from side to side, lifting his chin, working his mouth, intently going through all the shaving expressions in order not to notice where he was putting the tie. Only when the sober silk was draped casually over the photograph did he empty his pockets onto the dresser top. The pictured faces were safely masked behind the looped fabric. Not seeing the picture had become a ritual. His face in the mirror stared back at him without expression, the shadowed eyes barely noticing skin paler than usual for this time of year, wide mouth a bit more tightly clenched so that a little muscle below his left ear made a dancing bubble of flesh, jerk-jerk, twitch-twitch. All in all the strong, capable face he had become accustomed to, the dark auburn hair framing it a little untidy.

He ignored all of it as irrelevant. He avoided any thought at all about his appearance, or his body. Carolyn had liked his body. It was what she had probably liked most about him. He retreated into safer territory. He thought about

Vivian and Vivian's housewarming to which he had been summoned for the evening. Sweet sister Vivian, whom he loved with an accustomed patience. And her husband George, whom he loathed to precisely the same degree.

'What will you bet?' he asked the face in the mirror. 'What will you bet George has another obscure little wine?' No bet. George always had an obscure little wine. George collected obscure little wines and obscure little restaurants and some of the obscurer details of other people's private lives. Details about the wines or the restaurants or the people were George's conversational stock in trade, often communicated in the same tone a preteen might use on the phone with a friend – 'I know something you don't know.' Well, that was George. Badger poured himself an inch of Irish and carried it into the bathroom. 'To Vivian,' he toasted. 'To George.'

After showering, he selected another tie and put it on before the hall mirror as he phoned for his car to be brought around. He had been in the apartment almost half an hour. He had not looked at their picture once. Loss had proved to be something Badger had not handled well. Better not think about it at all.

Vivian's apartment had once been a warehouse. Now, after extravagant renovation, it had become an architectural gem featured on the covers of national design magazines. He had been there only once before. When the place was half-finished Vivian had insisted he meet her for an escorted tour among the ladders and stacks of Sheetrock. They had been alone except for the workmen and one elderly tenant who threaded his way among the construction materials with three self-possessed little dogs at his heels and an expression of eccentric glee on his face. 'I am at home,' he had called triumphantly, polishing his bald head with both hands, 'at home among the ruins.' Badger had watched in apprehension as the old man had approached a ladder to a balcony bedroom very much under construction, but he had gone up it like a monkey, carolling his pleasure at every rung.

'Who?' he had asked Vivian, pointing covertly.

'Oh, that's Myron Boyce,' she had told him. 'Professor Boyce. He collects things, I think. Art? Or artifacts? I can never get them straight. Both, maybe. I think he's an archaeologist. . . .' Badger considered this as an explanation for the old man's cryptic remark as she went on, 'I can never understand a word he says. At first I thought I was just ignorant, but now I think he does it purposely, talks crazy, I mean.'

Badger had watched the Professor scramble along the edge of the balcony like an aged but agile lemur, capering from time to time for the benefit of the workmen. 'Maybe he is crazy.'

'Oh, I don't think so,' she had said in a doubtful voice. 'Not a professor.'

Dear Vivian. Never an unkind thought. Often, never a thought at all, he told himself, immediately feeling guilty, though he had long ago realized he could tolerate the idea of George more easily if he could convince himself Vivian was not quite bright.

The parking attendant in the underground garage was bulky, wary, but polite.

'Yes, sir? Can we help you, sir?' The editorial 'we,' Badger thought. Like a nurse's 'we.' He discarded his instinctively flip reply as unduly provocative.

'I'm Badger Ettison, Vivian Victor's brother. That's Mrs. George Victor?'

The attendant nodded. He recognized the name. A man like this would always recognize the name. 'Certainly, sir. Mrs. Victor said you were to have one of their parking spaces tonight. Down there to your left, number fifty-three, just beyond Mrs. Victor's Porsche. Unless you'd like me to park it, sir? . . . Fine. If you'll come back to the elevator, I'll bring it down for you.'

'Very kind of you. Thank you very much.' Well, the place was certainly secure. Garage attendant on duty around the clock. Doorman at all times. Day and night porters. Elevator operators, too. None of this push-button

9

jazz. Lord. George must have robbed a mint.

George hadn't, of course. He had merely inherited a great deal of money. The apartment breathed money from the full-length triple-paned windows to the land scaped terrace outside them. Oddly muted, the sounds of traffic filtered up through the branches of flowering trees. A lovely hypocrisy. The hanging gardens of Babylon. A modern Tower of Babel. The babble greeted him as he entered a forty-foot living room: chatter, argument, expostulation, laughter, murmur of caterer's men, tinkle of ice, soft piano music from the library. Neither George nor Vivian played any musical instrument, but of course they had a piano for entertaining. Of course.

'Badger. Dear boy! How very nice to see you. How wonderful to have you with us once again.' George, face already flushed from too many glasses of whatever he was drinking, bellowing pleasure so that no one in the room could miss it, dropping into an only slightly softer voice for the intimate questions. 'How are you getting along? Do you feel you're beginning to adjust?' Badger felt himself flush, anger rising like a tide. George liked this ostentatious inquiry into privacy, this intimate questioning in public. He seemed to think the act of violation acquired some kind of cachet if it were done under the gaze of the multitude. Badger believed George to be the kind of man who could engage in rape in the middle of a stadium, but his mounting fury was muted as Vivian fluttered between them like a clothesline of flowery laundry, all flounces and ruffles in constant, billowy motion.

'Badger, darling! Do come in; don't stand there. George, hush. We agreed you were not to bother Badger tonight, and I was very serious about it. Now, Badger, come meet some very nice people.' He was drawn away, leaving George behind to put on his kindly, paterfamilias expression, one of his more ponderous poses.

'You know the Carvers, Badger, Myrtle and Dom. My brother, Badger Ettison. You all met that terrible New Year's Eve, remember? When it stormed!'

It *had* stormed. And they hadn't been able to get a cab, none of them. So they'd stayed until after dawn, ending the party with scrambled eggs and Bloody Marys, the snow coming down outside like a curtain. Carolyn had – No. He would not think about Carolyn.

'Where's Carolyn?' Myrtle asked. 'Is she here?'

'No,' Vivian said, too quickly, cutting off the kindly-meant idle question. 'I'll explain later, Myrtle.' She drew him away by one arm. 'Sorry, Badger. They didn't know. Come meet someone you've never met before. Mahlia. My neighbor. She's house-sitting for Myron Boyce. Remember the art expert I introduced you to? Or is he an archaeologist? I showed you his place when you came to see this one in process?' Vivian interrupted her chatter long enough to make the introduction. 'Mahlia Waiwela. My brother, Badger Ettison. Get Badger a drink, will you, Mahlia?' She was gone, and he turned to take a drink from the woman's hand with a sense of some terrible tragedy narrowly averted. At first he hardly saw her. She was merely a tall, slender figure in a white dress.

'What did my hasty sister tell me your name was? I can't have heard it correctly?'

She laughed. The laugh brought his eyes to her mouth, and then to her face, and he saw her as a person, not merely as the usual array of cocktail party weaponry: chatter guns, gesture cannons. This was a person. Her eyes were amber, the color of autumn beech leaves touched with gold. The color of brown sugar syrup. The lashes around them were, he thought, too long to be real, but then he realized she was wearing no makeup at all. He maneuvered to one side of her, peered along the smooth line of a lowered eyelid to find it flawless and without guile. Her hair was almost straight, a dark silken flow to halfway down her back; her lips were wide, neither full nor thin, simply a calm, sweet curve, as natural as bending grass. He cataloged her. A beige-brown girl of considerable quality. He asked again, 'Your name? What was it?'

'Wai,' she said, 'as in why. Wai-la. Waiwela.

Polynesian. At least Mother was. She used to say various things about Papa from time to time, so I can't guarantee his side of things. He was French. Very decidedly.' That explained the accent he had noticed immediately, a definitely French sound that combined with her soft, insinuating voice to make a more than attractive combination. 'But what did your sister call you? A badger?'

'A childish contraction,' he said, thinking it was a long time since he'd met anyone new and had to explain the name. 'Roger Ettison. Bad Roger Ettison, according to his older sister, who could not say Bad Roger without contracting it to Badger. It's the only name I've used since age three.' He brought himself out of this ancient fable. 'And you're here doing what – house-sitting?'

'I'm here to attend university. Postgraduate.' She half turned away, looking at him from the corners of her eyes. 'My field will be cultural anthropology. I intend to do my thesis on the quasi-kinship relationships among the staff of a major U.S. university and their effect upon achievement of tenure.'

This was said seriously, absolutely deadpan. For a moment he thought he had not heard her correctly, or that he had not understood what she had said. Then he saw a devil of light dancing in her left eye and was suddenly entranced. 'Tit for tat.'

'Turnabout is fair play,' she said.

'Enough of the pot calling moiety black.'

'Exactly.' She grinned, and inside him some chill ice dam gave way all at once, letting him smile and feel the stretch of facial muscles he hadn't used in months.

'Ah . . . house-sitting?'

'Well, Professor Boyce was about to move into the apartment next door when he got a wonderful opportunity to go on some cooperative expedition with the Chinese. Tombs, he said. Very ancient tombs. Full of marvelous art objects. Which is Professor Boyce's field, you know.'

'I didn't know,' he answered soberly. 'Had no idea.'

'You can take my word for it,' she said solemnly, sketching

an oath-taking position, right hand lifted. 'At any rate, there he was with this marvelous apartment full of all his treasures, and he had to go off and leave it and his three Lhasa Apsos for months and months. So. He knew I had no place to stay, and he believed me to be trustworthy, so he asked me to house- and dog-sit. Which I am doing. I met your sister in the elevator. I should say Ting, Ching, and Bing met your sister in the elevator. It took us fifteen minutes to untangle them and her.'

'Ting?'

'Ching and Bing. That's what I call them. Don't you dare tell. Their own names are unpronounceable. Ching's real name, for example, is Padmasambhava. I really can't say that, can you? And I simply won't do what Professor Boyce does. He calls them his puppsy wuppsies.

He laughed. The sound and feeling of laughter were startling, so startling that he stopped, swallowing the humor, though some of it remained on his face, quietly warm. 'Who, or what, is a Padmas . . . what you said?'

'Padmasambhava was a guru – no, more than a guru. By all accounts he was a sorcerer, exorcist, and magician, from Kashmir. He came to Tibet at the request of King Thisrongdetsan – that's Ting – to establish lamaism. Would you like to know more about him?'

He shook his head. 'I think that's all I can absorb for one night. Hold Bing's real name in reserve for an emergency.' He sipped the drink, made a face.

'You don't like that? I can get you something else.' She seemed genuinely concerned.

'Not at all. I'll pretend to drink it until the next waiter orbits by, then we'll see if they have some Irish. When I can get it, it's all I drink. Particularly when I'm with Vivian and George.'

She made a face of sympathetic understanding. 'You mean George's wines, don't you. Oh, I know. I'm so glad you said something. I thought perhaps it was my taste which had suffered – I worked for a wine importer for a while in Montreal, while I was an undergraduate. Vivian is sweet,

13

she really is. She's invited me to dinner half a dozen times since I've been here. But the *wines!*' She giggled, and he smiled with her. 'It wouldn't matter if he didn't spend so much for them. But they're all so exceedingly costly!'

'Exceedingly costly,' he repeated, mimicking her tone of voice, offended and haughty. 'You sound like some duchess, saying that. Or some elderly lady with a great deal of very old money.'

'I sound like my Aunt Irene,' she explained. 'On my father's side. She is elderly, extremely French, and has a great deal of appropriately aged money. How funny that you should know that.'

Badger, who had had a good deal to do with elderly ladies with old money, grinned at her. 'In my experience, old money simply means old enough that everyone has forgotten who stole it originally.'

'Then hers isn't old enough. I'm sure Great-Grandfather was the one. However, in Aunt Irene's lexicon, things are either reasonably priced or exceedingly costly. To Aunt Irene nothing is ever inexpensive.'

'Pity. When she feels that way, she can never buy a bargain.'

'A bargain would be beneath Aunt Irene. Not seemly.'

'How about you? Do you find bargains seemly?'

'Oh, well, I find them absolutely necessary. Aunt Irene may be very well set up, but she has not seen fit to share that state of affairs with the – dare I be honest? – possibly illegitimate daughter of her scapegrace younger brother, now deceased. Mother has always sworn that she and Father were well and truly married, in Father's church, at that, but evidently it was never proved to Aunt Irene's satisfaction.' She laughed about this, shaking her head, flushing a little as she did so. She might make light of it, he thought, but it obviously upset her. Seeing his concerned expression, she flushed a brighter red. 'No! Now I've made you uncomfortable. Don't be, please. A long time ago Mother told me it didn't matter what a previous generation was thought to have done. Or not to have done, as the case may be. I find that very comforting.'

He looked down, a little discomfited by this flood of personal history. She gave him no respite, however.

'What did Vivian tell me about you? Ah. I remember now. You solve problems for people.'

He bowed, making light of Vivian's typical slight inaccuracy. 'I do. No problem too large, no problem too small. All questions answered with a minimum of fuss. Also available for weddings, bar mitzvahs, and housewarmings.'

'Will you solve any problem at all?'

He bowed again. 'Well, there are some which haven't been offered me. Like achieving world peace, or solving the problems of population and drought in Africa. Aside from unimportant issues like that, yes. If I don't know anything about it, I'll find someone who does. So far I've been willing to tackle anything at all.'

'No, really, I'm interested. What kinds of things do you do?'

He thought for a moment. Much of what he did was dull and very complicated. 'Oh, let's say a manufacturer buys some small subassembly from a contractor. And let's say that contractor has trouble delivering on time, so the manufacturer is delayed and loses money. He might hire me to find out what the contractor's problem is and fix it. Or sometimes people just need information and have no idea how to go about getting it.'

Her face was flushed, and she lowered her gaze for a moment. 'I may want to consult you. Professionally. I'll pay your fee, too, so that you'll know I take it seriously.'

'I'd be honored.' Actually, her words chilled him. He had heard them before from cocktail party acquaintances. Too often they were preface to something better handled by a private investigator or an attorney. She was watching his eyes, and he made himself smile again. 'Would you like to make an appointment?'

'Yes. Tonight. For about ten minutes, just before you go home. It has to do with the Professor's apartment. Nothing better handled by the manager or the maintenance people, no – I could see you thinking that. I'll bet people approach

15

you all the time to do things you wouldn't do on a bet.'

He was stunned by this perceptivity. 'They do, yes.'

'Well, it's nothing like that. I'll probably leave before you do, so just knock on my door. It's just across the hall, on this same floor. Greenleaves two. That's what they call it. No numbered floors, you see. Each floor has a name instead. The floor is Greenleaves. Because of the terrace gardens, I suppose.'

'It eliminates worrying about the thirteenth floor.'

'I hadn't thought of that, but it would, if there were thirteen floors in this building. I don't think there are. But should I worry about it?'

'Only if you're superstitious.' He sipped his drink, amused by her serious expression as she considered this.

'I wouldn't call it superstition, but I am, I guess. I believe in things like that. Demons. Witches. My grandmama was supposed to be a witch. Spiritual influences. All that kind of thing. I can't explain them, but I do believe in them. Don't you?'

He wondered briefly if this were more of her devilment, not to be taken seriously, but then decided it was worth a serious answer. 'Not a lot. Perhaps not at all. Certainly not in thirteen being unlucky, or black cats.'

'Black cats and thirteens have nothing to do with my problem. You will give me a consultation? Is it a deal?'

'A deal.' He smiled, shook her hand, surprising himself when his own lingered on hers. Her skin was silky, yet there were hard pads of callus at the base of her fingers. Work? he wondered. Or play? He wanted to know about her, more, much more about her, but he was swept away into Vivian's circle of introductions once more.

She had evidently spoken to the Carvers. They lured him into their conversation but didn't ask him anything about . . . anything. They talked about real estate, and whether it would be worth it to have a summer place in Vermont. For a time they chatted about the recent plague of books and movies about demonic possession, and Badger saw Mahlia's head come up in surprise as she heard a few words.

16

'Some people really believe in them,' he said, loudly enough for her to hear, teasing her.

'Well,' said Carver, thinking about it, 'if I were going mad, I suppose it would be comforting to believe that something outside myself – something terrible and inexorable, before which anyone would be helpless – had invaded me rather than believe in my own madness. And if I were the parent of a mad child or the husband of a mad wife, perhaps I would rather believe in demons than that my loved one was faulty.'

'There is a tendency to believe in perversity rather than malfunction,' Myrtle Carver interjected. 'If my dishwasher doesn't work – which, by the way, it does not – I'm firmly convinced it's motivated by malice. I swear at it, kick it, and you can't tell me the thing isn't taking a vile pleasure in my frustration.'

'Paranoia.' Carver nodded. 'The true basis for religion, the most primitive of all faiths!'

'I can visualize that tribe of suspicious australopithecines trying to figure out spells to keep the falling rocks and burning trees and hungry bears off their backs.'

'They probably did. Thinking creatures have to believe that other things also think. If other things think, they are capable of intent. Because much of the universe is hostile to life – or at least thoroughly hostile to comfort – it seems plentifully endowed with malice. Malice, not malfunction. Ergo, every falling rock is out to git you.' Dom raised his glass in a toast to malevolent nature.

'So he creates spells to keep the rock spirits quiet.' Badger sipped his drink, amused.

'Exactly. And when he falls over a rock anyhow, it's because the spells weren't strong enough, or they weren't the right ones. How many thousands of years have men been searching for the right spells to keep things in place?'

'Since Solomon, at least,' said a voice from behind them. Mahlia. 'The legends say he was very good at putting malign forces in their place and keeping them there.'

'Of course.' Carver nodded. 'Solomon's seal. One sure

way of making things stay where they belong. Or, at least, where one puts them.'

'I want one for my dishwasher,' Myrtle said. 'Something malign has definitely gotten into it.'

Her husband shook his head at her in mock alarm. 'Not malice, dear. Simple malfunction, that's all. No such thing as demons.'

'But what if they are real?' Mahlia asked. 'Suppose most of the time it is just malfunction – of things, or of people, because there are all those mentally ill ones that no one can cure – suppose most of the time it is malfunction, but once in a while it *is* perversity, malice, a real demon in your dishwasher. How would you know the difference?'

'Easily,' said Myrtle triumphantly. 'If it were a real demon, the spells would work!'

'A perfect argument,' Badger said, taking Mahlia's arm and leading her away, toward the bar. 'It's always malfunction, except when it isn't. Spells don't work, except when they do. Demonic possession doesn't exist, except when it does. I can make very few certain statements under that reasoning. However, I can state with perfect certainty that your glass is empty *and* that I've had enough of discussion of malign spirits for one night.' He did not notice her flush. 'Let's get another drink.'

After that he caught glimpses of her from time to time, her face animated above the still column of her white-clad body, a dramatic contrast to her dark skin and nut-brown hair. She had a habit of pulling one long strand of hair from behind her ear, drawing it across her chin and twirling it there, a self-comforting little exercise the more engaging in that it was often her only movement. She would catch herself at it, flush, and push the hair back where it belonged, where it would hang, a separate little mink tail, waiting to be captured and twirled again.

Once she saw him looking at her and raised a hand in salute, tilting her head to one side like a surprised fawn. He decided she was lovely in an unassuming way, careful to carry the thought no further than that.

On her part, she watched him covertly, trying not to seem to do so, but sufficiently relaxed by the unaccustomed drink to forget her usual caution. He was very beautiful, she thought. Her artist's mind set him among the great Greek sculptures – Apollo as a youth, perhaps. Or that great face of Athena, which could be either male or female, being both strong and sensitive. He was not tall, only a few inches taller than she, but well built, lithe, moving with a natural grace that made her hands itch for a pencil. She wanted to see him without clothes. Suddenly aware of what she was thinking, she flushed bright red and went to the ladies' room. For shame, Mahlia, she told herself. But still she watched him.

There was a late buffet. The evening wore on. He found himself beside her on the terrace, heard himself saying, 'It's going to be early hours when this thing breaks up. Why don't we sneak over to your place and you can tell me your situation right now?'

She hesitated. What she was thinking was all there in her hesitation, in her embarrassed expression. He knew she had reconsidered in the intervening hours, and he suddenly did not want her to have done so. 'Come on. You said it would only take a minute.'

'It was presumptuous of me. . . .' He had caught her by surprise, before she had an excuse ready.

'It was nothing of the kind. Come on. Let's consult about your problem.' He nodded at the wrought-iron grill separating one section of the terrace from the other. 'Is it over there?' The door at the center of the grill stood ajar.

She led him through, more reluctantly than he wanted. They crossed the matching terrace, directly into the breathless hush of a museum. Color shone at him from every wall and floor. Track lighting picked out forms of jewels and gold, throwing dramatic shadows behind them. It seemed sacrilege to step on the glowing rug before him, like walking on a carpet of gemmy flame. He knew very little about oriental art, but the word 'treasure' breathed at him from every direction, from every gold-hued idol and Tibetan mandala.

19

'Good heavens,' he said. 'What a collection!'

'It's impressive, isn't it?' she asked, almost whispering. 'The first few days I was here, I tiptoed around as though it would all break or fall over if I coughed. This represents a lifetime of collecting. There are gifts from governments, gifts from ethnic groups – some of the rugs were given to him by the weavers in return for patterns he taught them – patterns that their ancestors had used. Can you imagine? He's a lovely old man. Almost eighty.'

'I met him,' Badger said, then almost shouted as something pressed firmly against his calf. The three dogs were behind him, silent as little shadows, giving him a thorough smelling. 'Ting,' he gasped. 'I presume.'

'Or Ching or Bing,' she said. 'They do everything together, so it doesn't really matter. Come on. The problem is in the bedroom.'

They went through the apartment. It was not quite as large as the one next door, but had the same feeling of luxury. The balcony bedroom he had seen before, in its half-finished state, was less museumlike than the lower rooms. Still, beside the bed a six-armed Siva danced on a tall pillar, starkly bright against the white wall, two hands up, two out, two down, hands and torso surrounded by a circle of jeweled effulgence. The bed was low, long, mahogany and cane, covered with hand-woven wool in shades of blue and violet. Mahlia stood beside the bed, gnawing on one knuckle.

'Ahhh,' she said, delaying, hesitant once more. 'You're not going to . . . Oh, well. Will you just hear me out and not ask a lot of questions?'

'If you like. Though usually I get answers by asking questions. I can be attractively persistent when it comes to asking questions.'

'Well, hear me out first.' Still with that doubtful face, she turned to face him. 'Someone comes in here, Badger. A man, perhaps fifty-five or sixty years old. There is gray at his temples. He carries a cane – maybe a cane. Maybe an umbrella. It has a silver handle, almost like an . . . oh, like a bird's head? At an angle to the shaft of the cane. I think that's right. . . .

'He comes in here. There's someone here. A young woman. Blond, I believe. Something is very wrong between them, and he hits at her, with the cane. Then he takes the handle in his fingers, and his fingers get all bloody. He flicks his hand, so. . . .' And she turned, her face drawn into a grimace of horror and disgust, flicking her hand at the white wall against which the idol stood. Badger's gaze followed the direction of those fingers, almost saw the blood drops flying away from them to spatter against the white wall. Almost he saw the pattern there.

Then Mahlia moved, drawing his eyes to her once more. 'You see? Now, either that *has* happened or it *will* happen. That's my problem. Has it already happened? I can't tell.'

Badger felt as though his mouth were full of sand. Was he to take this seriously? Was it a game? A kind of role-playing affair played with unsuspecting participants? No. Her face was serious, a little embarrassed, not amused, not focused upon his own expression or reactions. He struggled for a response.

'Ah. Mahlia. Do I understand that you have . . . seen this? Dreamed it? Or been told of it?'

She sighed, flushing, gave him an uncomfortable look that could have meant anything at all. 'You . . . you could say it was a kind of dream, yes.' She sighed again. 'Can't you just take it the way I said it? It happens. I just need to know whether it did or will – really, I just need to know whether it *did* happen. I thought of looking in the newspapers, but it could have happened and not been reported. . . .'

'Well, if that's all, I can tell you now. This place was originally a warehouse – for carpets, I think. There was no bedroom here until the renovation. Vivian brought me over while the work was going on. I met the Professor then, as a matter of fact. He was capering about up here like a mountain goat, and it wasn't half-finished. Nothing can have happened in this room before you moved in because it didn't exist. You're the first inhabitant. Except for Professor Boyce. How about him? Right age?'

'Bald,' she said, her eyes fixed rigidly upon his face. 'Totally bald, except around his ears. And he never moved in. So it couldn't have happened.'

Badger remembered the agile figure on the balcony, the clownish face, the hands busy polishing his head. 'Well then, it couldn't have happened. Not here. That is, if this is actually the place.'

'It's always the right place,' she said cryptically. 'Besides, it was the same. The statue' – indicating the dancing Siva – 'the bed, and the spread on it. The colors. Everything. This is the place. It hasn't happened yet.'

A weirdo, he thought. A crazy. Or, at the least, a very flaky lady. She had seemed so sane, so balanced. Even now, watching his face, reading him, she knew what he was thinking.

'I'm not batty, really.'

'I didn't think you were,' he said hypocritically.

'Yes. You did. Don't be concerned over it, please. I should have had sense enough to realize that the bedroom wasn't even here until the place was rebuilt.'

'This isn't some kind of game, is it?' he asked in annoyance. 'Not some kind of crazy game, or *Candid Camera* thing?'

'I wouldn't do that.' She turned toward the steps, slapping her thigh to bring the dogs after her. 'Let's go back to the party.'

She preceded him to the terrace door and left him there with a red-faced mutter. 'Sorry. Really. I shouldn't have bothered you.'

Since it was more or less what he had been thinking, he murmured only a polite negation. 'Not at all.'

He thought she had returned to her own apartment – to the Professor's apartment – but later in the evening he saw her across the room again, deep in conversation with an old woman who kept pounding her knee with one bony fist. Though he had been abstemious in recent months, his experieces during the early part of the evening seemed to call for more drink, a kind of preventive against thought. Mahlia was a flake. Enough. A pretty flake. Quite enough. A sexy, hell-on-wheels flake, and not something to fool around with in his present state of mind. Though he accepted this, he kept returning to it, one simple circle of thought. Attractive, but not for Badger, not now. Not now, not for Badger, though attractive.

Vivian kept George away from him.

He came to himself in a corner, starting from something which was half sleep, half a darkening melancholia that left tears brimming at the edges of his eyes.

He shook his head angrily. It took a special kind of boor to fall asleep at one's sister's party. He shook himself awake, had a cup of coffee, and began to make farewells. 'Nice to have seen you. Yes, we should make lunch soon. Call my office, won't you, when you have a free hour or so. I'll look forward to it.' Pleasant and meaningless. He wouldn't see any of these people again until Vivian next invited him. None of them were his kind of people. None. Particularly George.

Luck would not allow him a total escape. As he stood at the door saying good night to Vivian, George lurched up, putting one unsteady arm around each of them. Across his shoulder, Badger saw Mahlia approaching, half smiling as if to say a polite good-bye. He put on his company face, raised one eyebrow, nodded. No hard feelings, crazy lady. George was saying . . . Oh, Lord, George was saying . . .

'. . . sorry not to have seen more of you recently, my boy. I realize it was a terrible shock, Badger. . . .'

Don't go on, Badger thought desperately. Don't say anything else, George. Vivian was trying to hush him, but it didn't do any good. George was impossible to quiet.

'. . . terrible shock, your wife and child dying like that, but one must get on with life. . . .'

Mahlia's voice rose over it all in a knifelike edge of comprehension. 'But, your son's not dead.'

'*But your son's not dead*!'

23

Badger turned and fled. In the garage below he almost scraped the roof off the car as the door to the street rose too slowly. He did not know where he was going. He was not conscious of anything after that until he woke, curled on the bed in his own room, half-dressed, the picture of Carolyn and Robby clutched tight. The soaked mattress stank of alcohol. A bottle rattled beneath his feet. The clock on the bedside table gave him the time with digital precision. Eight-seventeen. There was no sunlight outside the windows. He had done it again, had one of those frenzied blackouts and slept an entire day away.

He set the photo on the table and looked at it for the first time in months. Carolyn. Blond, green-eyed, high-cheekboned, full-mouthed, like a princess from some English fairy tale, slightly turned away from the camera with that intriguing, secretive smile. And Robby, his tousle-headed form so full of life it seemed impossible he could be anything but alive. Four years old. A lithe, bronzed little frog shape in red swim trunks.

And all he could hear was Mahlia's voice, saying with complete conviction, 'But your son's not dead.'

'Damn you, woman!' he screamed into the pillow. 'Damn you. They *are* dead. Don't you understand! Why did you have to say anything at all! Why make one of your flaky, crazy remarks about my family. They're dead. Both of them. Get out of my life, my mind, my head. Get away from me!'

When he had yelled himself quiet once more, he still heard her. 'But your son's not dead.' How had she said that? 'But, your *son's* not dead?' Had that been it? Questioning. Horrified. Not a statement at all, just a shocked comment. 'But, your son's not *dead*?' A rising tone of disbelief. Shock and amazement. Pity and sympathy. Yes. That's what she'd meant. That's all she'd meant. He could forget about it. It hadn't meant anything. Not anything at all.

Staggering, he rose, undressed, got himself into the shower. Then he stripped the bed and remade it. Finally he put the picture in the bottom drawer of the dresser.

'Let's not play games with it anymore,' he told himself. 'Let's put it away. Let's not hide it and pretend we're not hiding it, let's just put it away and start to forget.' Knowing as he said it that it would not be that easy, had not been that easy in the eleven months that had passed. Amazingly, when he had eaten something, he fell asleep again and did not wake until morning.

2

Ron Frolius enjoyed few things in life. He found drinking overrated, and it escaped him how sex had acquired the reputation it had. He did enjoy eating. Molly, his wife, did well by him in that department, well enough he could over-look her infrequent demands upon him for the other thing. After all, the Bible did say to go forth and procreate, so he took it on occasionally as a kind of religious duty. The five kids served as proof of that, though they were grown up and gone. And not that she bothered him much anymore. She'd gotten real friendly with Martha and Simoney and that bunch of hens from around White Oak way. Spent a lot of time together, the dozen of them, gibble-gabbling in the par-lor, going for mid-night walks in the hills. It seemed silly to Ron, but Molly got a lot of enjoyment out of it. Since women missed out on things like plowing, they had to get their amusement where they could, which was just fine by Ron.

Plowing, though, that was just pure pleasure. Clean air. The pull of the tractor engine. Sitting up there under the blue sky with the land turning brown behind him in long furrows, as straight as a stretched fence line. Ron had won the county

27

plowing championship so many years running it had become almost boring, but plowing itself – well. It was God's gift to man, that's what it was, making him to earn bread by the sweat of his brow. The Bible said it was intended as a punishment, but Ron thought different. It was no more a punishment than making a kid toe the line about chores. It had to be done, and doing it right was just a pure joy.

He was sitting high on the tractor seat, the engine quiet while he had his lunch, looking over old Henry's house and buildings and the maze field. Henry Darinbaugh had no more interest in farming than he had in fixing up that old house. It was going to fall in around him one of these days. The house acreage was all gone to thistle and briar; the old barns and stables were gap-roofed and sagging. Ron knew if it weren't for him, the rest of the place would go to weeds and ruin, too. As it was, there wasn't much of it really wasted except the maze field. Every year he filled out the land use papers for Mr. Darinbaugh, and every year some fool county agent sent a form saying ten acres of corn. Ron never spelled it 'maize'; it was 'maze,' and nobody in the U.S. of A. called corn 'maize' anyhow. Maze field. That's what it was.

Not that it made any sense and hadn't ever, so far as Ron could tell. He mowed it himself, four or five times a year, just to keep it nice and flat the way old Henry wanted it. In the center of the field was a 250-foot-diameter circle, a tangle of little turf paths and asphalt lines, straight lines, curved lines, all full of corners and backtracks, leading into the center. If you started at the east side of the circle, you could walk around and around on every one of those little paths without ever stepping on one of the black-filled ditches. Or you *could* have, if old Henry hadn't put three iron gates in the way, big heavy things with locks big enough for a vault. Though, come to think of it, Ron wasn't certain Henry had done that. Might have been his father or grandfather. No one much did iron work like that anymore. All those fancy curlicues and twirly leaves. Could have been a hundred years ago, Ron supposed. The Darinbaugh family had been around as long as Ron's had, and that was some time.

On the hill straight across he could see the roof of the Shiel house, smoke rising from it like an endless strand of wool, pulling away into nothingness at the top of the sky. Jared Shiel and Henry Darinbaugh had been quite a pair in their day. Funny the way Henry had changed toward him after Henry's father died. Jared still hung around the place, sneaking and slying like some old fox. Story was he thought there was money buried on the Darinbaugh place. Ron snorted, thinking about that. Any money Henry had, he'd spent it twenty years ago. Buying books. Sending people all over the world looking for stuff. Lord, that house was full of stuff people had brought back.

'No sir,' Ron said aloud to the air. 'Henry hasn't got one dime except what I pay him for use of the land.' And then, after a moment, 'Speak of the devil.'

From where he sat, Ron could see Henry Darinbaugh now, fooling around behind his house. Henry claimed to have a kitchen garden there, but Ron had never seen anything growing in it except rhubarb. It was hard to kill rhubarb. The old man was more fretful lately, and more feeble and forgetful, too. He was only in his midsixties, not ten years older than Ron himself, but he had the appearance of a man twenty years older than that. Like he was eaten away, Molly said. Cancer, she opined, or something that acted like it. Whenever Molly talked about old Henry and how sick he looked, she got this funny look on her face, as though she smelled something bad. It wasn't that she didn't like him, either. Sometimes she seemed right fond of him.

Well, it was true. Old Henry had failed a lot just this year, just since that girl and the little boy came visiting. Like somebody had handed him a death sentence, Molly said. Though what should be so fatal about a pretty lady and a cute kid was more than Ron could fathom. Him and the little fellow had had a pretty good talk there while his mama and old Henry looked at the maze. Not that she'd liked it much. She'd been screeching and hollering and came back as pale as lilies, without two words in her mouth for the boy.

There Henry was, coming out of the backyard onto the

woods path. Ron lost sight of him for a few moments behind the trees, but soon Henry emerged onto the meadow. He had on those crazy spectacles and was holding on to some lumpy thing and an old book. Lord, that house of Darinbaugh's was a perfect rats' nest of old books, half of them chewed by bugs or mice. Old books and old pictures. There was one there old Henry said was his ancestor, from England, way back, all dressed up in religious robes with those very same spectacles on the table by him. Ron wasn't a teasing man, but he had said something about those religious folks not being supposed to have descendants at all. Old Henry had just nodded, serious-like, and said that had been part of the problem. Half the time, Ron didn't know what he was talking about, he was so weird.

But then, the whole place was strange. Whenever Molly went there to clean, she came back shaking her head sadly. 'He won't let me touch anything except his bedroom and the bathroom and the kitchen,' she said. 'And all the rest of the place stinking of mice. I probably have more sense about the stuff he has there than he has, but he won't listen when I try to tell him.' Ron didn't know what she meant by that, except that things lasted better if they were kept clean. The old house did smell, though. Ron knew that. The old man ought to have kin to take care of him. That is, he did have kin, but not what you'd call caring kin. Halfies-Annie Sudbury was his sister's daughter, for all the good that did him.

Below him in the maze meadow the old man approached the first of the iron gates, bending to unlock it with a large key. He sagged against the gatepost, leaning there for some time as though to gather strength. When he went on walking the maze, it was with a kind of dogged stagger. Ron watched curiously, wondering if the old man had been drinking. Ron had walked the maze a time or two himself, between gates, of course, even though he couldn't understand his own fascination with it. It was fascinating, however. He had to admit that. Like a kid's game.

The old man was plugging along pretty good down there, getting as far as the second gate in just a few minutes. He unlocked that one, too, but he had to lean against the gate again before trudging off along the grassy path. This time he stopped twice before he got to the last gate, stopped with his head down. Uneasily, Ron got down from the tractor seat. The old man oughtn't to be out in this sun. He started down the hill, not bothering to yell. Henry was deaf as a post anyhow, so no point in disturbing the peace.

Henry Darinbaugh was at the third gate, bending to unlock it, and fell against it heavily. It swung open, spilling him to the ground, where he made a feeble attempt to rise before falling back upon the path to lie limp and unmoving. Ron started to run, approaching the maze from the side and cutting across the paths toward the still figure. 'Mr Darinbaugh! You all right? Mr Darinbaugh?' Lord, suppose the old man was dead. What a fuss that would be. 'Mr. Darinbaugh?'

He knelt beside the still body and took the crazy spectacles away in time to see the old eyes flicker open. 'Mr. Darinbaugh? You okay?' He tucked the spectacles into his pocket to keep them safe.

'Ron.' The voice was too weak to hear easily. 'Ron. Waited too long. Lock gates. Promise. Lock gates.' There was agony in that voice, and Ron didn't hesitate. One thing Molly had told him. Don't argue with old people or sick people. It just upsets 'em.

'Sure I'll lock 'em up, Mr. Darinbaugh. Don't worry about them. Let's get you out of here and get a doctor.' He raised the limp old body easily and started out of the maze, suddenly aware of an electric heaviness in the air, a chill wind, as when storm pended. Uneasily, he looked, but the sky was as cloudless as it had been all morning. He did not see the key drop from Henry's lax fingers to the edge of one of the maze lines, black iron against black asphalt, invisible. The old man still clutched the book and a funny old bottle against his chest.

'Don't let . . .' the old man panted. 'Ron, don't let . . .'

Ron stopped, cradling the old body. Lord, he was light as a feather. Maybe there was something to that business of

Molly's about bein' eaten away, after all. 'Don't let what, Mr. Darinbaugh? Don't let what?'

'Don't let Annie . . . don't let her . . .' The old man's eyes fell closed, and his chest heaved once, only once.

Ron knew the old man was dead. His face held a kind of apprehensive fretfulness, the expression of one whose long-held plans have gone hopelessly awry. Ron was distressed by this. The dead were supposed to be at peace, but there was no peace at all in that face. Ron eased the body to the ground, then went to find a phone.

When the ambulance and the various officials attendant upon unexpected death had come and gone, he thought of his promise and walked across the maze to the third gate expecting to find the key in the lock. When he didn't find it, he was strongly tempted to forget the whole business, but a promise given was a promise given. He could not imagine why he was thinking of sex at that moment. He never thought of sex, and certainly not with this overpowering urgency. The fact that he did so now with such relentless, itchy insistency was infuriating, so much so that he went at once to his tool room and fetched three lengths of stout chain and three rusty padlocks, seeking to shut out the lewd thoughts by immediate, unrelated action. When the gates were secured, he stood there, waiting, though he could not have said why. Nothing. The momentary lustfulness had passed; the heaviness in the air was gone. The old book and bottle were still lying there, so he took them up to his house and put them on the mantel where the spectacles already stood.

It had been kind of a funny feeling, though, so he told Molly about it. She got that strange expression she sometimes wore, as though he had said something he didn't mean to say. All she did was shake her head, though, and take to watching him as though she were worried about him.

After that, there were still three hours until dark, so he went back to his plowing.

3

Vivian thought about it for a long time before calling
Badger. It was difficult for her to break the rule she had
established for herself some years before. After their mother
had died – some said from terminal astonishment at
Badger's unexpected arrival more than twenty years after
Vivian's birth – Vivian had mothered Badger as a matter
of course. He had been a very late maturing boy; clever in
many respects, but naive in others; deeply involved in a
lucrative career even before he left the university, but at the
same time oddly indifferent to women. Until Carolyn.

Vivian had never really liked Laura Beecham, née
Benedict. When Badger settled upon Laura's daughter as
the only woman he would consider marrying, Vivian found
herself not liking Carolyn, either. A half-humorous accep-
tance of her quasi-maternal role made her doubt her own
motives, however, and she examined them relentlessly.
Was it jealousy? Carolyn's glowing beauty was quite
enough to make most women hate her, but Vivian did not
think it was that.

She decided it was simply worry for Badger. At

twenty-eight, he had little experience with women, and she felt that Carolyn was a woman it would take a lot of experience to handle – perhaps one of those women who should not be taken too seriously.

Badger handled it very seriously indeed. Though perpetually impatient about almost everything, in this he did not hurry. Though he was abetted by Carolyn's mother to an indecent extent, he took no advantage of that. After eighteen months of single-minded, subtle courtship, he succeeded.

From the first, Vivian had watched the pursuit with troubled eyes. Badger hadn't noticed that of the year and a half he had spent in the effort, more than a year had been needed just to get Carolyn's attention. Though she did not seem to be a stupid young woman, neither did she seem interested in very many things. Carolyn shone as the sun shines, with no other activity needed. Badger's greatest ally in first getting her attention had been his own dramatic good looks, which only improved as he matured. Just as the sun needs an occasional cloud to show to best advantage, so Carolyn showed better when shadowed by those dark, elegant features. Vivian had observed this regretfully, without comment.

So much for the public Carolyn. Vivian sensed another, more secret Carolyn behind the lovely face. She could not have said why. Because she could not have said why, she said nothing.

Badger's initial understanding of his Carolyn extended no further than the honeymoon. He had not looked further than the wooing and the winning. When the honeymoon activities, at least those conducted in the bedroom, turned out to be a good deal more innovative than he had expected, he refused either to be shocked or to speculate about it. Her life, so far as he was concerned, began when they married, when she was twenty-two. When, on their return from an exclusive resort on the north coast of Majorca, where Carolyn had played endless tennis while Badger watched adoringly, Carolyn had returned to the club on Long Island to play endless games of tennis while others watched adoringly, Badger had found himself becoming slightly bored. His solution was to think of something else. His solution, whenever deeply troubled, had always been to think of something else.

He did not really evaluate their relationship again until the first year of marriage had passed and he began to want a child. By that time, his understanding of Carolyn had been reinforced by some intuitive slyness, and he approached the subject through vocal admiration of all of the women in their circle who had children. The young mothers certainly were blooming. Lovely. Maternity softened and beautified them. Et cetera. He spoke often of how handsome the children were, careful to speak of them impersonally, as possessions. He had heard others saying, he said, what a pity it was that the Ettisons were childless, saying this much as he might have said what a pity it was that the Ettisons didn't have a Mercedes. A few months of this kind of talk and Carolyn was pregnant. He had named the child before it was conceived – Robby, if a boy; Robin, if a girl – and amused himself by carrying on silent conversations with the baby-to-be while he shaved. A full-time, live-in nanny had been Carolyn's idea, but one that Badger had realized would be necessary after the briefest consideration.

And all of this increased understanding of her personality had occurred without his ever for an instant doubting that he loved her completely. He had chosen her; he had won her; she was his wife, the mother of his child; therefore he loved her. He had not doubted it for one moment since her disappearance. He did not doubt it now. All her little secrets, her long, whispery phone calls, her endless hours at the tennis club – none of it was important. He loved her.

Vivian had put all this together from things said and unsaid, from her observations of Carolyn, and from her intimate knowledge of the boy and the man. She knew a great deal more about Badger than he could have guessed.

Now, for the first time in years, she decided to interfere.

'This has to stop, Badger,' she said. 'I've gone along with this denial of yours for months now. Asking George not to mention Carolyn and Robby. Telling other friends to stay away from the subject. But running off like that at the party was the last straw. You aren't behaving like an adult, and it's time you must.' She waited, worried that he might hang up on her.

Finally, 'I know,' he said softly. 'I came to somewhat the same conclusion when I woke up last night.'

'I want you to have lunch with me' she went on, pressing her advantage. 'We're going to talk about this.'

'All right, Vivian. All right.'

The sadness in his voice hurt her. It had always hurt her. When he was fifteen, sixteen, with the face and body of a twelve-year-old, he had turned her inside out with that childlike, anguished sigh, but she steeled herself against it. 'One o'clock. Here at the apartment. George will be out.'

'So that's a start,' she said to herself as she hung up the phone. 'All right. It's long enough now. Time he got interested in someone else.' It was too bad Mahlia had made that remark just as he'd left the other night. They had been getting along so well until then. What had the silly girl meant? 'Your son's not dead.' Probably nothing. Just shock. Vivian had never mentioned the tragedy to her, and learning of a child's death came as a shock to any woman.

Well. There were other pretty women. Other good women. Better, thought Vivian with a hint of compression around her lips, than Carolyn. Though she could not, even then, have said what it was she hadn't liked about Carolyn.

4

He had lunch with Vivian. He talked about Carolyn and did not behave badly. He couldn't talk about Robby at all, but Vivian didn't force that. They made a date to have lunch again, to talk again. 'You have to,' she told him. 'You can't go through the rest of your life pretending they'll show up next week. It isn't going to happen, Badger.'

Soberly, he agreed. For the next few weeks, he took on more work than he could handle. He ate his work and drank it, falling into the bed each night too exhausted to think about anything. The days went by. He practised saying, 'My late wife, Carolyn,' in the shaving mirror. 'My late wife, Carolyn. Robby, my son who died. . . .'

Then the dreams began, as though his subconscious would punish him for believing they were gone. 'Daddy,' Robby said in the dream, demandingly but without fear. 'Daddy, come get me!' Mahlia was in the dream, too, in a wooded place, he thought, certainly somewhere with a soft greenness about it. There had been both terror and fulfilment in that dream, and he lay for a time curled around that latter feeling before he remembered who he was or where he was. Then he felt guilty. Mahlia hadn't belonged in that dream. Carolyn, perhaps. Not Mahlia.

He dismissed it, but during the day the dream came back to him, or rather the feeling of it, so that he slowed down, began to look around him at things he hadn't noticed for months. Faces of people. The shadows of trees on the street. A fat, happy little old woman leading a fat, happy little old Pekingese pup, the two of them yapping at each other in identical tones of voice. Shining pyramids of apples and oranges at the sidewalk shops. The sounds of life going on. Abruptly, without thinking about it at all, he called Vivian.

'I've been thinking about what you said, Viv. I do need to get out with someone. That woman you introduced me to? Mahlia? From next door. Would you have her phone number?'

He was prepared for coyness at this point, sisterly teasing, all very gentle, of course.

Instead, 'She moved out, Badger. Not a week after the party. She left me a little note with the manager saying she'd turned the keys over to Professor Boyce's nephew – evidently he's responsible during the Professor's absence – and thanking me for a nice time at the party.'

'Ah. Did she say why? Or where she was going?'

'Not a word. I was very hurt. I wouldn't have known she was gone except the manager told me when he gave me the note. I got a postcard from her a few days ago, thanking me again. It said she'd be in touch someday, when she got settled.'

'Postcard from where?' He was appalled at the abruptness, almost violence, in his voice.

'Don't bark at me, Badger! It was a Tahiti postcard, a joke, because she's from there, you know. But it had a New York postmark. She wouldn't leave the city. She's in school.'

After that he could only go on with inconsequential talk for a few moments before hanging up the phone. Gone. Gone five or six weeks ago. Why? Something to do with that crazy episode? Badger was angry with himself. She had taken the matter of her vision, or whatever it was, more seriously than he had, obviously.

'Well,' he said to himself. 'You could find her, Ettison.'

'No . . .' he answered. That was more commitment than he was prepared to make. More interest than he was prepared to show. Even as he made the decision, he had a hunch it was the wrong one.

5

Molly was darning socks, even though she told Ron often enough nobody darned socks anymore. It gave her something to do in the evenings, however, the ones she didn't spend wandering off in the woods on some mushroom hunt with her friends or having a chatfest at Martha's or Simoney's, both of them widows and alone too much, she said. Ron never minded her going, but he always preferred it when she was home, sewing. He liked the look of women sewing. His own mother had spent a lot of time that way. Whenever he remembered her, it was mostly with a lap full of mending.

'Damn Farmers' Feed,' he muttered.

'Got your bill wrong again, have they?' she asked, fully expecting a lengthy answer.

'If they don't fire that girl and get somebody who can add two and two, I'll take my business over to Ed Britter. He's not quick, Ed, but at least he doesn't charge you for fertilizer you never ordered.'

'Might be the stuff I bought for the vegetable garden,' she remarked. 'I got four sacks.'

'You did?' As usual, he was astonished she could have done anything without his knowing it, though he knew very little about what she did and almost nothing about what she thought. 'Why'd you do that without tellin' me?'

'You were at the hospital, tellin' the doctor about old Henry Darinbaugh, and I was in there with your list of stuff you wanted. Forgot to mention it later, you were so upset.'

'I was upset because of what the doctor said he died of. Wasn't his heart at all. Something like you said, Molly. A kind of cancer. Only the doctor said he'd never seen that kind before. He was all eaten out inside. No blood left in him, hardly. Got me feeling all squirmy. Well, it's over. No point in thinkin' about it.'

Molly heard this with a frown, shaking her head. She'd thought there was something odd about Henry Darinbaugh for a long time. He hadn't looked like a normal man, not a normal well man nor a normal sick one. Well, as Ron said, no point in thinking about it. She turned the sock right side out and frowned at the mended place. Somehow they never looked as neat as her own grandma had done them. Grandma had had a lot to teach her, and Molly'd paid more attention to some parts of it than others. Though who cared about how darns looked, she couldn't say. Nobody ever got to see the darn in a sock, anyhow. 'What'll happen to the place, do you think?'

'Halfies-Annie Sudbury'll get it. She's the only kin he had.'

'His sister's daughter, isn't she?'

'She's no chicken.'

'No, she's a tough old hen, that one. Old Henry's sister must've been a lot older'n him. Annie's fifty if she's a day. Got a hard, mean face on her.'

'She's a money sniffer.' Ron didn't need to specify further. Molly knew exactly what he meant. His own cousin Barbara was also a money sniffer. She had only to walk through a room and she could tell you what everything in it would sell for and likely what it had cost.

He'd only met Annie Sudbury a few times – and he'd kept it that way by staying clear whenever he could. She'd dismissed him the first time with a three-second look. She'd stared at the dog he had with him for a long, calculating time, however. The dog was a champion, being boarded for a friend, a very expensive animal. She's known it, somehow, just the way she knew that old Henry's books were worth thousands, just the way she knew what she could get for the land. Annie would always know where the money was.

'She'll want to sell the land, first thing. Most likely she'll plow the maze field, too. She was on at him that time about it, what the crop from that field would be worth.'

'You going to do it for her if she asks?'

'Maybe. If I get the money first. Or a legal paper takin' it off the rent for the land. I been cropping old Henry's land a good time, now. We got plenty of our own, o' course, but there's no reason to stop just because Henry's dead. Not until she sells it to some rich man.'

'Some developer, more likely. So he c'n cut it up in nasty little pieces. They'll have us surrounded on three sides soon. Still, Ron, I wouldn't be in any hurry to plow that field if I was you. Let Annie Sudbury get someone else to do it. You hear?' She knew he did. When Molly used that tone, she had a reason. Ron hadn't gone against that tone of voice for twenty years, and he still shuddered when he thought of the last time. Molly was just *right* about some things. She could smell trouble coming like some folks could smell storm on the way.

She stood up to put the mending basket on the mantel, pushing old Henry's book aside to make a place. The book and bottle Henry Darinbaugh had been clutching had been lying there over the fireplace since the old man died. 'What are you going to do with these?'

'Keep 'em,' he answered laconically. Privately he thought that Annie Sudbury would have enough old books and bits of gimcrack to satisfy herself; she wouldn't miss a couple of things. Besides, old Henry wouldn't mind Ron having a keepsake.

'Funny old bottle,' she said thoughtfully. She had not really looked at it before, but now her attention fastened on it with the beginning of a wondering suspicion as she turned it in her hands, tracing the design with a forefinger. 'Heavy. What's it made of?'

He shook his head. 'Might be iron, or lead. It's real old, too. The design on it's almost worn down.' He took the thing into his hands, impressed as he had been before at the heft of it, heavier than one would think possible for such a small thing, shaped like a slightly flattened tennis ball, with the neck of it stoppered tight. The design on the bottle flowed up into the stopper, too, all of one piece. It reminded him of something, but he could not think of what it might be.

'Keep it,' he repeated, apropos of nothing. He set it back on the mantel, not bothering to look at the book, full as it was of the old man's scribbles. Ron hadn't looked at a book since eighth grade, and if he never did again it would be soon enough. The newspapers and the county bulletins told him all he needed to know.

'I wouldn't mention it to anyone,' she said, catching his eye to be sure he heard her. 'Not anyone.'

He seemed not to understand.

'I mean it, Ron. You remember after Jared and Henry stopped bein' so close, Jared used to go around sayin' the Darinbaughs got so rich because they had a genie in a bottle? Remember that?'

'Oh, right. He did. I remember he did. You think this is the bottle?'

Taking the bottle once again from the shelf, she turned the heavy thing in her hands, letting the stopper swing loose at the end of its connecting chain. 'Nothin' in it now, for sure,' she said. 'Still, I wouldn't talk about it. Jared Shiel never had anything except what Henry gave him. He'd as soon steal as spit, and as soon kill as steal. Just smart to keep shut about it.'

'Well then, I will. Old Henry wouldn't mind me havin' it.'

Privately, hefting it in one hand and examining the curvilinear design more closely, she thought Henry would have minded very much indeed that anyone but himself was handling it at all.

6

Badger took on, for a small parts company, a quality control
problem that turned out to be industrial sabotage. He lived
the problem, and slept it, for two weeks with barely time to
eat and shave. The repetitive dream vanished in his
exhaustion, and he forgot he had wanted to call Mahlia.
Then it was over and he had one of those rare breaks
between jobs. One finished with no loose ends and another
not due to begin until the following Monday, five long days
away. On a sudden impulse he packed a small suitcase and
his fishing gear and took a holiday. Early Sunday evening
he returned to his apartment, pausing to pick up the Sunday
paper from the entryway floor. He flipped it open on his bed
as he started to unpack, his eyes running over it without
actually seeing it. The three-column picture on the third
page seemed familiar somehow. A dancing idol, framed in a
golden halo. On the floor, a body covered with a sheet.
Blood spots dashed down the wall, and his mind knew the
pattern of those dark blotches as though he had put them
there himself. VIOLENT KILLING SHOCKS EXCLU-
SIVE NEIGHBORHOOD the headline screamed. He

dropped onto the bed, scanning the text with unbelieving eyes.

'. . . identified as Virginia Gamble, sometime model, who had been staying at the apartment for only a few days, according to building manager Warren Guise. 'I understood she was only a temporary guest,' Guise said. 'In that apartment, we always check the air conditioning once each day, usually in the evening. The art collection there requires the humidity to be kept constant. When the maintenance man went in last night, he found her dead.'

'Lieutenant Barry Springer of the New York City Police, in charge of the case, had no information for reporters. ''We don't even officially know the cause of death yet. It's far too early to speculate about motives.'' '

Badger found himself staring at the picture again, his right hand moving as he had seen Mahlia's move, flicking the blood away. That story she had told him. Could she have been setting him up? For what? What craziness had he got himself mixed up with?

He dialed the police from the bedside phone. 'Barry Springer, please. Tell him Badger Ettison. . . . Barry? I see you have your name in the papers again. . . . What? . . . Oh, yes. I finished it up a week ago. Turned out to be someone hired by a rival firm. He told us the whole story as soon as he knew we had him. . . . No . . . Barry – hey, on that case in the papers today? Virginia Gamble? Is there an older man in the case, someone with gray or white hair at the temples? Maybe somebody who carries a cane or umbrella with a silver handle? Ah – I feel like a fool, but if there's somebody like that, check the handle of that cane for blood.

'No, I did not kill her, you idiot. Look, never mind. Just remember what I told you. . . . Sure, you too, at high noon on the Fourth of July. . . . No, I will not say anything more. . . . Okay. Sure.'

He sat staring at the newspaper for hours, until the print began to waver in front of his eyes and he lost track of who or where he was.

The phone rang, startling him out of his daze.

'Yes, Barry. . . . You did? Was there blood on it? . . . He did?' He listened, said reluctantly, 'Well. Yes, I'll tell you about it, but you're not going to believe it. . . . Sure you would, fella. Like you believe my fishing stories. Okay. Lunch tomorrow. At Sid's. One o'clock. . . . You got it.'

He hung up, sat for a moment, then began to tremble, tremble until his teeth chattered together, as though he had been caught in a cold gale.

'But your son's not dead.'

'But *your* son's not dead!'

'But *your* son's *not* dead!'

That had been it. That had been how she had said it. Exactly like that. *Not* dead! Robby. Four years old – five years old now. Not dead. Perhaps Carolyn, too. Not dead. Not dead. But if not dead, then what? Where? Why?

Would Mahlia know? Could she tell him, lead him to them?

Now he *had* to find her.

7

Annie Sudbury had greeted the knowledge of her approaching inheritance with a good deal of satisfaction. She had been counting on Henry Darinbaugh's dying for a number of years, observing his increasing weakness with impatience while taking informal inventory of the contents of the house during her infrequent visits. On being informed of his death, she went immediately to the Darinbaugh house, found it unlocked as she had expected, and removed to the trunk of her car some fifteen or twenty volumes that she had taken note of over the years and had had appraised *in absentia* by a rare book dealer in Albany. She could see no point in paying large inheritance taxes out of what could have been a gift from a loving uncle to his niece. After all, if he'd been in his right mind, he would have given them to her long since instead of holding those peculiar attitudes toward her. Peculiar attitudes indeed, as though he detested the very idea of blood kin. A strange way to feel toward one's sister's daughter, even for an eccentric, aged man.

The books were very old, concerned with esoteric subjects

that did not interest Annie at all. She thought them rubbishy, more untidy examples of Uncle Henry's senile dementia. They were genuine rarities, however, and worth a fortune, which pleased her enormously. There had been another one that might have been of even greater value, since the old man carried it around him most of the time, usually in his dressing gown pocket. When she arrived at the hospital she found the dressing gown there, part of the effects of the deceased. The pockets, however, were empty.

She returned directly from the hospital to the Frolius farm, where she confronted Ron and Molly Frolius with a demand for the return of any and all property of the late Henry Darinbaugh that might be in their custody. It was the wrong tack to take with the Froliuses. Ron turned a bland face, an uncomprehending stare, and disclaimed any knowledge of any item that had ever been the property of Henry Darinbaugh. Molly got a certain expression on her face that Ron saw infrequently but her female friends of the group would have recognized in an instant. It promised eventual anonymous retaliation, one of several lesser practices in which the group was expert.

'Old Henry had my Aunt Sophie's candle mold,' said Molly firmly. 'Borrowed it from me two years ago last fall to make candles from the beeswax in those two hives Ron set up for him. Bees was gone long since, but Henry never brought the mold back. Mark that down, Annie. I'll be wanting that when you clean the place out. Oh, and he had two bread pans, too. Gave them to him just last week with fresh bread in 'em. Likely I should come down and look around the kitchen down there. Lots of stuff got carried back and forth. Henry was no hand as a cook. I'll take a look and clear out my stuff. You can come along, be sure I don't steal the silver.'

'That's my log splitter down in Henry's barn,' said Ron. 'He got a load of logs from Joe Rencey in White Oak, and told me he'd pay to split 'em for him. I'll take a look around, too, Annie, and get my stuff out before the sheriff seals the place up.' Hidden in the fence row where he was making war against thistle, Ron had seen Annie's depredations among the books. 'Let's get on down there now. I'll take the truck.'

Borne along by their stubborn deafness and irresistible motion, Annie had only modest opportunity to mutter a few reservations before being escorted back to the Darinbaugh house where Molly and Ron felt she belonged. A truckload later – most of which actually belonged to them – they left her there, fuming, feeling she'd been outfoxed but having no reasonable complaint. They had moved her out of the Frolius kitchen so quickly she had no opportunity to see the old book on the mantel, and when she found some excuse to come there again, it had been put well away.

It remained for her to put old Henry's place in such shape as might increase its value on sale. Anyone sensible might have told Annie Sudbury that all the value was in the land and she might as well have burned the house and barns, but a lifetime of interfering with anything that was, in favor of something else that wasn't, led her into a flurry of house cleaning, junk hauling, and preparations to plow the maze field. 'It'll look better if it's plowed,' she said to Ron defiantly, he having suggested mildly that she just wait until the place was hers to dispose of officially. 'Like real farmland instead of some crazy place. You give me the keys to those gates, too, Ron Frolius. I did some pricing the other day of gates like them. That's a lot of fancy iron work there, and they'll bring a good price if they're cleaned up.'

'Well, horseshit, Annie, if you're going to sell 'em, whoever wants 'em will have to take 'em out of the ground, and whether they're locked or unlocked makes no never mind. You are the stirrin'est woman. Let the gates alone. Old Henry wanted 'em locked. You might let him get cold first.'

'Henry was senile,' she said viciously. 'And he should have died years ago. If you don't have a key, I'll bring the bolt cutter next time I come from town. But I want those gates down and put in the barn and the field plowed, and if you won't do it for a fair price, somebody else will.'

'Oh, I'll do it, Annie. Sure I will. For payment in

53

advance. I know you and your fair price. It's always fair before the job, then suddenly it's halfies after. They don't call you Halfies-Annie for nothing.'

'Ron Frolius, that's a damned lie. Nobody's ever called me that!'

'Nobody but Joe Harbite, over that cord of wood you said he cut too long for your stove, and Aldin Sourwood, over those fruit jars you said the lids didn't fit, and both the Misses Janberry over those dresses you had made that turned out the wrong color. And Wilma Nelson, and her brother Ed, over that porch addition.'

'And Mrs. Reverend Swall,' said Molly, peering through her bifocals at the needle she was trying to thread. 'When you told her you'd give her ten dollars at the bake sale for her double chocolate cake, then only paid her five. And most ever'body else in town. You've come by the name through a lifetime, Annie. No sense fussing about it.' She then said something guaranteed to make Annie Sudbury do the one thing she should not have done. 'Don't unlock the gates, Annie. That would be dumb.'

Annie didn't fuss about it. She just left, telling herself it would be a cold day in August before she hired Ron Frolius to do anything. Stupid old men, Henry and Ron both of them, and Molly not much better. She brought out the bolt cutters early the next morning and cut the chains on the gates. She'd get the ad in the paper over in Williston. One particular banker over there was restoring an old place and would pay thousands for garden gates, especially ones as old and unique as these. She stood looking at the open gates, feeling a suddenly icy wind in her face, all at once out of a clear sky, unexpected and unforeseen. She sniffed, scenting the wind. Money. Henry had had lots of it at one time. She wouldn't be surprised to find some of it buried around the place still. That's what old Jared Shield thought, Annie knew. He was always skulking around like some old crow, looking for pickings. Well. The wind made it too cold to linger.

Satisfied, she turned away, leaving the gates standing defiantly open.

8

During a crowded, noisy lunch at Sid's, Badger told his story to an accompaniment of vocal disbelief.

'Look,' he stated at last. 'I've told you the story, Barry. I left nothing out and I've put nothing in. I told you you wouldn't believe it. You insisted on hearing it anyhow. That's enough. I didn't make it up for your amusement. Or mine.'

Barry Springer took a large bite of his corned-beef sandwich and thrust it into one capacious cheek with his tongue, talking around it as he chewed, eyes squeezed half-shut with the effort. 'She was born in Tahiti?'

'That's what she told Vivian. She only said "Polynesian" to me.'

'Of a native mother and a French father.'

'That's what she said.'

'She told your sister she was educated in France after her mother died, from about age twelve until age eighteen. She mentioned her aunt to you, her father's sister, Aunt Irene.'

'There can't be more than a few million Aunt Irenes in France. Oh, all right. A few hundred thousand.'

'She knows Professor Boyce.'

'That's what she said. And Boyce is off in China somewhere, no one knows where, no one knows when he's coming back. Now I've told you everything I know, suppose you tell me.'

'What's to tell? The Professor had a nephew, Franklin Rendall. Rendall had a mistress, what one might call a semiprofessional. When Rendall ended up with the keys to the Professor's apartment, he decided to stash the lady there.'

'And?'

'And the lady saw it as an opportunity to engage further in the free enterprise system. Which her sponsor interrupted. Violence, as it so often does, resulted.'

'Your cynicism is disturbing, Bartholomew.'

'Shove it, Ettison. Nobody calls me Bartholomew except my mother. Anyhow, on receiving the tip from you, I went to the guy's house – up until then we had no special reason to suspect he'd killed her. Stashed her there, yes, but killed her, no. After all, she'd had a plethora of visitors. . . .'

'A plethora?'

'Well, what would you call it? A covey?'

'A bunch. Plenty.'

'Oh, she'd had plenty. So, I go to Rendall's place, ring the bell, ask to see him, and first thing tell him I have a warrant to search the place (which, by the way, I did *not* get by telling the judge I'd had information by way of a psychic experience) and that I wanted to see his silver-headed cane. He started crying. He confessed before, during, and after getting his rights, so I'm not worried about that.' He chewed in silence for a moment. 'And you say this woman friend of yours saw it before it happened?'

'That's what she told me, yes.'

'Well, according to Rendall, he's never laid eyes on her. He never went there until she sent him the keys.'

'She certainly never mentioned him by name.'

'But she saw the thing happen. Blood and all.'

'Silver-headed cane, gray-haired man, blood and all.'

'I'm not going to put it in my report. He was a logical

suspect, and I'd have gotten to him sooner or later. So I rushed it a little. So what.'

'So nothing. Put it down to one of those inexplicable events which happen from time to time.' Badger had no intention of leaving it there himself, but it suited him to let Barry believe it.

'I'd kind of like to meet her.'

'Why? All you'd do is mess up her life. I told you, she's troubled enough over it. The fact she left the place shows that.'

'I'd still like to meet her. But I suppose it isn't strictly necessary. Probably just foul up the details.'

'Likely. Yes.'

'You'd like me to leave it alone, huh?'

'I would, yes.'

'You buying?'

'I'm buying.'

'All right. I'll let it alone. But I owe you one big favor, count on it. And I don't promise not to ask for help next time I get a weird case. I might ask you to bring the lady around. See if she has a vision about it.'

Badger, who had no idea where to find the lady, smiled noncommittally. Thus far, he had had no luck. The university had no record of a student named Waiwela and no one there was cooperating in attempting to search records for women with French surnames. The day porter at the apartment house thought Mahlia had received mail under another name, a French name, but he couldn't remember what it had been. Neither could the mail carrier on the route.

'She wasn't a citizen,' Badger One had mused to himself. 'She had to have a visa.'

'Fine,' Badger Two snarled. 'Under what name? There's no visa in the name of Waiwela, I already checked that.'

'I imagine she was educated under her father's name, and kept that name for legal purposes,' Badger One continued.

'I imagine so, too. What good does that do us?'

'Not much.'

Meantime, he went into recurrent bouts of shivers,

dry-mouthed, staring at walls or innocent passersby with his eyes fixed as though catatonic. 'But your son's not dead.' It had become a refrain, like some TV commercial jingle, 'Da da dum *dum* dum.' Over and over, a tom-tom beat beneath consciousness. A day or two of this was enough.

'Okay,' he told himself at last, when nothing he had tried had given him so much as a clue. 'Enough of this lying about on the doormat, whining for someone to drop the keys in your lap. You solve problems for a living, fella. Solve this.'

The next afternoon found him at the university in white shirt, tie, shirt-sleeves rolled part of the way up his fore-arms, plastic pocket protector containing three ballpoints and a small screwdriver. A thick briefcase, obviously stuffed with parts and manuals. Nonchalant, bored expression. 'Somebody here call your computer's down?'

The woman at the front desk turned and bellowed into the silent, cavernous room, 'Somebody call the computer people?' The call echoed back between rows of filing cabinets. 'Everybody's gone home.'

'Well, shit,' he said. 'Does anybody know what the problem is? Something about some listing you got on data base? Graduate school, was it? Anybody here know about that?'

'Susan! Somebody's here about the graduate school listings.' Shrill screech, slithering into the spaces.

An echo came in response. 'Back here. . . .'

He ambled back. 'Hi. You the one with the problem? Yeah, well nobody else knows, either. How about I run a test, right? Can you print a list of names and addresses – ah, lessee, all the graduate students.'

'You want 'em alphabetized?'

'Sure, why not. And by department, if you can. Just set it up, if you want. I can wait while it runs if you want to take off. That'll show me where the problem is.'

'You want it, mister, you can stick around for it. I'm not putting in any overtime. This place wouldn't know overtime if it bit 'em. I thought you guys worked regular hours, too. What are you doing here this late?'

58

'Car trouble,' he said. 'I got in two hours late this morning. My lucky day.' He watched with concealed avidity as she set up the listing. 'Want to make it shorter for me, do just female students.'

'What d'you want? A date list?'

'Graduate students? Are you kidding? I met one once.' Which was more or less true.

She gave him a dirty look, hit a backup key, and snarled, 'Chauvinist.'

'Naw, I'd just like to get out of here before midnight is all,' he said mildly, watching the names appear on the screen.

'Lots of luck,' she said, hitting the print key as she rose, ostentatiously preparing to leave. 'The janitors'll be here in an hour or two. If you leave after they do, be sure to lock the door behind you.'

He gave her his lopsided, boyish grin. Unimpressed, she left him without a backward glance as a printer across the room exploded into action. He went to lean on it as if folded sheet after sheet into the bin. The entire run took only twenty minutes, and the stack of forms fitted nicely into the briefcase. He turned off the lights and was careful to lock the door behind him. By morning, no one would even remember he had been there.

9

Mahlia had searched for almost a week before finding a place to live, the ramshackle upper floor of a house in Queens, only a few blocks from the subway. It was the only place she looked at that had no feeling of heaviness, no shading of happening. Nothing had ever happened here. Nothing, so far as Mahlia could tell, ever would happen here. Certainly nothing in the near future. The old couple who lived downstairs spent their days in phlegmatic silence, walking the old dogs, mowing the minuscule lawn. She didn't know what they said or did when alone together. Not a sound came from the lower floor.

She had felt an ominous heaviness when she had first entered Professor Boyce's apartment. Looking around her, she had decided the feeling emanated from things, old things, valuable things. Surely they had seen time enough to be heavy with the bloody history of the race. So she'd discounted her foreboding, setting it aside out of pleasure in the beauty of the place. Now she was feeling guilt over the woman's death, though she knew nothing she could have done would have changed it.

'You cannot change it, Mahlia. It was, or will be, and that's all there is to it.' Her mother speaking, years ago, telling her of the ways of such visions. 'My sister, your Aunt Lualua, saw such things. Often she wept over them, but such is foolishness. Pretend it is television.'

Mahlia had been angry at that. Television indeed. The things she saw were not fictions to be so lightly dismissed, not even by a child of nine.

When challenged with Mahlia's anger, Mama had sighed. 'By the time you see what is to come, my child, it is very near. So little a way ahead that it has become a certainty. Like the bow wave that turns before the racing canoe, so these events turn before the present, to flow by us in their time.'

These words had been more comforting than the earlier ones. Mahlia thought of them often. 'Like the bow wave of the canoe. Already almost happening. Already determined, Mahlia. Pushed up before racing time into a kind of bulge you can see, that's all.' After all, some people were farsighted while others were nearsighted. An ancient warrior of her people would not have been dismayed because he could see the sails of war canoes farther out on the horizon than any other man could see, even though he could not stop their approach. So she rationalized it and learned to live with it.

Besides, the vision had been only part of the reason she had left. The other reason had been Badger Ettison. From the moment his sister had introduced him, the moment he had turned to her with that curious look, brows high in an expression that seemed to say, 'Tell me everything!' – from that moment she had been caught. Caught, eager, and behaving as foolishly as a child. For she had, indeed, told him everything, sought his help, confided in him. And he had done what every other man had done: disbelieved, become angry, mocking, finally distant – as though she had some peculiarly contagious insanity they feared.

And then to have run up to him as he left and blurted out that silly statement!

Except that it wasn't silly.

His son wasn't dead. It was horrible for him to believe that and it not be true. It wasn't a matter of vision. It was simply 'knowing.' There was no way to prove a knowing true, though she had never found one to be false.

Mama had said, 'Our family has always had that. Pay attention to it, but don't talk about it. People don't understand.' Well, they didn't.

And so she had run away. Not to see him again. Not to have to explain when she couldn't explain.

During the day she could forget about it. When night came, however, she found herself wondering about the child. She dreamed of the child and its mother, something happening, a frantic struggle with the child at the center of it. The dream child was nearby, but there was a vacancy where the child's mother had been, and Mahlia was gasping at some monstrous terror narrowly averted. 'Daddy, come get me,' the child called, urgently but without fear. There were great iron gates in the dream, terrifyingly open, and something hunting with an inexorable hunger.

In the morning the dream faded as she sorted out pens and notebook paper, subway tokens and book list. She was off to the library for another day of reading. Cave paintings today. The origin of all art, said Professor Boyce. The origin of man's perception of the world outside himself. She tried to imagine herself into that primitive world in which hunger and the hunter ruled all, spreading upon the rock walls visions of plentiful prey. 'Hunger and the hunter,' she whispered to herself, uncomfortably reminded of the dream she could not quite recall.

10

There were a dozen students with French-sounding names in cultural anthropology. He had hoped that one of them would show the Professor's apartment as a previous address. None did. There were no previous addresses at all. Everything was current. No old card with something half scratched out which patience and the laboratory could make legible again. No ledger full of erasures and corrections. Only this black on white, trim columns of names and places, chill and sterile as a phone book. Grumbling to himself, he flipped the anthropology department to one side and began to plow down the lists from other departments. She had said cultural anthropology, but it had been a kind of jest. Perhaps it wasn't that at all.

Economics. Political science – whatever that was. Fine arts. Literature. Languages. Sciences. Many women, many French names. He would have to hire help if something didn't break. Impossible to follow up on all these alone. Music. History.

History. Was that Professor Boyce's field? Was he a professor of fine arts or of history? Or of archaeology?

Which department would have claimed him? Cursing himself for having ignored so basic a clue, Badger thrust the lists aside and turned to the catalog he had picked up earlier. Would the old man be listed among the faculty at all?

He was. Not in archaeology. In fine arts; more specifically, the history of art.

So, he growled to himself. So, Mahlia Waiwela. So, dear crazy lady. The history of art.

And in the graduate school there was one woman, one, with a Gallic last name. Chalfont. With an address in Queens. Marie Chalfont, in Queens, by God.

11

He was waiting on the doorstep when she arrived home, head down, dragging a bit from the heat and noisy lurching of the subway, unable to become accustomed to the filthy, graffiti-smeared cars. Each morning's and evening's travel was like an assault, an agreed-upon rape that she forced herself to bear but could not ignore. The walk from the subway was a time of recovery, realignment. She did not expect to see anyone she knew so did not see him, found herself looking through him as though he were one of the scraggly lilac bushes along the walk.

'Mahlia,' he said, making it an accusation, forcing himself upon her. 'Or should I say Marie?'

'Wha . . .' she murmured, lost. 'Who? Badger Ettison? What are you doing here?'

'Didn't you expect me to find you? After what happened?'

What had happened? Her mind was full of plunging horses, speared bison. She couldn't, for the moment, think what he was talking about. 'Oh. You mean the woman. The woman who was killed.' Her confusion continued. 'But that had nothing to do with me. Nor you!'

'The police might have felt differently.'

'You didn't go to the police!' She was shocked out of her confusion, suddenly alert to him, to the meaning of his presence. 'You didn't!'

'I did, yes. However, the man I went to is a personal friend, and there will be no consequences. Would you have worried about consequences?'

'When your sister told me what you do – I thought it would be like telling a priest,' she exclaimed dolefully. 'I thought it would be in confidence.'

'I'm not a doctor, not a lawyer, not a priest. It won't cause you any trouble, though. The man I told hasn't even reported it, and won't report it. So, you see, no problem. Unless my finding you causes a problem. I can't guarantee it won't.'

The curtain at the front window was shaking. Behind it, Mahlia could sense two old pairs of prying eyes, two pairs of quivering ears. 'You'd better come inside,' she offered, reluctant. 'We don't want to talk out here.'

'If you like.' He was being careful not to seem impetuous, careful to move slowly. This was a rare bird, undoubtedly a shy one. It wouldn't do to scare it off with sudden, importunate movements. 'If you like,' following her up the creaking, bare stairs and into the barren little rooms, unable to restrain himself. 'Lord, how do you bear it?'

She stood in the center of the room, staring around herself. There was only the threadbare Hide-a-Bed and two straight chairs. Boxes of her books, of course, and the table covered with her reading and notes. Peeling plaster and stained ceiling, flimsy curtains yellow gray with age.

'Yes. Yes, it is ugly compared to the other place. Sometimes in the morning I wake and do not want to open my eyes. There is a stain on the ceiling over the bed which looks like some huge shark, come to swallow me.'

It was said in an uncomplaining, matter-of-fact tone, but for the first time during this encounter he thought of her as a living person rather than as quarry. Mahlia. He had forgotten who she was. 'Mahlia,' he said, testing the sound of it. 'Mahlia.'

'Yes?'

'You could have let me know where you were.'

'I . . . I didn't want to. I thought you would want to ask questions, talk about it. I don't want to talk about it, really. I'm tired of people asking questions, tired of being judged. You don't know what it's like. I would never have asked you for help, except I thought someone who does your kind of work . . .'

'Would be like a priest,' he finished for her.

'Yes. Like that.'

Not like that, she thought. I thought you would be different from the priests, different from other men. I thought. I was wrong.

She dropped the heavy bag on the table. 'Not that priests were ever much help, either. They seemed to think it was my soul at risk rather than my mind.' She sighed. 'But that isn't really why you came, is it?'

'No, not really.' She seemed about to weep, and he could feel her weariness. She had not been sleeping well. There were circles under her eyes.

'It's what I said about your child, your son.'

'You know it is!' He was hot with impatience, controlling himself with difficulty, but controlling himself, conscious of her weariness. 'You had to know. As soon as the other thing happened . . .'

'As soon as the other thing happened,' she repeated for him, 'you knew I wasn't a loony. Not a nut, not a crazy. Not bats. Not mentally ill.' She cast him a cynical look. 'Which, up until then, you thought I was.'

'I admit that. I'm ready to admit I was wrong. You've got . . . got something. I don't know what. Something other people don't have, don't know about.'

'All I've got is trouble,' she announced. 'All my life. Telling people things they didn't want to hear, wouldn't believe. There's no lead time, you know. By the time I see it, either it's already happened or it's so close nothing can change it. Sometimes only a few hours, sometimes a few days. This was the longest, but it was still as unchangeable as stone.'

'But you saw my son!'

69

'*No*. I *knew* you'd think that. I didn't see him. I simply know he isn't dead, that's all. It's another kind of thing entirely.'

'You know where he is!'

'How would I know that?' she asked, astonished tears hanging in her eyes. 'Look, Badger I'm tired. You're getting angry. I can hear anger in your voice. Lord, I've heard it so many times from people. Doubt, and anger, and hostility. Let me make some tea. We'll sit down and talk quietly like people if you'll promise not to yell at me, not to attack me. I've had enough of that. Truly.'

He sat down, unwillingly. In imagination this meeting was to have solved everything. Now there was this reluctant slowing and pacing, a gnawing disappointment that had to be hidden. He waited, chewing on his lip until he tasted blood, then forced his body to assume quiet where none was felt.

'Here,' she said after what seemed an interminable time, offering him a cup. 'You probably don't want this, but I do. Sit there, now, and let me tell you . . . .' She curled onto the couch, like a child, staring into the steamy depths of her cup as though to read some sign there he could not see.

'When I was six years old, I saw the neighbor's house burning down. I told Mama. She told me I'd been dreaming. I told the lady next door, and she cursed at me, calling me a little liar, making up stories. The next night the house burned. I woke up to hear the screaming and shouting. They didn't get the baby out in time. Next day the woman accused me of setting the fire, screaming at me, having hysterics, trying to claw my eyes out . . . .

'Mama said it was only grief, because her baby was dead and I was alive. I remember crying and crying. I used to play with the baby. I would never have hurt the baby . . . .

'Ever since then, I've seen things, sometimes. I can only see what has happened or will happen in the place where I am. If I am here in this room, I may see something that has happened in this room, but I will not see something which happened elsewhere. You have to understand that, Badger.

70

So, sometimes I'd see things – sometimes over and over – and tell Mama, and sometimes she'd say, "Yes, that happened her, right here, so many years ago." Then it wouldn't bother me, no matter what it was. It was just history. Something already over and done with.' She sighed again, and he made a sympathetic movement toward her, restraining himself. She didn't see him.

'It wasn't always bad things. Sometimes it was nice things. Someone getting married, or getting kissed, or finding something lost . . . That was sort of fun.

'When I was nine, we went to the beach. I saw a lady drowning. She had on a purple swimsuit, with pink ties at the legs. I found her. I told her I'd had this terrible feeling she was in danger, begged her not to go in the ocean that day. She laughed. She promised me. Later that day, they brought her body in. Mama told me then that it couldn't be changed. She told me then about her sister, my aunt, who had the same affliction. Those of us who see, we can't see anything, ever, until it's too late to change it.'

He puzzled over this, setting the story she had told him into an orderly array, so occupied by the puzzle of it that for the moment his own insistent demands were secondary. 'And that's what happened at Boyce's place?'

'Yes. I saw it. As I described it to you.'

'And you didn't try to change it, because you'd tried to change things before, and it hasn't worked?'

'Many times.' She sighed, leaning back into the sagging couch. 'It never works. By the time I see it, it's too late.'

'And you haven't seen my son, but you know he's not dead.'

'I know he's not dead. That's all I know.'

He stood up, walked around the little room, stood at her makeshift desk turning pages in her books without seeing them, stared out the window without seeing that. Then, 'Have you ever tried to have a vision?'

'No,' she said wearily. 'No. Of course not.'

'Would you be willing to try? Try for a vision. Of Carolyn? Robby? I must find them. You understand that, don't you?'

Without planning it, he put his arms around her and drew her close, momentarily dizzy with the wild, sweet scent of her hair, so long without holding anyone that he was confused in that instant about whom he was holding.

'If you came to my home – came to places my son used to be, do you think you could *see* anything?'

'Perhaps.' She trembled, half with tiredness, half from the tight possession of his arms. 'Perhaps I could.'

'Will you do it?' Whispering, insistently, his arms and voice demanding her compliance, her complicity. 'Mahlia, will you do it for me, please?'

Lost in that strong circle, she was unable to say anything at all except yes, yes, and yes, caught in such a turmoil of sympathy and fear it prevented any logical thought at all.

12

'I think the best place to start would be my apartment – that is, Carolyn's and mine,' he said. 'It's a fairly big place with a guest suite at one end of it, so pack what you'll need for several days.'

'Pack? You mean . . .' He had changed the subject so rapidly she did not understand him.

'Come stay with me. If you're going to see anything, you'll have to pick it up somewhere where Carolyn or Robby were. That means the apartment. Or possibly her mother's place, though Carolyn and Laura didn't get along well and Carolyn didn't like to go there. I'm not asking you to do anything but come stay for a while.'

'It seems an imposition,' she began in a stiff, uncomfortable voice. His sharpness reminded her she had decided to stay away from this man.

'Oh, hell, lady.' He spun on her angrily. 'Let's not waltz around with polite social chatter. You weren't like that when I met you.'

'You weren't yelling at me when we met!'

'I won't yell at you!' He controlled himself, stopped

yelling at her. 'I'm sorry. I won't yell. I won't bother you! You'll have better surroundings than this, and all I ask is that you tell me whatever you see! If anything!' He turned away, his face working. 'God, this is madness.'

She bit down her responsive hostility, looked at his troubled face, managed to say, 'Sorry. I am sorry. Of course you're upset, and I wasn't making allowances. It's all right. I'll get some clothes. I'll need all of those books, so it would save time if you put them in that box. Did you drive here?' She made a pretence of polite talk, shutting out for a time the doubts and small furies he had roused in her. He had been gentle enough in demanding her help. Why so relentless and brutal afterward? Because . . . because.

Because he could think of nothing but his missing wife and child. He had been driven to the edge of himself and left hanging there. She pictured him so, made an image in her mind of Badger on a high ledge, clinging with his fingertips over a great gulf of air. One could not expect politeness or gentleness under such circumstances. She held the thought as she carried her two small cases down to his car. At the door of the downstairs apartment she spoke soothingly to the suspicious face that peered at her over six inches of brass chain. 'Mail. Rent. Reach me at this number if needed. Back in a few days. Thank you. Yes. Fine. Thank you again.'

In the car she was swerved, caromed, dashed, and flung headlong into traffic, bringing her breathless at last to Badger's place with too little time for the transition.

He took her through the apartment as she caught glimpses of coved ceilings, high paneled walls, glossy old doors with hardware of brass and crystal. The guest suite had its own green-tiled bath, its own tiny terrace, its own minuscule sitting room with flowered love seat and graceful desk. Here among the bright chintzes he seemed for the first time doubtful, uncertain.

'Ah. Would you like to put your things away and then take a look at the rest of the place? Or what?'

She was moved to an irritated patience. 'I hardly know,

Badger. I've never done this before. Suppose you give me fifteen minutes to catch my breath, and I'll come out and take a look.'

He turned and fled, so abruptly as to seem rude, though she knew it was actual flight. She visualized him hanging by his fingers once more to evoke a more sympathetic mood. Then she collapsed onto the comfortable couch and stared blindly out the window over rooftops and water tanks, trying to make sense out of being there. After a few moments, she took skirts and dresses out of her bag and hung them in the closet, leaving the rest of the unpacking for later. She felt better when she left the room and walked back through the apartment, peering into each room in turn, preferring this solitary examination to whatever guided tour Badger might have given her.

Nice old rugs on hardwood floors. Nothing like Professor Boyce's treasures, but these, too, were soft and glowing. A few pictures, very modern, all sweeps and dashes of color that seemed about to say something, go somewhere, but did not, quite. One or two that did, indeed, go somewhere, and that somewhere a disturbing place from which she instinctively turned her eyes. 'These were hers,' she told herself. 'Carolyn's.' She did not ask herself how she knew. She simply knew.

There were one or two ostentatious touches: a leaded bevel glass screen in the dressing room, a sunken marble tub in the master bath. The king-size bed, a quarter acre of hand-woven spread, a soft film of dust on the fabric. Twin closets, his almost empty, hers overfull. He hadn't used this room recently? No, the one he had been using was near the kitchen – a small room with a Spartan white bath.

She paused, puzzled, then turned back down the hall in search of the boy's room, finding it across from the guest rooms. Bright curtains and rugs and a child-sized bed with a bedspread printed to look like a car. On the bed lay a stuffed animal, not a bear, a shifty, fuzzy-edged animal with a black mask. Perhaps a raccoon? When she looked harder, it was gone. Well. Had been? Or would be? And why had this back room been used for the child? Mahlia would have put the child's bedroom beside her own, to hear him more easily when he cried in the night. All children cried in the night. They dreamed of falling or of things coming after them. She was still standing in the doorway, musing, trying to see the stuffed raccoon again when Badger interrupted her.

'That was Robby's room,' his voice harsh. 'We had a nanny for him in the little suite.'

'A nanny?' She considered the implications of this.

'Carolyn had a lot of obligations. Little children aren't the most enthralling company in the world. Besides, it isn't as though we couldn't afford it.'

He has said that before, she thought. Said it more than once, to someone. As perhaps it had been said to him originally. 'Of course.' She nodded. 'It helps to know there was someone else here. Let's go into the living room. I've already been everywhere else.' She led the way, giving him time to settle himself, then perched on the edge of a chair, staring out the generous windows. Nothing there. He offered her a drink, she accepted absently, focused on nothing. So they sat for a time, sipping, not talking at all, but his eyes never left her face, demanding, begging. Finally, she sighed, half tension, half discomfort.

'Badger. I've got some reading to do. I'll just go back there and do it. I'll wander around in here, off and on. Try to ignore me, if you can. It will be more comfortable for me. I'd like to putter about a little, do some dusting, sort of earn my room and board. . . .'

'That isn't necessary. . . .'

'I know it isn't. It will make me feel better, that's all. Otherwise I'll feel as though I have to . . . have to see something, even if I don't.'

'Mahlia, I didn't mean –'

'I know what you meant! I know what you mean!' The anger, so well suppressed, rose all at once in a fury. 'I'm telling you how I feel. I'm not a tool. I'm not a screwdriver you can use to pry open some closed, hidden box. I'm me, and you'll have to consider how I feel about all this. I feel used!' She was close to panic, his silent expectation beating against her like the wings of some great shadow bird, impalpable but perceivable, a fluttering quake against her flesh as though the earth shifted. Anger was her only defence, but it met no opposition, could not refuel itself.

After a moment's abject silence, he said, 'I'm sorry. Truly. Please, do whatever will make you feel best. I'm asking a great deal.' Outside in the twilight the city lights came on, a few, more, many, checkering the skyline. They sat in the reflected shine of the city sky, a bruised luminosity that filled the room with an aching glow. His face brooded in shadows, and in the desire to stroke that face she wondered how risky involvement with this man would really be.

She shook herself, said instead, 'Did Robby have a stuffed raccoon?'

Badger gulped. 'Robber. Robby and Robber. He must have taken it with him that . . . that day. How did you know?'

'I saw it,' she said, dreading his response. It came at once, his face avid and threatening, but it was as quickly repressed. This time she kept her anger in control. He couldn't help it. She went on, gently. 'Nothing that will help us. Just a fuzzy image of the raccoon on his bed. On the pillow.' They sat a few moments longer. 'Let's let it go for tonight. Are you hungry? Can I fix you something?'

'I usually go to the little place on the corner.'

'Do it, then. Do what you usually do. Is there any food here? . . . Good. I'll fix myself an egg or something later. No,' she interrupted him as he began to speak. 'I don't want to go with you. I want to stay here, quietly. You go ahead.' She resolved anew to spend no more time in his company than necessary. Despite the anger he raised in her – or perhaps because of it – he raised other emotions as well. When he turned that burning face on her, she burned in response, melting. Dangerous.

He made no more protests but left like a chastened child.

She stopped in Robby's room on the way back to her own. The phantom raccoon was still missing.

In the days that followed she sometimes saw a little boy slipping around a corner or through a door, always just out of sight. Once she came into the kitchen and saw Carolyn there on the phone, a speaking shadow that began to fade as she stared. 'Mother,' the shadow was saying. 'Can't you let it alone!' Voices in visions were unreliable, tricky, sometimes clear and real, sometimes like echoes. This was real. 'Mother, can't you let it alone?' Let what alone? Mahlia wondered, staring at her own face in the mirror. In that room of chintz and wicker, she did look like an exotic, a wild brown orchid in a patch of sweet William. Let what alone?

That night she told him, 'I'm not getting anything helpful. Let's try some other place. Let's try her mother's place.'

'Carolyn didn't like to visit Laura,' he objected, shifting uncomfortably.

'You don't like her mother, do you?' reading his flush. While he wanted her to use every drop of perspicacity she had, it embarrassed him when it touched himself. 'Why not?'

'Oh, I guess because my sister, Vivian, doesn't like her much. Because Laura is one of those women who spend their whole lives acting a play with a cast of one. Everyone else is audience. Children . . . children move to center stage sometimes, even when one doesn't want them to.'

'And Carolyn did that? As she was growing up?'

'When she grew up,' he said bluntly. 'Carolyn was . . . is very beautiful.'

'I know,' she said, and he did not ask her how she knew. Progress. Perhaps in time he would trust her to do her best without his driving her. 'Nonetheless, I think we should go to Laura's house.'

'Miles's house, too,' he corrected her. 'Carolyn's father. A fine, good man, a little overadoring of Laura, in my opinion. He's the audience who never fails her, always ready with the applause, the standing ovation. I don't know what Laura would do without Miles.'

'How did Miles treat Carolyn?'

'As he treated Laura. No difference. No difference between them at all. He worshipped them both, always.'

'And that infuriated Laura? It would do that, I think, to the kind of woman you describe.'

'Perhaps it did.' He hadn't thought about this, but perhaps it did.

The Beecham house was on Long Island, elegantly laid out on several landscaped acres, every prospect ending in a predictable arrangement of trees and shrubs. It could have been a movie set, quite perfect, quite cold, but it was not this chill that made Mahlia shiver. It was something else.

They stood on the doorstep, the stone facade looming above them, unable to hear whether the bell had rung or not, taking it on faith. After a long time, the door swung open.

'Badger! What are you doing here?' Her eyes were set in graves of violet shadow, fringed with lashes like funereal grasses, a self-consciously tragic face, Helen made up as Hecuba. Unlined skin drew tight over bone, a face as unnaturally youthful as her figure. The clothes were as perfect as the face. She was obviously about to receive guests or go out; the voice was not welcoming. 'Why have you come here?' Shrill, obviously teetering at the edge of dismay.

'What's the matter, Laura?' Badger was surprised at her lack of composure, and it showed. 'Has something happened?'

The woman shook herself, then began to move sections of her face in a drill that ended in a smile of sudden and quite dreadful charm, all dismay and discomfort banished in the instant. Her face became wax with a mannequin's smile, too perfect, imitating life. 'You startled me is all. We haven't seen you in such a long time. Come in. Miles and I are going out, but we've time for a quick drink.'

She led the way to a dimly lit room overlooking the pool. 'We haven't met,' she said to Mahlia. 'I'm Laura Beecham.'

Badger made his own quick introductions. 'My associate,

Mahlia. Mahlia and I happened to be passing, and I decided to drop in for a moment. I haven't seen either of you in far too long.'

'I'll find Miles. Pour yourself a drink.' She waved at the bar as she left the room, and Badger moved gratefully toward it as Mahlia crouched into a chair. The room was peopled, crowded with ghosts, so tight around her that she could not breathe for their presence. Badger turned, saw her face, started toward her with an expression of concern . . .

And the ghosts vanished, all at once, as though someone had turned on a light.

The man who had erupted into the room seemed to have brought that light with him. 'Badger, my boy! I'm so glad to see you. So glad you felt you could come at last.' He was wide and ruddy, iron-gray hair bristling untidily from recent combat with a comb.

Badger was obviously embarrassed. 'I'm sorry, Miles. I haven't been handling things at all well. It was all I could do to keep the working days together. . . .'

'Don't apologize. Not for a moment. Believe me. I understand. We've had our own dismal days. One thinks, somehow, that the sun will never shine again, but one day it does. And that's good. And it should be. Carolyn wouldn't want us to be unhappy.'

'Not for a moment,' echoed Laura in a cold, quiet voice. 'Carolyn was very gay, always. Very happy.' There was almost satisfaction in her voice, a car passing over the corpse of some long-played mouse. Mahlia looked up, startled at the tone, more so at the brave, false smile. The woman was playing a role. Not grieving mother. Mahlia struggled to identify it, came up with 'woman made more beautiful by grief.' The room hummed for an instant, like a hive of bees, a single, ominous note, infinitely extended, fading into silence.

Miles put his arm around his wife, noticing nothing, squeezing her so gently she might have been labeled 'fragile.' There were introductions again. Miles poured drinks for them all. The ghosts slowly returned, and Mahlia kept them at bay, breathing shallowly, while the chatter went on. Carolyn was in the room. Robby was in the room. Doubly. Triply. A swirl of unreconciled, vertiginous motion.

'Miles,' Laura was saying, 'I hate to hurry Badger and Miss Wai-um, but we said we'd pick up the Luces at seven.'

'We'll get on our way,' Badger said, setting down his glass.

'Nonsense,' said Miles. 'You've hardly touched your drinks. You stay here and finish them. The sunset is gorgeous. Let yourself out when you've finished. After all, Badger, you're one of the family.'

Then, as Laura went upstairs to get her coat, he went on, 'I'd always wanted a son, Badger. When you and Carolyn were married . . . well, I had a son. I'd like to go on having a son, if you don't mind.'

Upstairs, with the door shut, Laura stared into the mirror. So he'd always wanted a son. Fat chance. She hadn't been one to make the same mistake twice. She leaned into the mirror, examining her hairline for scars. None. None under her breasts, either. That doctor had been as good as his reputation, and damn well better be. It had taken enough of Miles's money to hire him.

Miles. Miles was easy to handle. When she'd found herself thrown over by that ass Darinbaugh, she'd gone straight to Miles. 'I've always loved you, Miles. Marry me, Miles. Right now.' And he'd been so thrilled by her proposal he'd never thought to ask why, or why then. Never thought to ask why Carolyn was born so early.

She went downstairs, ignoring Badger's obvious discomfort at being expected to stay. Good. Next time he'd think to call first, and she could make some excuse to put him off. Miles might want a son, but she wanted nothing more to do with Badger Ettison. She gave him a chilly smile as she went out, Miles's arm around her.

'It's so good to see Badger again,' he was saying. 'Even though it brings it all back. Then I remember how happy she made us. Only one time she gave us any worry at all, that time she ran off with that Shiel fellow. One time. Only once in her entire life.' He wiped his eyes, helping Laura into the car. He had gone after Carolyn that time. He'd had to charter a helicopter to get into the place, but at least he'd had sense enough to take two sheriff's deputies with him. Miles was convinced they might not have gotten out of the place except for that. Michael Shiel might look like God's gift to women, but Miles knew that type when he smelled it, whether the bastard was the son of an old friend of Laura's or not.

He got into the car and took Laura in his arms, a little guilty for having thought of her critically that way. He held her so he couldn't see her face. A long time ago he had begun holding her like this, so he could talk to her without seeing her face. When he looked directly at her, he sometimes forgot who she was. He began to think she was someone else, and yet Laura hadn't changed. She was as young-looking today as the day twenty-nine years ago when she had said, 'Marry me, Miles.'

'Only one time in her life she caused us any worry,' he said again.

Laura disengaged herself. 'We're late, dear.' She patted his shoulder, wishing not for the first time that he had not gone after Carolyn that time. Life would have been so much easier if he had just left her there, with Michael Shiel. Twelve or thirteen years of Carolyn had been fourteen too many for Laura. Not for Miles. Miles couldn't see anything unless you rubbed his nose in it, and sometimes not even then.

For a moment something appeared on Laura's face that was not quite Laura herself, something quick and snakelike, a flicker and no more. In the instant, it was gone. Neither Miles nor Laura saw it. Since that night almost three decades before when Laura had wandered to the center of the maze field mouthing ugly curses against Henry Darinbaugh, since that moment when the thing had first found a place in her, she had never seen it and he had learned not to.

13

When Badger returned to the room he found Mahlia bent forward with her head on her knees, her shoulders heaving soundlessly. He patted her, uncertain what was wrong or what he could do about it.

'I'll be all right,' she said, voice grating. 'They're here, Badger. In this room. Shadows, one on top of the other, like a whirlpool. I can't sort them out.'

'Still?' he asked. 'With them gone?'

She raised her head. The room had emptied itself of the whirling shadows as a pool does after rain, from the turbid to the clear. 'You thought it was her?'

'It's just that you looked very uncomfortable when she came down the stairs. I thought maybe you were sensing something about her.'

'They were worse when she was here. More of them. Unsettled, twirling around. Gone now, but not far. I can still feel them.'

'Do you want to stay?'

'God, no. I want to run! That woman, Badger. There's something in her, inside her. It's like touching a snake. Like

83

looking down and seeing some huge spider crawling on your chest.'

'Well, Laura's not the easiest person in the world to –'

'I'm not talking about that! Oh, don't be stupid, please, I'm trying to tell you something! I'm not talking about any *personality* thing. It's something else. Something dreadful. I wish I'd never met her.'

'We'll go.'

'We can't,' she moaned. 'They're here. I need to see! You need for me to see. I'm tuned to them now – I don't see anyone else. You want me to see them so badly that I *can't* see anything else. They're going to be here, haunting me until it's over. I have to finish it.' She sighed wearily. 'Maybe another drink.'

'You haven't drunk that one.'

She looked at it, pale around the remaining bits of ice. 'I'd like a fresh one.'

He poured for her. She sipped, stared around her, looking for the invisible array, gradually relaxing as the earlier terror did not return. Evening shadows moved, tossed from branches of windy trees, moon shadows, nothing more than that. Quiet breathed in through a half-opened window, moving the curtain into gauzy wings against the dark. Dark. Against which forms were appearing, dimly at first, then more brightly. A child playing on the rug. Two women, confronting one another. . . .

'Badger. I see them.'

He leaned forward, watching her face as she spoke, looking sometimes where she was looking, baffled to see nothing when she obviously saw so much.

'Laura is sitting on the couch. Her face is very cold and angry. She says, "I want it back, Carolyn. Now."'

'Carolyn is standing by the mirror. She laughs. She says, "Mother, can't you leave it alone?"'

' "It's mine. Miles gave it to me. I want it back."'

'Carolyn turns to look in the mirror. She has on a necklace – oh, sparkling in the light. Stroking it with her fingertips. "It looks better on me than it does on you. Miles wouldn't mind. He's always like me better, anyhow.''

'Oh, Laura's face. Angry. Ugly. Like some demon mask. She's . . . she's saying – I couldn't hear. No. She says ''. . . wonder if he'd like you so much if he knew he wasn't your father.''

'Carolyn says . . . something. Calls Laura a liar, that's it. Angry. Robby looks up from his play. They hush, looking away from each other. Carolyn won't leave it alone. ''Liar,'' she says. ''You were always a liar, Laura.'' '

Mahlia looked around herself, dazed, eyes unfocused. 'I've lost them. Nothing. Wait. No, there they are. Laura says, ''I only married Miles because I was pregnant. It wouldn't matter now. Back then it did. Your father was a man named Darinbaugh. Henry Darinbaugh, from Baleford. I didn't want you, Carolyn, and neither did he. He told me any child of his would be in terrible danger. Aren't you curious, Carolyn? Don't you wonder why?'' '

Badger made a rough, unintelligible noise. She shushed him. 'Shhh. It's fading. I can hardly hear what they're saying. Carolyn grabs Robby up, starts for the door. ''Laura, you were always a liar.''

'She's running out. Laura is screaming after her. ''Better find out what the danger is, Carolyn. Maybe it's a genetic disease. Something you ought to know. Before it's too late.''

'Now Laura is standing at the mirror. She looks at herself. Strokes her hair. She's shaking, but she's smiling. She seems satisfied. Why? Why?'

Then Mahlia crumpled, the room, the images, the sounds all fading into a vague gray haze. Badger caught her as she fell.

She did not come to herself until they were half-way home. Even then it was a hovering kind of consciousness, a dreamy retreat. She heard his voice.

'I'm sorry, Mahlia. I think you blew a fuse. It's only strain. You'll be all right.' He was trying to convince himself, she could tell, but the dreamy withdrawal wouldn't let her speak except to murmur at him.

'Just sleep. Be okay, just sleep.'

She awoke in the late morning, still dressed in her slip and panty hose but with dress and shoes neatly set aside and the covers pulled over her. Assuming he had gone, she staggered out into the apartment in her robe, her body aching for food as though she had run a marathon.

He was sitting at the kitchen table, whiskery, an empty coffee cup before him and evidence of more than one pot brewed during the night.

'You seemed to be sleeping well when I looked in on you.' He shrugged, rubbed his chin. 'At least you look rested.'

She nodded, half-shy, half-angry. The night before had faded into a kind of dream embarrassment, barely remembered. 'I seem to have passed out,' she said. 'That's never happened to me before.'

'If it had ever happened to me, you couldn't get me to do it again – not for any reason. I've been sitting here kicking myself. Part of me is concerned enough about you to call the whole thing off. The rest of me simply wants to get on with it. I've been thinking, most of the night.'

'I've never believed she was dead. She wouldn't have died that way. Oh, a car accident, maybe. Victim of a murder, maybe. She's so lovely, and not too sensitive to how people feel. Women like that do get murdered. You read about it all the time. . . .'

'Surely not all that often, Badger. Surely –'

'What I'm trying to say is there were reasons I didn't believe she was dead. Don't believe she is dead. That kind of death just doesn't equate with what I know about Carolyn. You saw what really happened. She had one of her fights with her mother, certainly not the first, probably not any more vituperative than most. When Laura had a drink or two, she could let go and play wicked witch with the best of them.'

Mahlia, remembering what she had seen the night before, did not think Laura had been alone in playing wicked witch. Certainly Carolyn had not been Snow White.

'So, in the middle of this argument, Laura got mad enough to tell the family secret. Carolyn isn't Miles's biological daughter. As though anyone cares, these days. The real father is someone named Darinbaugh who lives in Baleford. There's a Baleford in upstate New York, and I'll give you odds that's where Carolyn went.'

'And Robby?'

'Well, Carolyn would have gone to find this Darinbaugh character, immediately and without thinking how upsetting that might be for Robby. She didn't really see Robby as a little person – he was more of a pet to her. Now we have to follow her, don't we? There's nothing for us to do but follow?'

He leaned toward her, grasping her shoulders in hands that were full of nervous strength, trembling but hard upon her; his skin where it touched her own above the low neck of the robe burned like fire. She shivered in response, but he took it for another kind of trembling. 'You're cold. I had the windows open in here to air it out. . . . Well? Will you help me follow her . . . them?'

She could not answer him. The sense of threat, of danger, was smothering. She avoided the question with another. 'Why would she have run off like that? Without telling you?'

'Oh, my dear, that's the least of it,' he said with weary patience. 'Not only why she ran off, but why did she come back and fake that accident? Carolyn is the only one who could have done it. It wasn't enough to run away. She had to make us think she was dead.'

'All right,' Mahlia agreed. 'So it was more than merely running away. But why take Robby? She wasn't used to caring for him – someone else did that. You said she wasn't really concerned with him as a person. Why take him?'

'There's only one reason I can think of. Robby talked. Like a little parrot, repeating things he heard. He would have heard everything at Miles's place. If she took him wherever she went afterward, heaven knows what he saw and heard. If she had left him behind, he would have told me everything.'

'Whatever it was. . . .'

'Whatever it was, it was so important, or terrible, or frightening that the only way she could deal with it was to disappear. And she would have known I would follow them forever, if necessary . . . unless they were dead!'

Follow her forever. The words hummed in Mahlia's mind, and the tingle of her skin where his hands rested turned to a soft, shameful burning. Oh, shame. Here she was tingling at his touch, and he thinking only of his wife, his child. She flushed, turned away from him, making him release her. 'And you want me to help you follow.'

'I want you to help me follow. Yes. And I'll try to be patient, and not yell or badger you or use you as though you were some kind of battering ram. I promise.' His voice was almost tender, and she shivered again, biting her lip as she set all the liquid feelings aside.

'All right. If you'll keep your promise, I'll do what I can. When do you want to leave?'

'As soon as I can get the car serviced and pick up a few things. Can you do without all your books for a few days?' He was trying to make a small joke, trying to be light and easy for her, and she responded with a tremulous half smile.

'I'll take a couple. Thick ones.' He accepted this, leaving her with what she considered an impersonal pat, as though she had been a puppy he had stroked on the street. Sighing, she refilled her coffee cup and went back to the bright little rooms to shower.

The phone rang while she was washing her hair. She answered to hear the breathy annoyance of a very well recognized voice.

'Mahlia? I have been pursuing you over six counties since very early this morning. I have just arrived. I have learned of my idiot elderly nephew and his so violent affair in my apartment. Foolish old fart! At his age!'

'Professor Boyce?'

'Who did you think? Genghis Khan? We have this in common, Genghis and I. We have both spent the latter part of our lives in a most mysterious East. Ah. Child, I have seen such things! There was a jade carving of a goddess would take your breath into your throat for a thousand years. They would not give it to me. I was annoyed. I was hurt.'

'When did you get back?'

'Did I not say? Just. Within the day. I have been trying to locate you since last night. At last, I bethought me, you use that Gallic name in your dealings with academe, so with proper reference to it I was given a number in the benighted boondocks of Queens. Why did you not fly to Ultima Thule and be done? The woman there – though it may have been some other primate taught vestiges of human speech – gave me this number. Where are you?'

'Are you home? With the dogs?'

'My puppsies have greeted me with such joy! Ah, little loves. They say you ungratefully left them to the middle class attentions of the manager's wife, who has fattened them abominably upon meat scraps and buttered toast. Sanbandarong has gained half a pound.'

'Can I come to see you? Right now. I have to talk to you.'

'Well, of course, my child.' The self-amused old voice dropped abruptly into concern. 'Are you all right, Mahlia?'

'Not really. I mean, I'm all right, but I'm not all right. Look, I'll be there within the hour.' She rubbed at her hair with the towel, rummaging through the still half-packed suitcase, slipping into a loose cotton dress and sandals, her bare brown legs smooth as silk above them. She would have to let her hair hang, it was still wet. She repacked the suitcase, put the two thick books into her carryall, and carried bag and suitcase to the door, where she left the one with a note. Badger could pick her up at Professor Boyce's when he was ready to go. Meantime . . .

Meantime, the Professor was the nearest thing to a tahua she had. Not a priest – not like those priests in France who had seemed either to flee from her as though they smelled brimstone or to hover over her like some bird of prey, a soul to be saved by any means at all – and not a doctor, but a wise old man for all his outrageous, dramatic talk.

He met her at the elevator, escorting her in a wake of dogs

to the door of the apartment, standing there, blocking her way, not letting her enter until she had seen it – the newest acquisition, a shining jade figure almost two feet tall, slim, incredibly graceful, a drop of opal water falling from one raised hand.

'You said they wouldn't give it to you!' she exclaimed.

'They wouldn't give me the other one,' he said, preening. 'This one, of course, what could they do? We have discovered a Praxiteles of the Orient.'

'Praxiteles didn't carve in jade.'

'How would we know? If he had done so, they would have been like these. Ah, Mahlia. How dreadful a thing for you, though you had prudently fled long before. Why?' Suddenly he was beaky-nosed peering into her face, intent as though he held a magnifying glass. 'I say, why? How did you know to run?'

She sighed, already half in tears.

'Ah. So. Emotion. Well, you will come sit with me in the room of the quiet Buddha and tell me all about it.'

When Badger came to pick her up two hours later, she had told, cried, been dramatically denounced for drama-tizing herself (a guilt the Professor seemed not to share), and he had packed a small case. 'Ah,' he said upon being introduced. 'So you are the neighbor's brother? You are more sensible-looking than one might have hoped, and I seem to remember remarking so when I saw you last. I am going with you.'

Badger tried polite bafflement and followed it by outright anger, to which the Professor presented a placid face and a hand that, when it was not polishing his bald pate, waved in Badger's face.

'Young man, young man. Here is my charge, my child, my student, in this country because I seduced her here, all adrift in your behalf, and you would deny me the right to go along on this endeavor? Ha? What if she is mad? Had you thought of that? You'll need a witness to her delusions or we'll never get her properly confined. Say she is not! Worse yet! Who is to confirm this wild tale should the proper authorities need to be summoned? No. I am set. Determined. I go with you.'

'Mahlia . . .' Badger pleaded, looking at his watch.

'He's ready to go,' she said implacably. 'You're the one who's holding us up.'

There was only one further delay – that occasioned when Badger found that the Professor intended to bring the dogs. Once that point had been made clear, they departed. Mahlia silent, yet somehow more relaxed in the front seat beside fuming Badger. The Professor, no less loquacious while travelling than while at rest, with Ting, Bing, and Ching around and upon him.

14

It was almost noon the next day when they arrived in Baleford. Darkness and repeated encounters with road construction had delayed them. They had spent the night in a motel not far from Baleford, but the morning brought more road construction involving a lengthy detour, and then a last delay occasioned by their driving through Baleford without noticing it. They had to turn and go back.

'So this is Baleford,' said the Professor, looking about him at the three buildings within sight. One of the three, labeled in faded red and black paint as 'Sourwood's,' appeared to be a kind of general store cum gas station, where they inquired for Darinbaugh.

There were two men seated on the porch of the place, one silent and saturnine who stared beneath black brows from eyes so dark that they seemed to be all iris, shadowy holes sucking the questioner in without offering anything at all.

The other man was round and forthcoming. 'Darinbaugh, huh? Well now, I 'member only one person askin' for Henry Darinbaugh in twenty-five years. Now all of a sudden ever'body wants Henry Darinbaugh. Too late, though. He's dead.'

'Oh, Lord,' Badger murmured hopelessly. 'When did he die?'

'Few weeks ago is all. Some folks say heart and some say he starved himself, and some say Halfies-Annie – that's the only kin he had, poor soul – killed him for his woodpile.'

If the talker was immoderately amused at this, the other was no less irritated. He sneered, stared at each one of them as though to memorize their faces, then demanded, 'What business you got with Henry Darinbaugh?'

Badger stiffened. Beside him, the Professor broke in with easy loquacity. 'Boyce is my name, sir. Professor Myron Boyce. I don't think we've had the privilege of learning yours.'

A moment's flash of demonic anger crossed the heavy face. 'My name's my own business.'

'Then I'm afraid our business is our own business.'

'Henry Darinbaugh didn't have any business that wasn't my business,' the other replied ominously, trying to stare them down. 'He owed me, Henry did.' They did not retreat. The Professor regarded the man mildly, Badger with growing anger, Mahlia with wonder. Unable to dominate them, he sneered again, made a rude gesture in Mahlia's direction, then stalked around the corner of the building, spitting copiously as he went.

'Don't let old Jared Shiel bother you,' the talker went on. 'Him and Henry Darinbaugh used to be real close, thirty years ago. Time and the devil, you know that sayin'? Time and the devil comes between friends? Well, did with them. Some say Jared sold his soul, so maybe it was a real devil did it, though I'd be inclined to lay it to ordinary meanness. Now he doesn't want to hear spit about Henry Darinbaugh, and I don't suppose Henry wanted to hear spit about him.

'Now, if you was to go out the road here about half a mile, you'd come to a bridge going off to the left. If you was to take that bridge, you'd come to a silo, half tumbled down, and just beyond that another road going off right. Nobody there now, though, 'cept maybe old Henry's niece, Halfies-Annie. Place isn't even a little through probate yet, but Annie Sudbury just can't wait. If you was wantin' to make an offer on something old Henry had, now'd be a good time to do it. Once the courts are through with it, it's as good as gone.'

'Ah . . . Mr . . . .ah . . .' Mahlia stumbled.

'Name's Aldin Sourwood. Tenth one of that name. Been Sourwoods here for 'most as long as there's been Darinbaughs. Old Henry's family and my family came on the same boat, back in the sixteen hundreds, if you can believe it. At least, that's what they tell us.'

'Mr. Sourwood, does the niece come from around here? I mean, would she know about Mr. Darinbaugh's affairs?'

'Halfies-Annie? Does a pup drink buttermilk? There's no affairs around here Annie doesn't know about, you can believe that. If old Henry had any, Annie knew about 'em.' He smiled a slow, reflective smile. ''Course Henry might have tried to keep some things private. In that case, it'd be Ron Frolius or Molly, his missus, who'd know about it, 'cause they took care of the place for him and kept quiet about it. And in that case, you'll likely not find out about it, either.'

Badger was hardly paying attention as Mahlia repeated the directions once more, but he found the bridge, the broken silo, the ponds, and then a high, ancient gate with stone pillars at either side and a dark, furtive ruin glimpsed between them. With a collective sigh they left the car once more, Ting, Bing, and Ching scurrying off on business of their own while the humans stretched and stared, wondering what to do next.

They stood in a cobbled courtyard, long stables to their right, half doors missing or hanging in rotted fragments from rusted hinges. Inside, the stems and tangles of greenbriar mixed with blackberry filled the stalls and protruded above the eaves, broken rafters making only a symbolic sketch of roof against the sky.

To their left were the remains of other outbuildings, one

recently patched with bright new shingles. Through a narrow window they could see stacks of salvage neatly arranged and labeled for sale. The Professor leaned against the glass to peer at wood and metal, drying racks and beehives, old hinges and latches, chairs with broken legs. 'Early Colonial,' he muttered. 'Absolutely authentic early Colonial. Good Lord.' Just inside the window was a painting of a brown-robed friar standing amidst an alchemical litter, a pair of odd spectacles on the table beneath his hand. 'Now what? That would have been thirteenth century. Surely not!' Shaking his head, he moved back out into the sunlight to stand beside Badger, staring at the house.

Low fieldstone walls crouched in the shadow of a ruined barn, dwarfed by the high-pitched, bulky roof. 'My God,' the Professor said. 'The roof is thatched. Where would he have found thatchers in New York?'

They shifted uncomfortably while the little dogs ranged back and forth around them, silent as small shadows about their affairs. When the voice interrupted, the dogs were as surprised as the people.

'Something I can do for you folks?'

They turned to confront a rangy man in clean, worn overalls and a faded shirt who regarded them calmly from equally faded blue eyes. 'Somethin' you wanted?'

Badger stepped forward, holding out his hand. 'We're trespassing, I know, but we came looking for a Mr. Henry Darinbaugh. The man at the store told us he had died.'

'That'd be Aldin Sourwood? Right. Well, he told you fact. Henry Darinbaugh died, and his niece will inherit the place soon as the law gets through with it.' He stood silent then, looking them over, while they tried to decide what to do or say next. It was Mahlia who broke the silence.

'Are you Ron Frolius? You looked after the place, I guess? Well . . . you might know whether a tall, blond woman with a little boy came here. It would have been about a year ago. In the springtime. This is Badger Ettison, and his wife disappeared about then . . . and his son . . .' She let her voice trail away, meeting no encouragement.

The man was looking at her very intently, examining her from feet to head, face a little puzzled.

'Foreigner, are you?' he asked finally. 'You got a little accent there.'

'Not really,' she said slowly. 'I came to New York from Montreal. They speak French in Montreal. But Canada isn't really foreign.'

'S'true,' he admitted, sucking a tooth. 'People there came from the same places the people here did. How about you?' He turned to the Professor, who was pointedly ignoring him as he examined the worn carvings above the windows of the house.

'Me? Why, Mr. Frolius, I'm as foreign as the moon and as domestic as cheese. I've been everywhere in the world and seen everything there is to see, but I'd still like to know where a man living in New York State finds thatchers in the twentieth century.'

'Found 'em next door to my place,' Ron replied. 'Me and my brother Wilson and his boys. No trick to it. All we had to do was look at how they did it before, and we've done it twice. I figure it only needs it once ever' twenty years or so. Now it'll never need it again, likely. Halfies-Annie's goin' to sell it, and whoever buys it'll tear it down. All mice and dust inside.'

'When was it built?' the Professor asked reverently. 'I'd swear it was seventeenth century.'

'Well, you'd swear right. Been here a long time, that one. Built it up in 1690, old Henry said. Same time my ancestors built the mill. Mill burned down in the eighteen hundreds sometime, but the Darinbaugh house kept standin'.'

'And you say it will be torn down? That's sacrilege! That's immoral! Why, it ought to be preserved. It may be the earliest building this side of the Hudson!'

'Don't know who's goin' to preserve it,' Ron said. 'Nobody knows it's here. Old Henry kept himself to himself, pretty much.'

'Look,' said Badger, unable to restrain himself. 'This is all very interesting, and I'm sure the historical society of wherever the hell we are will be delighted about this find, but we came to find out about my wife and child.'

Ron nodded, as though agreeing with some suggestion made previously. 'You come on up to my house and talk to Molly. Maybe we can help you out some. First road to the right, up the hill.' And he vanished behind the stables, obviously into some runway through the greenbriar known only to himself. Badger raised his hands in a gesture of frustration and climbed back behind the wheel, waiting in a finger-tapping impatience while dogs and people assembled themselves.

'Calm, my boy,' the Professor urged. 'Calm. Nothing gained by this agitation. We progress, we progress. One thing leads to another. Day to night. Shadow to substance. Come, Padmasambhava! Come, Thisrongdetsan! Come, Sanbandarong! Mount thy steed!'

They left in a flurry of dust, not seeing Jared Shiel where he had hidden among the briar on the far side of the court-yard, close enough to hear everything that had been said. He stared after them for a time, face graven in an expression of fury, then turned away through the thickets toward the Shiel house upon its wind-curved hill.

Ron Frolius was waiting when they arrived. A short, plump woman stood beside him, hands rolled into her apron in a gesture that Mahlia recognized from her years in France. So the farmwives of Aunt Irene's estate had stood, respectful, quiet. So Mahlia thought. For a moment. Until she saw the woman's eyes.

Molly Frolius had eyes that were wild, intent, and power-ful. And yet, Mahlia found herself thinking, half-hysterically, that they held one of the most detached expres-sions she had ever seen on a human face, though she had seen tigers look out at her from photographs or the television screen with precisely that calm, emotionless ferocity. Not bears. Bears were more curious than that. Though why such a plump little body with such round cheeks and a kindly mouth should have eyes that stared at her like those of a predatory beast, she could not say. Feeling like prey, she shivered. Hunger and the hunter, her mind said, apropos of nothing.

'This is m'wife, Molly,' Ron Frolius said, nodding toward her.

The woman smiled. The tiger look was gone, replaced by a friendly warmth. 'You come inside,' she instructed. 'Let the doggies run around out here. There's nothing can hurt them, and I'll shut the storm door so they can see we haven't left them. I've got some ice tea, and Ron says you're lookin' for the woman was here last year. My, isn't that awful! Disappeared, with your little boy? Just awful!' She chatted them inside, disposing them about the kitchen table as though she had known them for years. 'Now, Ron says you want to know about the blond lady. You mind just tellin' me a little bit about it?' Again, just for an instant, that predatory look of disinterested calculation.

'Carolyn Ettison was . . . is my wife,' Badger began a little hesitantly. 'We have a little boy, Robby, who would be about five now. A year ago, my wife found out that . . . that she is related to a man named Henry Darinbaugh. We believe she came here to meet him with Robby, and right after that she disappeared. Until just recently, we thought she was dead . . . she and my son. But now we're not sure.'

'I'm sure,' said Mahlia. Molly turned her tiger's gaze upon her, and Mahlia shivered but refused to be subdued. She tried to adopt a bland, distant, faintly tigerish expression of her own, needing to let this strange woman know that she, Mahlia, was no inconsiderable creature to be stared down in this way. 'I'm sure, Mrs. Frolius. The little boy is alive.'

'Is he now?' Molly breathed, smiling slightly, as though she had recognized some kinship in Mahlia's expression. 'Is he? And you're sure of it?'

'He is. I don't know about Badger's wife. But his son is alive. I know it!'

'Do you? Well, well. You all have some more ice tea while I get us some cookies. Just baked this morning, and they're Ron's favorite.' She rose and disappeared into the pantry, from which crockery noises came.

Molly returned with a plate heaped with oatmeal cookies, fat with raisins and nuts. 'When Ron told me the woman had been here, I had a trouble hunch. I just knew someone would come lookin' for her sooner or later. Ron, you tell 'em what happened.' There was nothing in her face but housewifely concern. For a moment, Mahlia thought she had been imagining things. This was only a farmwife. Yes. No. No! Mahlia sat down, shaking a little, making herself listen.

'She come along here last year,' he began, rustily clearing his throat and looking at Molly from time to time for approval, in the manner of a man who spoke little and not often. 'Her'n the little boy. His name was Robby, he told me that. Told me his daddy did big secret work. Told me his mommy came to find him a new grandaddy, which didn't make a lot of sense. Anyhow, while him'n me was havin' this conversation, old Henry was talkin' to his mother when suddenly the old man turned yellow as cornbread, Henry did, and I thought he'd fall down right there. We was all there in the courtyard, and I started to go catch him before he folded up on the cobbles.

'Well, he pulled himself together and waved me to go on about my business. Then he talked to the woman and talked, on and on, and I was tryin' to keep the little fella interested and away from 'em. Didn't look to me like the kind of talk you want a little fella in on. She kept arguin' and arguin' with old Henry, and finally he throws up his hands.' Here Ron thrust both hands high in a gesture of despair, dramatic, unlike his phlegmatic self.

'He threw up his hands like that, then takes her by the hand and drags her through the woods to the maze field. Well, never mind about what that is, I'll show it to you pretty soon. Anyhow, I follow along with the little guy, and when Henry and the woman start into the maze, him'n me stand there at the edge of the woods and watch.

'Well, Henry unlocked the gates, and he started in, with the woman comin' after him, and he had those old spectacles on his nose, trottin' in there 'round and 'round. They

100

went 'round in the maze, you understand? Not across it, the way you'd go ordinarily if you was just lookin' at it. He comes pretty close to the middle, not right in the middle, you understand, but pretty close, and he stops and gives those spectacles to . . . what was her name? Carolyn? Well, she puts 'em on, and she peers and peers like at something there in the middle, and then she lets out a screech that'd wake up a man six days dead.

'Well, he grabs at her then, and I grab at the little guy to keep him from runnin' to his mommy. There's old Henry shakin' her like you do a kid that's having a tantrum, and talkin' to her loud, almost yellin'. Then she comes runnin' out of there across the maze like the devil was after her.

'She goes by me too fast to catch, grabbin' up the little boy as she goes, and I hear their car start up right away. Meantime, old Henry's locking the gates one by one, comin' across the maze to do it. He found the spectacles where she dropped 'em, and he comes up to me panting and white, clutching his side. I thought he'd die, right there.'

'What did he say?' Badger asked from a dry throat. 'Did he say anything?'

'Said . . . What was it? I told you, Molly. What was it he said?'

'You told me he said something about Laura Benedict having a beautiful face and a lying mouth. And something about her child being damned and wishing to God he had her here to make her pay for it.'

'That's right. And after a little bit he said, 'Poor child, poor little boy.' He was talking about the little fella.'

Badger leapt to his feet with a muttered obscenity. 'This is crazy, damn it! This is the silliest story I've ever heard. Carolyn came here with Robby; she met Henry Darinbaugh and talked with him. Darinbaugh was upset. I'd be upset, too, finding out I had a daughter I'd never known about. So then they argue, right?' Ron nodded. 'And he takes her somewhere and shows her something, after which she runs away screaming. It doesn't make sense!'

101

Ron shook his head stubbornly, refusing to be angered by this. 'Hey, now there, mister, I didn't say it made any sense. Matter of fact, when I told Molly about it, I said, "Molly, it don't make any sense at all." I just told you what happened, that's all. I'll take you out there and show you where it happened, too, soon's I take care of a couple of things.' He left the room, very erect, much in possession of himself and his offended dignity while Mahlia and the Professor stared after him and Badger went on fuming.

'Do you understand any of this?' he asked Molly, who regarded him calmly as she continued chewing on a cookie.

'There's not much I know,' she said with a sidelong tigerish look at Mahlia. 'I used to work for Henry Darinbaugh's daddy. Henry was real set on marrying the Benedict girl, that is up till him and his daddy had a long yellin' match one night and Henry sent her packin'. I guess we can all figure out she must've been pregnant at the time, though this is the first I've heard of it.' The last of the cookie was nibbled up as well as the scattered crumbs from her ample bosom. 'Mahlia, will you help me clear these glasses? Ron'll be back in a minute.' She led the way, Mahlia coming thoughtfully behind.

The occasion seemed a contrivance of Molly's to get Mahlia away alone. When they were behind pantry doors, Molly fixed her with that fierce stare and said, 'Girl, you're all mixed up in something here that's none of your business. Your mama or somebody must have told you it's better not to get involved, but here you are in the middle of this and it's none of your affair!'

There was no reason Mahlia should have answered her. No reason at all. 'I know,' Mahlia said, whispering. 'I didn't mean to.' She could not keep silent when this woman asked her a question.

'What was it? Something about the little boy?'

She was unable not to answer. The words were squeezed out of her like toothpaste from a tube. 'Badger thought he was dead. We were at a party, and we'd been drinking. His brother-in-law said something about his wife and child being

102

dead, and I didn't think. I said he wasn't dead. That's all.'

'I suppose you just knew that, right? Surely you did. Well, that's the way of it, isn't it? Don't I know that from experience. But that isn't all. There's more to it than that. Why would he take your word, out of nothing?'

Mahlia struggled, gave in. 'Oh, there was something else. I kind of . . . predicted something. And it did happen. So that's when he remembered what else I'd said. . . .'

'Gave you a little what-they-call credibility, did it? Oh, yes, he'd remember. That one has a mind like a trap, nothing gets loose from it. And you're in that trap now, child, like it or not. But you're not pulling out of it, either, are you. You want to go on . . . because of him, is that it?'

Mahlia flushed. 'He . . . he . . .'

'Oh, don't "he . . . he . . ." at me. He's a man. Obviously. More of one than I've seen in some time. All nervy and twitchy like steel wires humming, and the power flowing through him and you quivering. And you're a pretty thing full of life and juice who's been savin' it up for something. Why? Girl your age ought to have sixteen lovers to the acre.'

Mahlia could only shake her head miserably. Not sixteen lovers, not six, not one. Why go into it. Why talk about Mama's cautioning, 'Don't get too close, Mahlia. When they find out what you are, they'll mistrust you, draw away from you, hurt you.' Why talk about Aunt Irene. 'Nonsense, girl. You're no different from any other adolescent chit, full of fancies and dirty little lusts. Do you think I wasn't young? I can remember. Keep away from the boys, Mahlia. Those from good family won't have you, and those from bad families you wouldn't want.' Or the priests to whom she had gone for some feeling either of understanding or absolution. 'These fancies come close to sin, Mahlia, if not something worse. Pray to God to forgive you, to turn your mind from these wicked fancies. . . .'

She shook her head again. 'There hasn't ever . . . ever been anyone, that's all. But Badger, he . . . he . . .'

'There you go again. He knows what you can do, but he

accepts it, is that it? He believes you. Believes in you. Well, of course. Why wouldn't he? And that would be mighty attractive to a little girl who's been warned off and warned off. Oh, don't look at me like that, girl. I can read you in your face. So, now what's to do except go along with it? Ahh? Oh, girl, girl, I wish I'd had the rearing of you. Twitchy as a siskin, you are, and a match for that man, both of you jittering around like summer lightning. . . .

'Well, it's against my principles and all good sense, but I'll help as I can. Old Henry Darinbaugh had some things with him when he died: a book – funny old thing full of scribbles, some of it not in English, either – and a pair of spectacles and a bottle. You tell Ron you want those three things. That's all we've got, but the old man was carryin' 'em when he died, so they must have been important. And if you ever set eyes on Halfies-Annie or Jared Shiel, not a word, do you hear!'

Mahlia felt tears welling into her eyes, a hard lump in her throat. 'I . . . I feel all lost. I don't know what to do. What . . . why . . . are you like me? Can you see things? Do you just know things?'

The woman became quiet, almost wary, gave her a side-long, conspiratorial look. 'Don't be silly, child. Of course not. Would I admit it if I could? There was a time women got hanged by the neck just for being suspected of that, you know. Time changes; time stays the same; that's what I say. You go on, now. Remember, you ask Ron for the things old Henry had with him when he died. Don't worry about your Badger. He's a strange one. By this time he'd be disappointed if you didn't do something strange, too.'

When Ron returned, noticeably washed and combed, Mahlia asked him in a small voice if she might have the things the old man had with him when he died. 'Spectacles,' she said, quavering. 'And his book, and the bottle.'

Ron cast Molly an accusing glance, but she refused to look up from the darning she had put in her lap. 'Molly told you,' he said. 'But if she told you, it must be all right. The things are here in the drawer by the sink.' He opened the drawer and put a towel-wrapped bundle in Mahlia's hands. The Professor peered curiously over her shoulder as she unwrapped it. The spectacles were prismatic, faceted, and thick, and Mahlia shook her head over them, holding them before a page of the book and trying to see through them. Beyond the lenses the world shattered into something totally strange. The book was old, brittle, with pages that seemed to be of parchment rather than paper. The earliest pages were crabbed in Latin, and the Professor took this and the bottle from her unresisting hands. She continued to turn the spectacles in the light as Ron said, 'I thought of something else, Molly. If that lady was old Henry's daughter, then she's his heir, too. Or the little boy is. Halfies-Annie would be out of it for sure!'

'That's true.' Molly nodded thoughtfully. 'And we should be sure to let the judge over at Williston know. At the very least, it'd hold things up a bit and give 'em time to settle.' She rose, putting the darning aside and putting on a heavy sweater which she buttoned to her throat. 'Now you all come on, and we'll show you where old Henry died and where the young lady got so upset.'

They stepped outside into an icy wind. Ron muttered something about a wind change and went back to find a coat. The Professor wondered briefly how Molly had known what the temperature was before leaving the house as he and the others fished wraps from the car before setting off up the bare hill. The sky was bright with sun, but the chill wind blew into their faces freighted with a faint sulfurous stink. Mahlia had smelled something like it at the house on Long Island, and she wrinkled her nose in distaste.

Ron began to curse as soon as he topped the rise and looked down at the maze field. 'That damn-fool woman. She's cut the chains and got those gates standing open. Molly, Halfies-Annie's got those gates open. She's down there now with some guy and his kids. I'll bet you beans she's tryin' to sell those gates. He's got a truck. Damn fool!'

They watched the scene below: Annie in her usual jeans

and battered hat, the man in expensive country clothes, and two children about eight or ten, impossible to say whether male or female. Spread upon the meadow grass was the maze, gleaming lines of black asphalt and green turf. The tall iron gates stood open, and upon the unimpeded path the children were playing at maze walking. They had gained a position just short of the third gate, only a little way from the center of the maze.

Mahlia began to choke, unable to catch her breath, filled with a sense of overwhelming panic at some impending horror. 'Get them out of there,' she gasped. 'Get them out. Now.' Molly turned to her with an expression of awakening awareness and began running down the hill.

Annie Sudbury stood near the first gate with her prospective buyer as they discussed the merits and value of antique ironmongery. 'Five thousand seems a lot,' the man was saying while Annie waited impatiently to close the sale. Annie didn't think five thousand was much. She'd priced gates in Albany last week that weren't half as complicated as this one, and she knew to the penny how much the man would pay. He was a banker, for God's sake. He should be above bargaining like this.

There was shouting from the hill behind her, but she was so concentrated upon the sale that she did not turn. The banker did, however, peering in puzzlement at the oddly assorted group plunging down the hill toward him. There were distant shouts of 'Don't!' and 'Get the kids out of there!' He turned to see what mischief the children had gotten themselves into and was pleased to note they were playing quietly in the maze, walking to the center of it. Good. It must be a mile or more into the middle and the same distance out again. They'd be tired enough to be quiet on the drive back.

Mahlia fell behind the others in the downhill run. Her heels were sinking deeply into the damp pasture ground, and she stopped to pull off her shoes. Something at the center of the maze caused a queer distortion, a kind of boiling, a troubling of the air. Without thinking she raised

106

the spectacles as she would a pair of binoculars, holding them across her eyes with one hand as she teetered on one foot trying to remove a shoe. The boiled air trembled before her as though she had moved within arm's length of it. She stopped, mouth falling open, fascinated. Below her on the slope, the Professor looked back, saw her expression, and turned to struggle toward her, the little dogs growling at his heels, tails down and teeth bared.

Annie, her attention gained at last, turned grumpily toward the Froliuses, moving across the maze from the first gate to its entrance. The banker looked once more toward his children, thinking to tell them to come out now, for the group on the hill were still yelling, 'Get the kids out of there!' But Jimmy and Peggy had already reached the center and turned to come out. They were coming out.

Coming out.

He watched without belief as they came out, running the maze like automatons, moving faster than human beings could move, like maddened things, starting to howl as they moved. 'Peggy,' he called, suddenly fearful. 'Jimmy! What's the matter? Kids? What's the matter?' He moved toward them, but they were running too fast for any mortal to intercept, like lines of fire, shrieking fire upon the maze, too rapid to follow. 'Jimmy!' he screamed. 'Peggy!'

Mahlia had fallen to her knees, trembling, shaking, her face ghastly white. The Professor snatched the spectacles from her nose and perched them on his own, turning as he did so. Below him was the maze; within it two children running, their shrieks rising in a frenzy of pain and fear, and following behind them . . .

Following behind them.

He could not think in words what it was. Fang, his eyes said. Fang, maw, eat. Red. Horror. Tangled, his eyes said. All tangled in a squirming mass. Dripping. Full of eyes. Coming out, his eyes said. It's been trapped in there, and now it's getting out. Following the kids out. Making the kids lead it out. Fast. Too fast. They shouldn't have gone in there. They shouldn't have unlocked those gates. . . . The

107

lenses fell from before his eyes, and he focused on nothing but the screaming children, their father trying to reach them in slow motion, the woman standing there with her mouth open, Ron and Molly running, running – God they moved so slowly – and Badger beside them. The kids were almost at the entrance to the maze, and the woman was standing there, staring up at the hill, not seeing what was coming, coming, coming. . . .

The children burst from the entrance of the maze like projectiles, flung through the air to fall on the turf like broken dolls. One moved feebly, the other not at all. There was a moment's quiet before the turbulent air reached Annie Sudbury. The Professor dropped to his knees, fumbling to hold the glasses steady.

The turbulence touched Annie's jacket tangentially, grabbed at the sleeve of her coat, twisting her around, only a little. It left her, the wind, then came back, like a cat attracted to a rolling spool, touched her again until she spun around like a top, frantically grabbing the air, trying to stop herself. This time the turbulence was going with her, spinning around her, yarn upon the twirling spool, engulfing it. The Professor shuddered, found himself choking on his own breath, gargling saliva as he tried to shout. To what? Warn her? She could not have heard him. Through the boiling air he could see her whirling, arms outstretched, cheeks flattened away from her lips, the lips themselves drawn back into a terrified rictus while booming, thunderous words poured through her.

'MY ANNIE,' howled the enormous voice. 'MINE.'

She screamed. He heard it, then realized it was not Annie he heard but Mahlia, who crouched beside him with maddened eyes, watching as though she could not turn her face away. No, he could not have heard Annie's scream, but he could see it, see the mad struggle of that flailing body as it tried to pull free of the wind. Blood began to pour from her nose, from her eyes, from her ears, blood pouring out in trickles, in streams, forming a cloud in which she spun. She struggled once, twice, jaw jerking wide in spasms of shrieking which could not be heard over the thunder of the wind. Beside him, Mahlia gagged, fell forward on the grass, her eyes white and blind.

Annie Sudbury was being consumed by the word that thundered through her, spun her, whirled her like a dervish. 'All . . . his . . . blood . . . *mine*. All his blood . . . his child . . . his child's child's blood . . . *mine*. MY ANNIE. MINE!' The woman became a fountain, spurting into a cloud that spun into somewhere else, a cloud that coalesced, giving momentary shape to the hugeness, the horror, the thing beyond description, which faded in that moment as a thunderstorm fades with a final mutter, into silence.

He dropped the glasses, even in that instant careful to protect them with his crouched form. Mahlia lay still beside him. He reached for her, pulling her half-upright, patting her face. Her eyes focused slowly, still full of horrified disbelief. Of all those upon the hill, only they two had seen what had come from the maze. Below them, Ron and Badger reached the crumpled children as their father emerged from the maze like a battered marathon runner. Molly had turned toward the place Annie had been, mouth open as though about to call a name.

Ron's shout came from below on still air. 'Ambulance! Get the operator and tell her ambulance!'

Taking the glasses in his handkerchief, Professor Emeritus Myron Boyce pulled Mahlia to her feet, half pulled half pushed her into reluctant motion as they staggered voicelessly back the way they had come only moments before.

Below, beside the maze, Molly stood up from her examination of the children, her face feral and watchful. A shoe lay nearby, Annie Sudbury's shoe. Leaving Ron and Badger to tend the banker and his children, she moved along a trail of spun-off garments. At the end of that curving trail was a crumpled thing, brownish, dry like a piece of old rag-clad hide. It rolled as she touched it with her foot, feather light, staring up from black sockets in which the dried eyeballs rolled left and right as though looking at her. Molly's heart lurched; she spoke angrily to herself, then took off her heavy sweater and covered the thing. The cold wind had gone. Gone with whatever it was that had brought it. Gone with whatever had been Annie Sudbury.

Thougthfully she moved back to Ron. She would help him with the victims until the ambulance came. After which it seemed there was something she would have to help see to.

15

Neither Mahlia nor the Professor were up to much in the way of helpfulness, and Ron was kept fully occupied by the paramedics, the patrolman, and two or three assorted officials who showed up in response to various radio messages for help. Badger and Molly kept themselves busy with the children and their father. The state patrolman opined the kids had been hit by lightning. He collected Annie Sudbury's shoes, which were charred some on the inside, and said she'd probably been hit by lightning, too. There had been a nasty cold wind there for a while, and lightning had been known to strike from a clear sky. Badger, wisely, did not ask when or where it had been known. He kept his mouth shut, fed Mahlia hot tea, kept the children warm and their father quiet until the ambulance got there. The kids were burned around the legs and feet. Badger didn't think it was lightning. He thought it was friction. He knew what he'd seen, and he'd seen two kids moving faster than anything living could move, like streaks of fire. When the ambulance left, they were quiet in morphine-induced unconsciousness.

Their dad, according to the paramedics, was having a psychotic episode, thinking he'd seen things. 'Stress-induced,' one of them said wisely. 'I've seen it happen. People go crazy for a while.' Each of them, thus warned, did not go crazy even for an instant, and nothing at all was said about demons or fangy things which bled people dry into a whirlwind of air.

Even the paramedics had a little trouble with what was left of Annie Sudbury, though, as one said comfortingly to the other, it wasn't any worse than the old mummies archaeologists were all the time digging up. Molly, remembering those rolling eyes, said nothing. When the ambulance left, and the patrol car, and the hangers-on, they all retreated to the kitchen except for Ron, who went out to see to the cow. Seeing to the cow was a constant refuge in time of trouble and probably served as the primary motivation for having a cow at all, as cheap as milk was. Ron was no dairyman, but it was soothing and comfortable to have a cow to see to.

Mahlia swallowed a gulp of hot tea, a little color in her face for the first time since it happened. 'I saw it,' she said in a trembling voice. 'I don't care what anyone says. I saw it.'

'There, there, girl,' the Professor hummed, patting her ponderously. 'No need to become defensive about the whole thing. You saw it, and so did I, and the rest of them felt it or saw the results of its passage. I don't think we need to go through some obligatory obeisance to rational disbelief. Not at all. I'm a rational man, known to be so, needing no verification of that fact at this juncture. . . .'

'What!' Badger demanded. 'What did you see?'

'I saw something that looked very much like Kachang-inda-chamgunga, the Demon of the Pit.'

'Matuku-pago-pago,' said Mahlia. 'Star-Eater.'

The Professor nodded. 'The pit devil is Tibetan. He has counterparts all along the Hindu Kush. Star-Eater is Polynesian, of course. The Canadian Indians called it Wendigo, I think. I agree with you, Mahlia. Not dissimilar.'

'The cold wind,' she said. 'Matuku brings a cold wind.'

112

'Which would be scarcely noticeable in the Hindu Kush,' he remarked in a dry voice. 'Chamgunga brings a smell of death. We noticed that, too. And its speed of motion is said to be faster than living creatures can achieve.'

'What in hell are you two talking about?'

'In hell? Obviously not in hell, my dear, would you say?' Bowing in Mahlia's direction. 'No, obviously out of hell and here, now, somehow trapped by someone in the middle of that extraordinary maze. For how many centuries, I wonder?'

'Since the sixteen hundreds, I imagine,' said Molly, warming their tea. 'That's when old Henry Darinbaugh's people first came here. And that maze was built right away. Used to have wooden gates and cows grazing on it, Henry said.'

'The picture!' exclaimed the Professor. 'The picture down there in the outbuilding. A man, dressed in friar's garb, with alchemical equipment and – heaven save me – holding spectacles like these!' He took them from his pocket and stared at them in wonder. 'When I caught sight of it, I said thirteenth century. Would the family go back that far?'

'That was Henry Darinbaugh's ancestor,' said Ron, wiping his feet at the back door and bringing with him the unmistakable aroma of cow. 'He told me so himself. Old Roger, he called him. Bad Roger and his legacy'

'You're joking.' Badger shook his head. 'That's my own nickname, you know. Bad Roger. Shortened to Badger. What was his legacy?'

'Probably the creature we've just seen,' the Professor commented. 'And I imagine the friar's name was Roger Bacon. Who, in his late twenties, became enamored of strange studies and arcane knowledge. He repented later in life. Having seen what I have seen, I can imagine why. Where'd you put that book, Mahlia? The one Ron gave you?'

'In my shoulder bag.' She rummaged it out and passed it to the lamplit place where he had retreated. 'I looked at the

113

first few pages, but my Latin isn't that good. The kind I learned didn't look like this. . . .'

'Latin. Well, he would have written in Latin. Or in that tortured form of Norman English, with the spellings any which way. Give me a minute. I'm no Latinist, but it's an inescapable part of my field.' They sat as it darkened outside, Myron Boyce polishing his head from time to time, Badger mostly silent, Molly and Mahlia rising after a short time to prepare food for them all. Not that anyone was particularly hungry, except Ron, who was always hungry, but it was suppertime and when suppertime came, people ate. It was one of the verities, like cows and plowing.

They had food on the table before the old man closed the book and sat in the lamplight massaging his eyes. 'Well?' asked Badger. 'Well, anything there?'

'Oh, yes, lad. Surely. Superstition, and alchemical formulae, and prayers to God, and in between all that, a few words about devils. Roger was an experimentalist – not a patient man. Not what we'd call thorough. More interested in results than method. He experimented with optics, thus the spectacles. He was imprisoned late in life for having heretical ideas and opinions, but he died in the church.

'It seems that in his relative youth, however, he sent agents looking for all kinds of arcane information. One of the things he wanted was a formula or artifact reputed to exist called "The Seal of Solomon." According to this book, he received a metal bottle which was said to have inscribed on it "The Seal of Solomon." I imagine this is the bottle, the one Henry Darinbaugh had.'

'Look,' Badger said in a tightly controlled voice. 'I've been willing to accept that Mahlia may have some gift or talent for precognition. I've never believed in it, but there are reputable people who do. I've been willing to believe she has some kind of hunches which tell her things are true or not. I had a great-aunt like that. Strange it might have been, but when Aunty Ada said something was true, it almost always was. But if you think I'm going to buy some story about a genie in a bottle, you're out of your minds.'

114

'Ah' – the Professor polished his head – 'so no genie. No demon. All right, my boy. Treat the whole matter scientifically, if you like. You know what has happened; that is, you know what you've seen for yourself. You know what others whose word you trust have seen – me, for example. At least I can be trusted to report faithfully what I believe I have seen. After considering that, you can take this book, here, and can read what your poor, benighted, unknown father-in-law wrote.

'He thought he had a demon. His family back for about seven hundred years thought they had one. They believed Friar Bacon caught it – the same Friar Bacon who in his misspent youth fathered a natural child who was fostered in the Darinbaugh family and came to be its heir. So says the book. *And* they believed the Darinbaugh family kept this demon, first in a bottle, then in a maze. It seems Henry Darinbaugh could see the thing through those spectacles. He gave them to Carolyn, and she saw something. Mahlia put them on her nose, and she saw it, and then I saw it. Now you figure that out any way you want to. Take the glasses and have them analyzed. Take Molly's cookies and have those analyzed. Maybe she put something in them to make us more credulous than we'd otherwise be.'

'Oh, pooh,' said Molly, unflustered. 'Why would I do that?'

'I'm only saying he can subject the matter to analysis,' the Professor said in a mollifying tone. 'As any proper scientific mind would wish to do. Now, I haven't had a chance to read this book carefully. The writing is eccentric, the text is faded, and parts of it are in an unfamiliar language. However, it seems to say that some early Darinbaugh, having arrived in this country and prepared the maze through some arcane knowledge we're not privy to, decided to let the thing – whatever it is – out of the bottle in order to see it and talk with it. The book seems to say that the family amassed quite a fortune as a result of those conversations. Evidently the thing – whatever it is, and I'm not saying it's a demon at all, my boy – had some limited ability to foretell the future.'

'People,' snorted Molly. 'Always prying, poking, opening up things that should be closed.'

'Having put the whatever-it-is into the maze, the family had evidently kept it there for hundreds of years. Now it doesn't matter what you believe, my boy, or what I believe. The fact is that *they* believed it. They believed they had something, something dangerous and secret, and they passed it from father to son for a very long time. . . .'

'Until Henry Darinbaugh,' said Mahlia in a dreaming voice, peering into a vision only she could see. 'His father didn't tell him until he was past his youth. Then, when Henry was planning to be married, his father told him, and showed him, and Henry told his father the thing was a devil. He called it the curse of the Darinbaughs. He swore he would never marry or have a child to carry the curse. He told Laura he could never marry her. Never.'

'Curse?' Badger asked. 'Curse?'

'Blood,' said Mahlia, her voice breaking. 'Didn't you hear the voice out there on the maze? Blood. All the blood of the person who had imprisoned it, all down the ages, forever. Every child, every grandchild, right down the line. So, if it was Roger Bacon who caught the thing and put it in the bottle, the Darinbaughs were cursed as descendants of his through his natural son, and Annie Sudbury was a descendant of the Darinbaughs, and Carolyn was Henry Darinbaugh's daughter, and Robby is her son.' She began to cry, unable to go on.

Nothing but this could have caught Badger's attention. His mind was suddenly full of the banker's children, Peggy and Jimmy, their bodies flaming, running, screaming. Then it was Robby running, screaming, his tiny body on fire from its passage through the unyielding air. 'Oh, Lord,' he muttered. 'Robby! Darinbaugh thought he'd limited the risk to himself. . . .'

'Exactly. He planned to rebottle the thing. Here . . .' The Professor leafed through the book. 'Here's what he says. "I, Henry Darinbaugh, writing these words as warning for whoever may read them after my death, had completed my

116

studies and was prepared to risk all in the recapture of the creature into that receptacle it had originally occupied. Imagine my horror to learn that the weakness of youth and the perfidy of a beautiful woman had led all my vows into perdition. I have met my daughter, my grandson. I curse Laura Benedict forever, beautiful and false, a wanton liar and seductress.

' "I have told my daughter to flee, without leaving any trace behind. I have told her I must not know where she has gone, for the curse of the Darinbaughs knows what I know. I have told her to go far, for if I am not successful, it will hunt her down after I am dead. It knows, now, that I have a child, and a grandchild. Perhaps if she had not come here – ah, but this is fruitless. I must succeed in bottling it up once more, as Friar Roger did, as Solomon is said to have done, after which I will drop it into the depths of the sea. If I am successful, I will publish a notice in the *Times* and the girl may come out of hiding. If I am unsuccessful, God help her, for I cannot." ' The Professor plumped the book down on his lap. 'Dramatic, isn't he? I like the bit about the wanton liar and seductress, as though he had nothing to do with it.'

'That's not what he meant,' said Mahlia. 'Before he sent her away, he asked her if she could possibly be pregnant and she said no. I can see it. He's pleading with her, and she's shaking her head, hitting at him, screaming, 'No, no, no.' She knew she was. Even then. That's what he means by a wanton liar.'

Badger took the book from the Professor's hands and puzzled out the words for himself.

'So,' the Professor continued, leaning down to pat a small dog that had appeared from nowhere to nuzzle his leg, 'you do not accept a genie from the bottle, nor Matuku, nor Chamgunga, nor Wendigo. Very well. Do not accept them. Tell us then what it was almost killed those children this afternoon, what it was pressed Annie Sudbury dry as a squeezed sponge. Tell us what it was we saw.'

'What we saw,' Mahlia cried, the tears running down her face. 'What we saw.'

Badger could only stare at her uncomprehendingly before returning to the book. The Professor gave her his handkerchief, then rose to help clear the table. He found himself at Molly's elbow in the pantry, her fierce yellow eyes fixed on him.

'You got anything to handle a situation like this? A traveled man like you? Any little thing you haven't mentioned?' Her voice was only a whisper, but as commanding as the crack of a whip.

He gazed into those eyes without fear but with considerable understanding of the power resting there. 'A few bits and pieces from Tibet,' he whispered back, refusing to grovel before her though his guts told him obeisance might be very sensible. 'Old Tibet, before the Communists sanitized it. A few protections, maybe. But any little thing to bottle a demon? No, lady, Lord love you. And you?'

She actually smiled. 'You tell me something first, scholar man. Are there any here would bring harm if I tried? Any who would tattle to the papers or the TV? Stir up a storm?'

He looked at Mahlia and Badger, considered briefly. 'None. They have better sense, woman. And so do I.'

'If that's the case, then I might could try to help you. Or some I know might could. Seems first you got to find the thing, though.'

'Well, and if I find it, where would you be?'

'Here. Waiting for a phone call from you.'

'Could you get there quickly? May not be any airlines where we're going.'

Her lips quirked into a wicked, triangular smile. 'Oh, Simoney, Martha, and me could get there, maybe with some of the others.'

'Other members of –'

'Well now,' she went on briskly, interrupting him. 'Twenty-five years ago there was a girl named Laura came here to visit Henry Darinbaugh. Story was, she was Jared Shiel's sweetheart first, in Paris, when Jared and Henry were whooping it up over there. Jared was a widower then, with a ten-year-old son. Then somehow Laura got to be

Henry's girl. That's where the money was. Jared never had a dime but what Henry gave him. Then Henry's daddy told him about that thing in the maze, and Henry sent her away. Seems he didn't send her away quite soon enough, doesn't it?'

'No. No, like many of us, he was a little late.'

'Well, the point is, she was quite some article. I saw her the last night she was here, wandering around on the maze field, screaming curses at Henry Darinbaugh. Not exactly to my taste, if you know what I mean. Us country folk are a little simpleminded. We usually expect the black cow to drop a black calf, and more often than not she does. That woman was a black one for sure. What her calf was, I couldn't say, but I've suspicions. Just a word in your ear, that's all.'

'I'll keep it in mind,' he said soberly, looking back at the table where Mahlia and Badger were isolated each in singular misery.

'Those two young'uns are like moths. Each burning, each circling. You goin' to be able to keep the two of them from burning' up?'

'Lord love you, lady,' he murmured, casting a quick glance over his shoulder where the two sat, eyes fixed upon one another as they pretended to look anywhere else at all. 'Ask me can I stop a comet – or Matuku-pago-pago on a rampage. That isn't the way I'd planned to end an illustrious life, either, but what can I do? Ride it out, that's all. Ride it out.'

'Well, if you need help, this is the number,' she murmured in return, giving him a Farmers' Feed receipt on which the number was scrawled. 'Put that where you won't lose it or the doggies chew it up.'

'Ah. Well,' he said. 'If we were to need help, I'd keep that in mind.'

16

Badger would not allow them a respite.

'Look,' he said in a reasonable voice, only his stance betraying the unreasonableness of his demand. 'We've learned everything we can learn here. We've been to Laura's place, and mine. Presumably we have to find another place, somewhere Carolyn went after she left here. Right?'

'If you want me to try to see anything . . .' Mahlia faltered.

'Well, I do, of course.'

'That's not the point, Ettison. She's tired. I'm tired. The puppsies are tired.'

'I don't give a damn who's tired. No. I didn't mean that. I do care, of course, but you and Mahlia and the dogs can sleep in the car while I drive. That way we'll be there first thing in the morning.'

'Be where?' Mahlia asked wearily. 'Where, Badger?'

'She went two places I know of. She went to the bank to cash a large check. She went to the boat, to the *Carolyn*. After the accident, I told the yacht broker to put her up for sale, but last I heard she's still at the moorings.'

'There wouldn't be much chance in a bank, Badger.' She rubbed her eyes, trying to consider the idea without prejudice. 'I've never seen anything in a crowd. Once on a beach, but it wasn't crowded.'

'All right, then the boat first. There'll be no crowd there. She loved that boat.' Realizing as he said it that she had really loved the parties they had had on it, loved showing it off.

'We might as well,' Mahlia said, rising unsteadily. 'We've presumed on Molly's hospitality long enough.' She took the woman's hand, then, moved by the understanding in those wild yellow eyes, leaned forward and hugged her, like hugging some great, dangerous animal one did not really believe, despite the risk, would eat one. 'Thanks. It would have been nice to meet you without . . . without this.'

'I know, child. Don't worry about it. We'll see one another soon enough.' She helped them collect their scattered belongings, including the things that had belonged to Henry Darinbaugh, and saw them out of the house.

'I feel like a blood hound,' Mahlia laughed tiredly as they drove away. 'Some slobbery creature with my nose to the ground.'

'You don't look like that,' said Badger, wanting to touch the hair that streamed around her. She looked so alive, so *present*. Then they were on their way south once more, and he had to give all his attention to the driving.

Except for thinking. Thinking. Carolyn had cashed a large check the day she had disappeared. Large enough to buy plane tickets almost anywhere in the world. She could have gone anywhere, anywhere at all. If she had wanted to. If she had been convinced she had to.

He tried to visualize what it was she had seen, what it was old Henry Darinbaugh had said to her. 'See that thing? That thing will eat you up!' Like a fairy story. 'The bogeyman will get you!' And yet Mahlia and the Professor and Molly – don't forget Molly – seemed to believe the thing real. A real bogeyman. What had Boyce called it? Matuku. Wendigo.

He imagined the most horrible thing he could think of,

then tried to guess how Carolyn would have reacted.

Not with panic. No. He had never seen her in a panic. Whenever there was any threat, she became wary, calculating, a sly intelligence driven ruthlessly to the heart of the problem, like a stake. He had been somewhat shocked by this attribute of hers. And yet, why not? He was not shocked to find it in others, men, friends – people like Barry Springer. Barry could be as ruthless as they come. No. Carolyn wouldn't have panicked. She would have protected herself.

And Robby? Robby would have had to be hidden, too. Hidden safely, because otherwise the demon might find her through the child. Demon. Good Lord, he was taking this seriously. Demon.

Well if not demon, what?

'Extraterrestrial,' he said suddenly, almost shouting.

'Pardon me?' said the Professor. 'You said?'

'Extraterrestrial! That's what the thing is. A visitor from space.'

'You find that easier to believe?'

'Ah, yes. I do. Much easier. Some other planet of some other star. . . .'

'Or some other continuum, perhaps. Some other dimension.'

'I could go that far, yes.'

'Acting and appearing in all respects similar to the appearance and acts traditionally ascribed to demons?'

'Why not?'

'Under another label.'

Badger gulped at that. But what was it, after all, but another label? 'I . . . er . . . ah . . .'

'Exactly,' said the Professor in a grumpy tone. 'A rose is a rose is a rose. A genie – or one should say djinn – is a Matuku is a Wendigo is a Chamgunga. Fact is, something is loose upon us, my friend. Doesn't matter what the hell we call it.'

'Except that we summon it by speaking its name,' said Mahlia in bell tones, thrumming alarm, high priestess on the front seat. 'Follow. Do not summon.'

123

'Yes, well,' the Professor agreed, 'that might be a good idea.'

'Can't you describe it better?' asked Badger somewhat plaintively. He had asked this question before.

'I'll tell you,' the Professor said, tilting his head back and pulling his green eyeshade over his eyes. 'Next time, you wear the spectacles.' In a moment, snoring sounds came from the rear seat, one, then two, three, four. One bass, three tenor. Professor, Bing, Ting, and Ching.

The Professor ignored an important fact, as did Mahlia. Badger had not seen it. Badger had seen two children moving improbably fast, had seen their injuries later. Not pleasant, but he had seen worse during episodes of routine smash and stomp violence on the streets. He had not been facing the right direction to see Annie Sudbury's end, and what he had seen had been the dessicated corpse of someone he had never known who was in no sense lamented. He had not seen the thing, the whatever-it-was. Though he had begun to accept on faith that the others had seen something, he was not yet a believer. He felt no fear. He was worried about Robby, fearful for him because of what he *had* seen, but he felt no sense of imminent destruction.

Because he had not seen, he did not ask the obvious question. If they were successful in finding Carolyn, might not the thing, the whatever-it-was, follow them to her?

He did not ask. No one else had yet thought of it.

'When will we get there?' Mahlia asked sleepily.

'By morning.'

'If I can't see anything there, I don't know what to try next. I keep thinking about your little boy.' She sounded pitifully worried and concerned, and he choked over a sudden lump behind his breastbone. All this time, doing so much for him, mostly uncomplaining. The danger he had put her in. The trouble. And she worried about Robby.

'I know,' he said, taking her hand. 'So do I. I keep having this dream. He keeps calling me.'

'I know. He keeps calling, "Daddy, come get me." I know. I hear him.'

He tightened his grip upon her hand, wanting to stop the car and take her into his arms, wanting to cry on her shoulder, hold her while she cried. It was an unfamiliar emotion, a sharing of sympathy so great that it frightened him. He released her hand, slowly, so she would not feel rejected. Oh, he did not reject her. Not at all. No. Except . . . except for Carolyn, he would not let her go at all.

Except for Carolyn.

He shook his head. It was too late. He was too tired. The Professor had been right. 'I can't drive any farther,' he said, voice thick. 'There's a motel just ahead. We'll stop there.'

No one objected. Once they were separated, he lay rigid upon his bed, fighting the wild desire to leave it, to knock on her door, just to talk. Just to talk.

And she, curled into a sodden lump around her own pillow, hearing the small sounds that came through the wall, sleepless, wondering what he was doing, what he was thinking.

Until at last exhaustion broke them both and they slept.

The boat, thirty feet of shining mahogany, was moored at the end of a long pier. They stood staring at it.

The Professor harrumphed. 'It would be interesting to know how these visions of yours operate, Mahlia. Is it geographical? In which case, we'll perhaps need to take her out to whatever place she was found. Or is it topographical, connected with the material surroundings? Climb aboard, my dear, and let me make us some tea. I suppose there is some tea aboard, Badger?'

'Nothing, I'm afraid. There's a little store up by the harbor office, though. Go on aboard. It'll just take a moment.' He was gone, leaving them to find the cabin and slump on the couches cum bunks while the dogs whined plaintively from the deck above.

'Anything?' he asked in a gentle voice.

'Oh, Professor Boyce, I don't know. I've never been so mixed up. You know that woman, Molly? I think she's a witch. She said some very strange things to me.'

'Wouldn't surprise me,' he said. 'Very sapient, that one was. Close-mouthed about it, though. No covening and dancing about widdershins.'

Mahlia shook her head. 'She knew, though. I could tell. She knew all about me, just by looking at me. She knew about Carolyn and Robby, too. I could feel it.'

He patted her. 'So? Doesn't it make you feel happier, somehow, knowing that someone else is as crazy as you are? Hmmm? Why, that would gratify me immensely. It's never happened to me.'

She flushed. 'Don't tease. . . .'

'Who's teasing? Trouble with you, child, is you've been sold a bill of goods by your kinfolk. Mama told you to be still about it, and Aunty told you it didn't exist. Why don't you just accept it? Badger does.'

'Does he? Really?'

'Well, of course he does. And not just because it may lead him to his son, either. He's a true pragmatist, which is very rare. He believes what he sees. And I believe it. And you believe it. And Molly knows it. So – relax. Here comes Badger now. I do believe the nice man has brought food for the animals. Heavens to Betsy, isn't that a thoughtful personage. Look alive, girl. Put the kettle on.'

When they had drunk their tea, they left her alone. She lay wearily on a bunk, letting the sound of the wavelets splatting the side of the boat lull her almost into sleep. A ghostly sound came from above, and she looked up. Carolyn came down the ladder. Beautiful. So beautiful. Wild golden hair; face like a goddess. From above a child's voice said, 'Mommy?'

'Just a minute! I've got to get the bag, then we'll go.'

'What's this place?'

'It's noplace. Just a shallows.'

'What's a shallows?'

'A place we can get off the boat and let the sails take it away.'

'Why?'

'I've told you why! Because we have to get away without anyone knowing!'

'And we're going to ride horses.' This was said sadly, but with some satisfaction. After all this disruption, at least there would be horses. 'Out in Colorado.'

'Going . . . to . . . ride . . . horses . . .' said Carolyn's ghost, fading up the ladder toward the deck. 'In . . . Colorado. . . .'

17

When she told Badger, he sat down upon the other bunk, mouth slightly open, eyes focused on some other time or place. 'Colorado,' he mused. 'I've heard her talk of . . . No. It was Laura. I've heard Laura talk of it. Carolyn had a vacation trip there. With . . . with some school friend, I think.'

'I don't want to see Laura again,' said Mahlia. 'I won't.' She shuddered in revulsion.

'What this?' the Professor asked in his usual rumble. 'Something I don't know about?'

'Like snakes. Like something crawling on me. I can't stand her.'

'You don't need to,' said Badger absently, shutting off the little stove, the lights, fastening the windows shut. 'Come on. You can wait in the car.'

'Call her,' Mahlia suggested. 'Ask her by phone.'

'No. I want to be where I can see her face. Laura lies. I want Miles there. He'll tell me if she won't.'

Nothing she said could dissuade him, and nothing he said stopped her feeling that something venomous was threateningly close to her.

129

'What?' the Professor rumbled into her ear as they spun through the darkening streets. 'What?'

'Just that constant slithering,' she whispered. 'Something disgusting and verminous. I don't know what. Oh, God, why did I get into this?'

'You know as well as I do,' he rumbled, patting her knees, her shoulder, her face, a vast series of bear pats, both bruising and calming. 'This is a pleasant neighborhood, Mahlia. What is this place?'

'Where they live. The Beechams. That's their house just ahead. There are lights on.' She trembled uncontrollably, smelling something harsh and mephitic around them, and he put a heavy arm about her, squeezing her until her ribs creaked. She did not protest.

The porch light came on as they drove up, and Laura and Miles came to the door. They were dressed up, obviously expecting someone else, as obviously confused when Badger got out of the car.

'Badger, my boy. Well, I'm delighted to see you, but this is most unexpected. We thought you were our cocktail guests.'

'Miles, Laura. I won't keep you a minute. You'll have to take what I'm about to tell you on faith, I'm afraid. At least for now. There's a chance that Carolyn and Robby aren't dead. We've found – ah, we've found a witness to their disappearance. Or part of it, at least.'

'Who?' asked Laura in an icy voice. 'Who?'

'It doesn't matter who, Laura. . . .'

'It very much matters, If you think we're going to be led on some wild goose chase, you're mad. Probably some con man wanting money. . . .'

'Laura!' Miles's voice cut into her expostulation like a whipcrack. 'Go on, my boy. What do you need from us?'

'It seems Carolyn may have gone to Colorado. I heard something about Colorado from you, Laura. Long ago. When Carolyn and I were first married. You said something to her about 'that time in Colorado.' A vacation trip? Someplace she went with a school friend?'

'Shiel,' snarled Miles in a voice so unlike his own that Badger turned, stared, totally surprised. 'Michael Shiel!'

'Now, Miles. That was years ago. A childish escapade.' Laura, as surprised and shocked as Badger, tried to calm him.

'That was no childish escapade. That was seduction pure and simple, Laura, and I told you so at the time.' He turned to Badger. 'Michael Shiel is the son of an old friend of Laura's. When Carolyn was just fifteen, he talked her into running off with him to this crazy camp in the mountain. He was twice Carolyn's age, and I could have had him prosecuted then. Oh, no harm done,' he said. He had seen Badger's confused shock and waved a hand, dismissing it. 'No harm done, my boy. I fetched her out of there soon enough. But there could have been harm if she'd stayed. An ashram, for the love of God. Isn't that what they called it, Laura? An ashram. I've read about ashrams, and that place was no religious house. It was a den of iniquity.'

The old-fashioned phrase seemed to anger Laura. She blazed at him. 'I've told you, Miles. Carolyn was in no danger at all. And it's silly to think she's gone back there. Ridiculous. She's dead. Anything else is foolish. Wishful thinking.' She looked at the jeweled watch on her wrist. 'Now, we have company coming. I think this is enough discussion of –'

'Laura!' This time the voice roared. 'Mind yourself! What are your saying, woman? You think the Shaws and the Luces are more important than this? What's come over you?'

Mahlia, who had smelled the stench of it as they drove up, could have told him. It was not entirely Laura who was speaking.

Badger ignored her. 'I think I've met Shiel. His father, I mean. Do you know where the place is, Miles? I'd like to get a plane out of New York tonight, tomorrow morning at the latest.'

Then they were gone, Miles muttering something about an atlas in the library. Laura stood where she was, staring at

Mahlia through the windshield with a hard, hateful look that disfigured her face into a raging mask. The Professor heaved himself out of the car with a muffled exclamation.

'Ugly,' murmured the Professor, just loud enough for Laura to hear. 'Such an expression makes you look ugly, madame. Do not let your guests arrive and see.'

'Who the hell do you think you are?'

'Who I think I am doesn't matter. At this moment, however, I need to find out who someone else is. I'm going to ask you a question. Just give me a one-word answer. When you were up at Baleford, pregnant with Carolyn, did you stand in the center of that maze field of Darinbaugh's? Right in the middle of it? It's important that you answer me.'

The woman turned and moved away, peering down the drive as though willing the arrival – or perhaps the delay – of her guests.

'I'll not tell you anything.'

'Your silence is answer enough. You stood there. And you felt something, did you?'

'Don't be a fool,' she said, turning her harpy's face upon him. 'Don't be a damned fool.' She moved away, toward the door.

The Professor heaved himslef back into the car. The little dogs were whining, ears down. 'She smells of it,' he said. 'The Demon of the Pit.'

'I know. I smelled it, too.'

'Is it here?'

'Yes.' She shuddered, burrowing into his side. 'Feel the cold. Listen to the dogs. It followed us.'

'Wendigo. I wish I'd had more time to read these books. There might be something in them to help.'

'Just stay away from her,' moaned Mahlia. 'Don't get close to her. Don't let Badger get close to her when he comes out.'

'Something's going to happen? You see it?'

She nodded, hiding her face, trying not to see what she had already seen.

Badger and Miles came out of the house. 'I can't find the

name of the place, Laura. Some fellow flew me up there, and I wasn't paying attention to the route. In the mountains, I know. In some national forest. Laura! Do you remember the name of the place?' Miles shook her gently, demanding she respond.

'No,' she said. The word boomed like a drum, a single word, then echoing, a string of no, no, no, no, no popping back at them from every side like a machine gun. 'No,' she said again. The word left her lips in a scarlet flash, breaking into lightning strokes which curved and circled around her like a cat-o'-nine-tails, lashing at her. 'No!' screaming it this time, the lashes punishing her, her dress falling away in shreds.

'Laura remembers the name of the place?' Miles's voice, but not Miles speaking. He stood frozen in place, unable to move or speak, as paralyzed as the others. *'Laura, tell me the name of the place!'* Miles's voice enormously amplified, thundering at them from the vacant air. The cold increased. Around them leaves shriveled and blackened, falling from the trees in crisp shreds. Stems cracked like firecrackers. A tree exploded. *'Laura, tell me the name of the place!'*

'No!' she screamed once more, the last word she would utter in her own voice. She began to spin, the blood leaving her in a cloud, and not only blood but streams of oily black, which fled in all directions from her collapsing body.

'The place is named Lhamballa.' Laura's voice, but not Laura's voice. Something read information from a disintegrating brain and transcribed it in Laura's voice. *'Lhamballa. Come to me, my Laura. . . .'*

Another tree exploded, closer. Miles and Badger fell to the ground as the very air creaked with cold, Miles thrashing there, gasping, only the whites of his eyes showing. 'MY OWN LAURA!' The voice was enormous, Laura's voice, amplified and deepened. 'MY OWN LAURA!' The blood spun out of her into that same amorphous cloud that had surrounded Annie Sudbury, that same shapelessness assuming shape so that for one instant it could be seen without the strange spectacles of Friar Bacon.

133

Badger saw it, limned in blood, lit by inner fires, swelling into a monstrous, threatening coil of tentacle and fang. The oily blackness gathered and fled into it, the blood fled from the spinning woman to enter . . . a void. A place of darkness, a place of nothingness.

Then silence. The drive was splattered with jagged chunks and splinters of wood. A great, shattered limb was driven through the front door of the house. Miles lay on the gravel, eyes rolled back, chest heaving in long, stertorous breaths. His right hand was clamped between his left arm and his chest as though to quell some horrible pain. Badger crawled toward him. 'Miles. Miles.'

Where Laura had been was only a heaped shadow from which bare teeth grinned at them, a skull's grimace between parchment lips.

From far down the drive car lights made a pendulum swing, marking the turn.

'Badger!' the Professor demanded, 'You and Mahlia get him inside. I'll forestall the people coming.'

He went down the drive, waving the oncoming car to a halt. Mahlia could hear him murmuring there as she and Badger struggled with Miles's heavy form.

'Heart attack . . . we have a doctor and ambulance coming. Do you know how many guests were expected? Would you mind stopping at the foot of the drive and telling the others as they arrive? Very grateful. Yes. I'll let you know.' The Professor's voice faded as they entered the house and moved Miles to a couch. Badger went at once to the phone while Mahlia covered the stricken man, wrapping him warmly against the room's chill.

As the Professor entered the room, Badger turned from the phone. 'I got Dr Wilson. He lives just down the road. He's calling for an ambulance.'

'What did you say about . . . about her?'

'I told him Laura had burned up. He thinks I'm crazy. What am I supposed to say? Eaten by a devil, for God's sake?'

'We'll say something about lightning, no doubt. That

134

seems to be what we say in these cases. My God! How many more . . . Never mind. Stay calm. Don't say anything unless we have to.' He pressed trembling hands against his forehead. 'Is he warm enough?'

'I think so. I'm going out to throw something over . . . over her.' Badger started for the drive, turning back from the open door, retching. 'Lord, she's looking at me.' From the drive the shadowed sockets of the skull seemed to stare at them accusingly.

'It's not looking at anything. Nothing at all. Here, I'll do it.' The older man picked up a small rug from the floor and went out to cover the remains.

Badger was muttering. 'I didn't believe you. Not really. I thought you were making parts of it up. Lord. That thing . . . Mahlia. It *followed* us here!'

She took hold of him, for he seemed about to shake himself into pieces. His near panic prevented her from showing her own. 'Probably, yes. Though maybe it . . . well, I think it already knew Laura. It might have come here anyhow, because it knew her.'

'Knew her?' He fell silent, thinking. 'Of course. From years ago. Did the book say anything about Henry telling her.?'

'He didn't tell her.' The Professor came back into the house, pushed the splintered door as tightly closed as possible behind him. 'Henry Darinbaugh didn't tell her anything. However, I'm fairly sure she stood right in the middle of the maze, pregnant as she was. Pregnant women are vulnerable.'

'Standing in the middle of that field would have **app**ealed to her sense of drama.' Mahlia muttered. 'And she *was* vulnerable. The Professor's right. Pregnant women are, and men who have just killed, and babies who have not been named yet.' And babies in utero, she did not say, shivering at the thought. Babies not yet born.

'I have no doubt Matuku managed to find a way into her, a home for at least a part of itself. The tip of a tentacle, perhaps.'

'But if it followed us here, it will go on following us. If we find Carolyn, it will be right after us. If we find Robby, it will be right there!' He turned as though seeking an exit that he couldn't find. 'Right there. No matter how fast we move.'

'Laura already told it where the place is.' Mahlia wanted to believe the thing had left them, though all her perceptions told her it had not. 'Laura told it the name of the place.'

'Only the name,' said the old man. 'Not a location. Not a set of directions or a map. I doubt she knew the way there herself. If she did, the thing is on its way there now.'

'No.' Mahlia said, shuddering. 'It isn't gone. I can feel it, still here.' She moved to the window, carefully not looking at the covered pile on the drive. 'There's a siren coming.'

'Following us,' muttered Badger, not hearing her. 'How can we get away from it? And I have to find Carolyn. She's alone, lost, frightened. And Robby. I have to find Robby. . . . Lhamballa. It sounds like Tibet.'

'I think it was supposed to sound like that.' said the Professor. 'Invented to sound like that. Hush now, Badger. The ambulance is here.'

Then they were surrounded once more by all the uniforms and men taking notes, pads and pencils and incredulous looks.

They handled it as they had handled it before, all the conjecture and mystery, one fact mixed with a dozen guesses, talking volubly, telling nothing.

Paramedics, shaking their heads, the doctor's car careening into the drive just as the ambulance was about to leave, someone being sick in the bushes after looking into what was left of Laura's face. Then silence. Alone. They had promised to come in the following day to sign statements. None of them believed they would do so. They would not be near enough to do so. Badger was on the phone to Vivian.

'She'll get in touch with Miles's brother. She's met him a time or two. I told her Laura was dead.'

Neither of them said anything at all. They stood in the

shadow, one lamp alight in the corner, a swamp of ominous darkness outside the windows, very much aware that something lurked there. The dogs whined at the door.

'Ah. My puppsies. Poor beasties to be forgotten so. How did you get out of the car? Tsk. Agile wee creatures.' He went to the phone, murmured into it as the dogs circled the room, growling softly, the hair on the backs of their necks high. Mahlia watched them transfixed as they trotted through Laura shadows, Carolyn images, pictured Robbies.

'I've got to get out of here,' she said. 'I can't stay here any longer. Whether it's out there or not, we have to leave.'

'My place,' the Professor announced, hanging up the phone. 'Probably the safest place we could be just now.' He herded them to the car, all of them trying not to peer around them for the threat they felt was there. The dogs knew it. They fled to the car, ears down, to crouch whimpering on the floor.

At the end of the drive an oak tree made harsh lace against a streetlight. As they passed it, it exploded, fragments driving across the windshield in a blizzard of leaves and splinters. On the main road, they drove beneath trembling, tossing branches. Frost slithered across the windshield with an audible crackling. Badger couldn't see. He stopped, took a scraper from the glove compartment.

'No,' whispered Mahlia. 'Don't get out of the car.'

'Listen to her, Ettison.'

They sat cowering in the cold as Badger turned the defroster on. It was icy in the car. The dogs whimpered, growled. After a time clear spots melted on the windshield and they went on.

Cloud followed them, black and roiling, a rolling storm. In the city it lifted a little, just above the tops of the buildings, always at the same distance. Passersby took cover beneath awnings, in doorways. Trash blew around them like snow. When they reached the apartment building the garage attendant gave them a curious look as they packed into the elevator, dirty, disheveled, the dogs circling and howling like miniature wolves.

Then they were inside the Professor's apartment with the door shut behind them, and the cold storm moved away like a burden shed.

The Professor nodded at the glowing mandala on the wall. There a multiarmed god crouched upon a recumbent demon, around them a host of winged warriors. 'The Demon of the Pit conquered by the forces of enlightenment. A very powerful protection.'

'Powerful enough to keep that thing out?'

'Powerful enough to make it not want to come in, at least for a time.' He moved to the kitchen to put food and water down for the dogs, then stood watching them in dismay. They circled, whined, sniffed at the glass. Their tails and ears were down. Once in a while they growled. Despite his urging, they would not eat or drink.

'So. The small ones tell us it has not gone far,' he said. 'Nonetheless, we must sit and cogitate and make sensible decisions. I do not think it will hear what we say in here.'

'Talk!' snarled Badger. 'What good is talk? I can't imagine what there is to say. We daren't leave here to search for my wife or child, or that . . . that thing will come after us like some monstrous hound.'

'And we daren't sit here for too long,' added Mahlia, 'or it will grow impatient and find some way to make us move. Probably some unpleasant way.'

'True. But there is a source of help.'

'Why didn't you say so?' Badger rose, his face avid.

'Sit down!' the Professor roared at him. 'I didn't say so for obvious reasons. I can't deal with this volatility of yours, my boy. If you want my help, and the Lord knows you need it desperately, you're going to have to settle down and act like some aged academic with no more juice in him than a dried apple. I need you cold and logical, Ettison. Cold and logical, yet willing to set disbelief aside.'

'Set it aside?' He mocked laughter. 'Having seen what I've seen? How can I disbelieve?'

'How can you disbelieve? Well. I've placed a call to a coven of witches, asking for their help.'

'Don't mock me, Boyce. You're an old man and I respect your obvious experience, but don't mock me or patronize me.'

'I tell you not to disbelieve. You say you will not. I make a statement and you disbelieve it. I say again. I have placed a call to a coven of witches, asking for their help.'

'Don't be silly,' Badger said feebly. 'This is serious.'

'As I am well aware. Stop this thrashing about. Be cold. Calm. Icy. Take my word for exactly what I say, and Mahlia's for what she sees. Trust what we are. If I say witches. I mean that. Isn't that so, Mahlia?'

'I – I believe so,' she faltered. 'Molly is, anyway. She's bringing her friends, Martha and Simoney.'

'Amity, Verity, and Patience will undoubtedly wait at home.' said Badger viciously. 'Do you expect me to –'

'I expect you to if you ever want to see your son alive again.' said the Professor, suddenly chill. Accustomed to occupying center stage, he had had enough of Badger's drama. He was about to be more specific when a soft knock at the terrace window stopped him. He spun, choking back a startled exclamation, to confront a dark shadow of merely human size.

'Molly,' said Mahlia with wonder. 'How did she get out there?'

'I rather think she came that way.' The Professor opened the sliding doors, letting the three women slip through. Molly wore the same dress they had seen her in last, covered with a dark coat, her hair in a kerchief. Martha wore blue jeans and a checked shirt straining across her ample breasts. Simoney was thin as the broom she carried, and as beautifully disordered as a plum branch. Badger stared at them as they were introduced, still disbelieving, closing his eyes, clenching his hands, scarcely feeling the pat Molly dropped on his head.

'Shock,' she announced to the others.'Simoney, for heaven's sake, girl, put the broom outside and bring the picture in.' The younger woman flushed and did as she was bid. Molly commented, 'She's young. Too young, really, but Amity and Patience are down in Orlando visiting Mother.'

'What about Verity?' blurted Badger, trying not to dissolve in a fit of unbecoming half laughter.

'Bursitis,' said Molly flatly, 'which she hasn't learned to control yet. You find our names amusing, young man?'

'They seem . . . well, it's a cliché, isn't it?'

'It's a symbol. Jargon, if you like. In our circle, there are some fifty names which are recognized as appropriate. They mean something. More important, they unmean something. There are certain kinds of attitudes you will not find among us. For which, young man, you should be very grateful.'

Mahlia said, 'Molly, how did you get past the thing out there?'

'By being sneaky, child. It's not interested in us. We knew it would follow you before you even left Baleford, and we began to plot against it then. So, Ron Frolius will just have to get his own supper for a few days. Let's see if we're in agreement on this. You, boy, get your face out of your hands. You're supposed to be smart as a whip, now act it!'

'We've talked it over,' said the bulky Martha, taking off the heavy checked shirt to reveal a lighter one beneath. 'The thing has to be bottled, you know, and we haven't the least idea how. Old Darinbaugh's bottle will hold it, sure enough, but how you get the thing in or the stopper in behind it – well, we haven't a clue. It's out of our line of work.'

'Which is what?' demanded Badger, red patches appearing on his cheeks.

Martha turned toward him, examined his fretful, nervous face, and abruptly grew three feet taller. 'Healing,' she said in an organ voice, like some great goddess speaking from a mountaintop. 'Forgetting. Fruitfulness.' When his mouth opened in shock and awe, she became her own size again, almost playfully. 'Most of what we do is undoing black deeds the other side gets up to. Which is the heading this comes under.'

'Ah' – he gulped – 'but you don't know how to proceed.'

'Haven't the foggiest,' she said cheerfully, fixing him with yellow beast's eyes. 'Nonetheless, we've come up with a twist to gain a little time. Him.' She pointed to the picture that Simoney had set against the wall; the dim, brownish picture they had seen at old Darinbaugh's place, the one of Friar Bacon in his laboratory. The painted eyes looked at them across six hundred years. 'I figured we'd recall him for a bit. He's the one the thing out there has a grievance against, so old what-you-call-him should go haring off after the Friar.'

'I'm afraid I didn't follow that,' said the Professor, polishing his head with both hands.

'We'll call him up,' said Martha, plumping a heavy carpet bag on the floor. 'His shade. His semblance? Whatever. That thing out there will sense it, never fear. Then, we slam the old Friar back where he came from, six hundred years or so, and old greedy-guts out there should go swirling away after him. The trick won't hold him forever, of course, but we'll put a bit of a twist on it.' She wound up and swung at an imaginary golf ball, stocky body uncoiling as she drove the spectral ball a few centuries into the past.

'Wait a minute!' Badger had suspended his captious disbelief, but none of his alert intelligence. 'If you can do that, why can't you ask the Friar how he bottled the thing in the first place? He did it, didn't he?'

'We assume so,' breathed Simoney in her bee's voice, softly humming, so that one had to concentrate to hear her. 'But it doesn't work that way. We'll have only time and power to call up – oh, a very slender semblance. No – no thickness to it, you understand. Not the whole person. Not that we couldn't call up a real person, but it would take months of preparation!'

'A few weeks,' corrected Molly. 'Which we don't have, so it doesn't matter. And there would be implications to our doing that. Meddling. Not wise. What we will do is a bit of temporal TV. Real enough, I hope, to suck that critter out

141

there away, like a greyhound after a mechanical rabbit. When he catches up with it, the real Roger will have moved on, of course, so old demon won't be pleased, but logic says it should take him a while to find his way back.'

'Back from . . .'

'From six hundred years ago and however many thousand miles the earth will have moved since the semblance left the here and now. Oh, he'll find a way. Never imagine he won't find a way.'

'Blood,' hummed Simoney. 'He'll smell it.'

'What should we do?'

'You should pack your bags and be ready to leave. Charter a plane or something. The minute we get the thing decoyed away, you should go.'

This time Badger didn't argue. He went to the phone and made the arrangement. He also made a quick phone call to Barry Springer. 'Barry, that favor you promised me? Will you run the names Michael Shiel and Jared Shiel through, both originally residents of Baleford, New York? . . . Right. There may be something in Colorado. See what you can do? . . . I'll call you in a day or two.' He hung up. 'All right. There'll be a plane waiting for us at the airport. My bags are still packed. If the others are ready to go?'

They nodded, and Molly smiled, satisfied. 'Well then, time to get cracking. Martha, you got that chicken?'

Martha had, a live one, which had its neck wrung in a forthrightly farmwife manner and was then bled onto the painting of Friar Bacon. Molly muttered and chanted as she wiped the blood off on tissues which she heaped in a priceless Sung dynasty bowl, the Professor not even protesting. Simoney crouched over the bowl, crooning to it, accompanying herself on a tiny tambour no larger than her fist.

'Blood turn blood, year turn year,
Open a door for the forefather Friar.
Open a door and bring him here,
Blood turn blood, year turn year.'

The air in the room curdled, like fresh milk on a hot day,

seeming to solidify in places, to thin in others, as though a fabric were stretched between strong fingers.

'Contagion.' muttered the Professor to Mahlia, who gave him a wild-eyed look and did not answer. 'The semblance they're calling up will be bloodless, I guess, so they're creating a stink of blood around it. It wouldn't mislead a biochemist for a moment, but a blood stink is a blood stink so far as demons are concerned.'

Martha nodded as she put the last of the tissues in the bowl. 'Has to be warm-blooded, of course. Strange the way all earth creatures are more alike than different. We're using tissues because they're light. Minimizes displacement.'

'Between then and now?' asked Badger incredulously.

She nodded again as Martha wrapped the remains of the chicken in a plastic bag and stowed it in the carpet bag. 'Supper,' she commented, then, 'Fire-place,' hefting the picture across the room to the hearth. 'Fire.' She had it going almost as soon as the word was spoken and was rummaging in the carpet bag for herbs and resins. They chalked a pentacle on the floor as the Professor stared and made mental notes and Badger simply watched, suspending all judgment. Mahlia swayed in her chair in time to Simoney's chanting. It seemed she had heard it all before, in some time past.

'Time turn time, and herbs in the fire,
Blood turn blood, and year turn year,
Open a door for the ancient Friar,
Open a door and bring him here.
Shadow turn shadow and light turn light,
Open a door but only a crack,
Day turn day and night turn night,
Open again and let him go back'

The atmosphere in the room changed again, accumulating, dispersing. It was as though there were other places in the room, gathering; other places, retreating; other places – other times. Mahlia shook her head, trying to clear it. Around Martha and Molly and Simoney a pale fire seemed to burn.

'Open the door,' whispered Molly. Simoney carried the bowl out onto the terrace and set it down as Martha quickly chalked another pentacle around it. They retreated into the room, closing the door tightly behind them as Simoney went on singing, more loudly now.

'Time turn time, and smoke of the fire,
Blood turn blood for devils to smell.
Open a door for the ancestor Friar,
Open a door for the devil as well.
Shadow turn shadow,
Light turn light,
Open a door, but only a crack.
Welcome his coming,
Welcome his flight,
Open it wide and let him go back!'

An explosion of flame and scent erupted on the hearth; Molly howled a word in a voice that did not sound like her own. Outside on the terrace a spinning cloud formed above the bowl.

The figure solidified out of mist, just as it appeared in the picture, brown robe, rope girdle, eyes fixed on some distant thing beyond their sight. The image may have been only a semblance, but it was a semblance that lived, for its eyes widened in surprise. Molly howled the word once more, and the bloody tissues rose to hover about the Friar's figure as moths do to a flame. He had heard that sound! His eyes peered through the glass at them, widening still further, mouth beginning to open, not quite aware. . . .

And at that instant Matuku came, boiling over the edge of the terrace, its passage marked by shattered limbs of trees, tumbled plants, a stench of rotted, sulfuric breath that reached them even through the glass.

The word was howled for the third time. The figure before them began to turn, to bring the strange spectacles it held toward its eyes . . .

'MY ROGER,' boomed a great voice. 'MINE.'

The image faded into itself, growing smaller, like something seen through the wrong end of a telescope, compressing into itself, away and down, the cold stinking wind pouring after it through some tiny hole in the fabric of being and time, down and away. There was an abrupt popping as that hole closed.

'Now, get out of here,' said Martha, 'quickly.' She was lifting Molly with one arm, holding a flask to her lips. Molly's face was drained, appearing almost bloodless. Simoney sighed and put her drum away.

'How long do we have?' Badger thrust his arms into his coat and pulled Mahlia to her feet.

'Lord, boy, who knows! Two days? A week? That at the outside, I'd say, and the thing could be back within the hour. I don't know how time twists around in its innards.'

Mahlia knelt beside Molly, whispering 'Will you . . . are you coming with us?'

'We'll be nearby, child. Go on now. Don't waste any time.' As they left the room, she cried, 'Don't leave any more trail than you can help.'

'What did she mean?' Mahlia asked in the elevator. 'Don't leave a trail. What kind of trail?'

'Telling people things, I should imagine,' said Badger. 'She means not to tell people where we're going, what we're looking for. What did old Darinbaugh's diary say? "The thing knows what I know." It must have some capacity for reading minds. So, we get on the plane. . . . Lord. I had to tell the charter company we were going to Colorado Springs. It's the closest airport to –'

'Let's concentrate on moving,' the Professor demanded. He did not know how Matuku thought or learned things, nor how it could be locked up, but he thought, almost with panic, that he had better find out. Lord, he would have to find a way.

'Books,' he muttered. 'The ones Molly gave me up in Baleford. Be sure we get them out of the trunk of the car and onto the plane.'

18

Once on the plane, however, the Professor could not focus
on the books. He had not felt this weary in many years, not
even during long, harsh expeditions in wild parts of the
world. He stared out the window of the plane, waking with a
start from a dream in which Simoney waved at him from the
wing. The flight attendant put breakfast in front of him, but
he was not hungry. He glared out at the paling sky. It had
been only last evening that Laura Beecham had died.

In Colorado Springs they checked into the Antlers Hotel,
a vast Victorian pile that peered down its gray stone nose at
the upstart urban renewal around it.

Badger went to buy maps.

'Best place to ask would be the Forest Service,' the clerk
said, making no attempt to follow Badger's pointing finger
on the quadrangle map of the Pike National Forest. 'Two
dotted lines should mean a jeep road. Sometimes they do.
Sometimes it means there was a road there when they
printed the map, but it washed out ten years ago. Sometimes it means there's a new four-lane highway through
there.'

'Are there private places?' Badger was doubtful this could be the Lhamballa he was looking for. 'I'm pretty sure it's a private place.'

'It could be,' said the clerk. 'An old mining claim. A ghost town somebody bought up. National Forest's all peppered with bits and pieces of private stuff. Best place to ask is –'

'I know,' said Badger. 'The Forest Service.'

At the Forest Service office, he found two uniformed Rangers deep in a conversation about baseball. 'Sorry to interrupt,' he said in a voice that conveyed no such sorrow, 'but I've got to get to a place called Lhamballa, and –' He stopped abruptly. The expression on the two faces before him told him he had just sprouted another head. 'Sorry. Did I say something wrong?'

'Lhamballa,' said one, shaking his head. 'Are they expecting you up there?'

'I doubt it very much. Nonetheless, I have to get there.'

'Last I heard, they'd taken to shooting at people who "had to get there." I'm Dave Walters, by the way.'

'Badger Ettison. Ah, I've got a bit of a problem. I believe my wife is there. We've just found out she has a health problem which needs treatment. Well, I think she's there with an old acquaintance of the family, and I obviously have to get to her.'

Walters shook his head. 'You can try. I'll tell you frankly, though, it's not going to be easy. The only traffic in and out of there is by their own helicopters. There is an old trail that leads up to the cirque, but –'

'Cirque?' Badger asked, baffled.

'Look here on the map. A cirque is a rounded, cliff-edged scoop taken out of a mountainside by a glacier. Right here, see the topographic lines? See that curve? Well, that's a cirque. Now, you should be able to walk right up to the front of a cirque, except in this case a fairly large mountain fell across the access. See those lines jigging around there, up and down, up and down, no system at all? You can't cross that. It's boulders the size of buildings. Can't get across

148

them and can't get through them. Over here, though, along the north edge of the cirque, right at the bottom of the cliff, there's a path. It's steep, winding, and rough, but it's there. You can try that. Have you done any climbing?'

'Quite a bit of hiking. No rock climbing.'

'You don't need rock climbing. Just good sense. Take it easy. I've got no idea what your wife is doing up there, but I don't mind telling you I'd be very worried if she were mine.'

'What is the place?' he asked belatedly. 'Some kind of hermitage?'

'Some kind of nut cult,' said the other Ranger. 'Like something out of an old movie serial. Skulls nailed to trees. "Keep Out" signs with dead bats nailed to 'em. Girls disappearing.'

Walters shook his head, cautioning. 'Ben, you don't know the disappearances have anything to do with Lhamballa. Kids disappear all the time, everywhere. As for the rest of it, they want to be let alone, that's all.'

'Sorry. The whole place makes me think of that Manson thing more than anything else.' Ben made a face as though he tasted something rotten.

'How long has it been there?'

'Oh, it's been there as long as anyone can remember. It was gold mines up there first. I don't know when they played out. Even then they told stories about the place – miners disappearing; people vanishing into the mountain. A lot of fairy tale junk. Then it was a bunch of survivalists, old people mostly. They thought the world was coming to an end, so they were going to hide out up there and wait for the second coming. Died out, about twenty years ago. Or maybe the mountain trolls got them, too.' Ben snorted.

'After they were gone, this Shiel guy showed up with a deed to the place,' said Dave. 'He bought a lot of construction materials and had them flown in. Then he brought in his own choppers, and the only people to go in there since have been invited –'

Ben interrupted him. 'My sister works at the airport. She

says every month or so a bunch come in, sometimes kids zonked out of their skulls on happy dust, sometimes fat-cat types. Funny combination. The chopper from up there picks them up and brings them back.' He thought about this for a while, sighed, and then pulled the map closer.

'Well, if you're determined to get there, here's the route.' And he began to draw lines on the map while discoursing about the kind of vehicle that might make it to the trail.

Badger went to rent something with a four-wheel drive, after which he returned to the hotel to phone. When the last conversation was over he sat unmoving, staring at the phone.

'What is it, my boy?'

'I was talking to Barry Springer. He got a report on Shiel. A bunch of minor drug charges. Felonious assault. Contributing to the delinquency of a minor – more than once. Dropped. Kidnapping. Dropped, because the parents wouldn't prosecute after they got their daughter back.'

'That's why Miles was so upset.' said Mahlia. 'About Carolyn having been out here once before.'

'That's why I'm so upset now,' he replied 'Under the circumstances, I can understand the remoteness of the place appealing to her, but why in God's name did she come to him instead of me? I could have found a hiding place equally remote. Oh, I don't know. This whole thing is a nightmare. I mean that literally, I don't think I'm awake.'

'Still, my boy, we have a direction to go. We do need a vehicle, however.'

'There's a Bronco due back about noon,' he said. 'Nothing with four-wheel drive is available sooner. We've got an hour or two to get anything we may need. You need shoes, Mahlia. Those will cripple you on rocks. And some jeans and a warm jacket. You need anything, Professor?'

'Information, my boy. This whole matter is about as confusing a condition as I can remember. You know, it wouldn't be amiss to have a few tactics in mind for staying alive, if what your New York police acquaintance told you about Shiel is true. If, indeed, they do shoot people as the

Ranger alleged, it might be wise to think up a cover which might keep us alive.'

'I can't go as anyone but myself. If Carolyn's there, she'll know me at once.'

The old man frowned. 'I'll try to think of something.'

By three o'clock Badger had driven them some sixty miles, the first fifty on paved roads, the next seven on a so-called improved road, and the last three over a rough track that looked rather more like a stream bed than anything else. The dogs, weary of being thrown about, had sought refuge in the Professor's lap. Mahlia had pulled her seat belt as tight as possible and was bracing herself against the dash. They were too tired to talk, and Badger drove with a kind of focused ferocity that discouraged communication, stopping only at long intervals to check the map and the Ranger's notes.

'Next turn should be it,' he grunted. 'There'll be a lake below us to our left and the rockfall to our right. The trail should start right there, and we should be able to see the cliffs above timberline.'

Timberline. Mahlia shuddered as though a cold wind from some vast height had blown down upon her. High and cold. Like that mountain range the Professor spoke of, home of the Kachang-indachamgunga. The natural hunting ground for such a being. Even in the warmth of the South Pacific, Matuku was known as Star-Eater, Shark-of-the-Skies, a creature of cold outer space.

They rounded a corner, coming to a jolting stop at the side of the road as Badger pulled the aging Bronco between two towering pines. The lake lay below them, glittering like heaped tinsel in the sun, surrounded by low walls of willow and an interlaced network of shallow beaver ponds. On their right lay the evidence of a mountain's collapse, broken pillars and boulders fallen in wild disorder from the cliff face ahead of them. Above those cliffs towered snowy peaks, blue and white against a bluer sky. When they emerged from the car it was onto a carpet of wild-flowers, nodding clumps of columbine, white heads of bistort, spikes of magenta elephantella, the tiny ears and trunks in profiled rows along the stems. As the Professor declaimed upon each, its growth and antecedents, its kin in wilder parts of the world, the dogs roamed among the clumps, jaunty tails aloft like plumes. They waded through marsh marigold to drink from a tiny stream.

'Snow melt,' said Badger. 'Probably safe enough to drink if you're thirsty.'

Mahlia knelt to scoop the icy water into her mouth, shivering. The trail led away before them, a narrow defile between the cliff on one side and the rockfall on the other, stretching precipitously upward. Badger had already climbed a hundred feet along it and was turning to stare impatiently back at them.

Mahlia stumbled, teetered, realized suddenly that she felt dizzy.

'Take it easy,' advised the Professor. 'Your body will catch up to the altitude in a few minutes. Don't push it.' He plodded after her, seeming not to notice the slope, the altitude, his white hair ruffling around his ears. They walked among gigantic boulders, occasional lodgepole pines struggling though the mass to rise like cautionary fingers. 'Be still,' the fingers admonished. 'Shhh. Don't let them hear you.' The way was marked by deer droppings and an occasional beer can. Soon even these markers were left behind and they wound their way upward on a trail only marginally smoother than the rockfall itself. They could hear water running deep among the stones, unseen, a liquid gurgling that provoked thirst by its very inaccessibility. A single harsh cry came from above, and they looked up to see circling wings, dark against the sun.

'Eagle,' said the Professor.

Mahlia sighed. She had never seen an eagle before, except in zoos, and it would have been nice to stop and look at it. It would have been nice simply to stop.

The Professor seemed to read her mind.

'Badger. Hold up. My artificial hip is complaining of too much strain. We need a bit of rest, drink of water.'

'I'll go on ahead,' he called, not looking at them. 'You can catch up to me later.'

'Badger!' It was an imperative. 'Better we stick together. One man, arriving alone, might be easily disposed of. Beside, we need to talk.'

'More talk!'

'There's been very little. I went to the library this morning while Mahlia was shopping, to look up the file on this place. No one was here at all from the time the miners left until about 1938. Then a religious cult was founded here shortly before World War Two by a man named McCloughlin. He was an Englishman, an expatriate who had traveled quite a bit in India, Nepal – all that part of the world.'

'I don't see what this has to do with –'

'You will. Now, there was a rumor that this McCloughlin had collected rare art works in India. I think it likely that the man had picked up some scrimshaw of no particular value. Nothing indicates he had any particular taste or acquisitive sense. However, if I, as an eminent art historian – which I am, no question about that, eh, Mahlia? – were to assert that this McCloughlin was thought to have had some things of real value? Wouldn't that make you curious if you were an inhabitant of Lhamballa?'

'The cover story you were talking about!'

'Exactly. So. You are seeking your wife. Well and good. But Mahlia and I, acquaintances of yours, are seeking a treasure – not to own it, merely to locate it and evaluate it. Keep that in mind. Now. One more thing. We don't mention Matuku. We don't mention Darinbaugh unless we must. We are ignorant on both those topics – we know only what anyone might have told us. Understand?'

Badger shook his head obstinately. 'No.'

'Then you're not thinking. If Carolyn is here, she's not here alone. Michael Shiel runs some kind of cult. His father was an enemy of Henry Darinbaugh *and* was Laura Beecham's lover. We don't know what's going on, and we don't know how Carolyn fits into any of it. We don't know

153

enough to appear to know anything. Our best bet is to be ignorant. You're looking for Carolyn. Her mother told you she might be here. And that's all.

'Now, we've had our drink and our sit-down. Shall we go?'

Badger nodded, accepting the Professor's reasoning despite himself, frowning, beginning the climb again.

'I didn't know you had an artificial hip,' said Mahlia, showing a certain troubled concern for him.

'Believe me, child, it normally doesn't bother me at all. I'm very agile. I can't run, and I can't leap. I can do almost anything else. Don't let it concern you.'

She nodded, but it did concern her, and she found herself watching him, waiting for him to limp.

The sun was low, shining into their faces when they reached the top of the fall. A chipmunk showed a striped head among the rocks, and the dogs darted off in full cry. The human searchers kept their eyes on the path, up the last few lung-tugging steps. Then they looked down into a verdant valley, centered on a lake green with huge, tropical-appearing leaves. 'Spatterdock,' said the Professor. 'Indian pond lily.' Around the lake were isolated stands of lodgepole pine and spruce, and among these . . .

'Cabins,' said Mahlia, not sure she had really seen them. The log walls and shingled roofs did not make them easy to see.

'And there're the choppers,' said Badger, pointing beyond the lake to a flat, flower-speckled meadow where one large helicopter and one small, buglike one rested. 'And what in God's name is that?'

They had not seen it at first, partly because it was stone against stone, gray on gray, and partly because it was so improbable. A temple, one facade above another, pillared corridor above pillared corridor, the whole crowned with a grove of stupas as though it had been in India or Cambodia rather than here in these Colorado mountains.

The Professor peered at it through his field glasses. 'Someone must have been building this thing for decades. It certainly isn't recent. The pillars have lichen on them. Did the Rangers mention this to you?'

'Unless they've actually been up here, they couldn't have seen it.' He turned, peering up at the high ridgeline beyond the head of the cirque. 'It's at the foot of the cliff. From up there, one couldn't see the foot of the cliff.'

'We don't like people seeing the foot of the cliff,' said a voice behind them. They turned to be confronted by a rifle barrel poking from a rock cleft, well hidden from anyone coming along the trail. The man who held it regarded them with a kind of sour glee. 'We don't like people trespassing, period.' The gun swung wildly to cover the dogs, returning from their hunt. The Professor whistled sharply, bringing them to his side, though they seemed more inclined to take on the rifleman than to obey.

Badger's first inclination had been to snarl as the dogs were doing. The eager expression on the rifleman's face made him change his mind. Instead, he clenched his teeth and used his mildest voice. 'We don't intend to trespass. I've been told my wife, Carolyn Ettison, may be here with an old friend of her family's. Michael Shiel.'

The man before them did not reply. He bit his cheek in what seemed to be a facial twitch, fiddled with the rifle trigger, clicking his fingernail across it repeatedly in a little tic, tic, tic of annoyance or thoughtfulness. His face was not reassuring, being made up of equal areas of deep, pitted scars and long, narrow ones. One eyebrow had ben cut in half so that it tented in what should have been a quizzical expression but in fact appeared arrogant and threatening. 'Shiel,' he said at last. 'You know him?'

'My . . . my in-laws know him,' he replied very carefully. 'My wife's mother thought she might be here with my son. Robby. He's about five.'

'A kid?' No mistaking the mocking incredulity of that word. 'Here in Lhamballa? Not likely, mister. Not for long.'

Mahlia slumped to the ground, half sitting, eyes resolutely fixed on the broken rock between her feet. She felt the

155

Professor's hand on her shoulder but did not look up. When the rifle-bearing guard had first spoken, the world around her had shifted alarmingly, everything within sight suddenly moving, as though seen through thick glass or water, and ghostly images flowed by. 'Here in Lhamballa,' he had said, and a child had run past him screaming, a young girl, white-faced with terror, crowned with lilac blooms. 'Not likely. Not for long.' Her face had been covered with blood from a cut on her forehead; her white dress was stained with blood as well, and she stopped, panting, to hold herself between her legs and scream soundlessly into Mahlia's face before running on. Mahlia panted a little, tried a quick glimpse at the mountainside. It had shifted back. The pursuing black figures were gone. She struggled to her feet, hearing Badger say:

'My wife. Carolyn. Is she here?'

'I couldn't say,' the guard replied with a sidelong sneer that could have meant anything at all. 'You can ask Shiel, though. Since you're such a good friend of the family.'

His stance as he followed them down into the valley was almost playful. A cat with a mouse, Mahlia thought. The path was smoother, worn down by much use, running between small garden plots where robed workers looked up without interest as they passed. For a moment the workers were gone. White-clad processions marched instead, a ghostly glimmer of torchlight, dreamed against the sun. The valley was full of phantoms, but in a moment reality came into focus again.

'What can they grow here?' she asked. 'It's so high. So cold.'

'Lettuce,' the Professor answered absently. 'Peas. Spinach. If they start things in a greenhouse, they could grow quite a number of short-season crops. Or it may be make-work. Just to keep them busy.'

Badger was stalking beside them, examining the face of every woman they passed, receiving in return only glances of dreamy anticipation that had nothing to do with reality. They were seeing something else, doing something else.

Mahlia's skin quivered, and she looked away.

They mounted the steps of the temple, a flight almost a hundred feet wide at the bottom, narrowing to half that at the top, to stand in a sheltered porch. Roughly carved pillars supported the stories above and heavy oak doors stretched in a long line to either side. There were no windows. The guard went crabwise down the porch, stopping to knock at the end door and murmur something they could not hear. He beckoned them then, his sneering smile more evident than before.

'Here's your old family friend. Michael Shiel.'

He was incredible, fantastic! Incredibly handsome. Fantastically dressed in a long, full robe quilted from ribbons or strips of cloth, a garish coat of many colors which should have appeared clownlike but did not. A fretful murmur came from the room behind him, and he shut the door firmly as he moved toward them into the light, eyes slitted and hands thrust deep into pockets. Though he and the guard were unalike in feature, their sneering smiles were kin.

'Well, well,' he said. 'So it's little Carolyn's husband, Beaver. Or Squirrel? Some animal name, isn't it? Who are these? Your keepers?' The mockery was intentional, designed to elicit anger. Behind them Mahlia could hear the tic, tic, tic of the guard's fingernail on the trigger of his rifle, the half-muffled snigger.

Badger was astonishingly calm. He might not even have heard Shiel, so little attention did he pay to it. He looked once at the Professor, then said, 'Badger Ettison, Mr. Shiel. This gentleman is Myron Boyce. Professor Boyce is an expert in the field of art history. When he heard I was coming here to look for Carolyn, he asked if he might come along. It seems there's rumored to be an art treasure here, something quite valuable collected by the man who built the place. . . .'

Whatever Shiel had expected, it was not this. His brows quirked, two tiny lines between them, almost annoyance. He was one, Mahlia thought, who did not like surprises.

The Professor picked this up smoothly. 'Mr. McCloughlin was said to have some priceless eighth-century Cambodian sculptures. I quite understand your reluctance to have half the museums of the world trespassing on your privacy, but there's more than one of them would pay millions. Millions. Wouldn't you say so, Mahlia?' The Professor turned to her, bland, poised.

She took a deep breath before answering him, The little girl had just run down the cloister in which they stood, still crowned with purple flowers, face a white blur, without expression. 'Certainly,' she said, carefully not looking to see where the child went. 'The recent wars in Cambodia have destroyed so much. Conservation efforts came much too late. Authentic antiquities are simply priceless. . . .'

Badger again. 'If the carvings aren't here, at least the Professor can tell the art world so and keep them off your neck. If they are here . . . well, he can appraise them for you, and I suppose that hasn't been done recently. That's not why I came, however. Has Carolyn been here?'

Dark eyes regarded them without expression. His face might have been carved from stone except that when the word 'millions' was said, there was a flicker. Only a flicker, but unmistakable. 'Carolyn? Why, yes, Ettison. She's here, as a matter of fact. I'll . . . have someone scout around and find her for you. Meantime, Denk can take you down to one of the cabins and rustle you up some supper. You'll do that, won't you, Denk?' Eyes locked on eyes, and it was Denk's that fell from the contest. Evidently this was not what Denk had expected, either.

'Sure, Michael.' He shifted from foot to foot uneasily, starting as Shiel spoke again.

'I'll want to talk to you about these sculptures, Professor. Are you talking about something pretty big?'

The old man smiled charmingly. 'Quite small, actually. I shouldn't wonder if old McCloughlin stole them. I doubt he had the kind of money necessary to buy them. I take it you don't know where they are?'

'There was a lot of stuff here when we took over,' he said,

waving vaguely at the valley as though all of it had been awash with artifacts. 'I never paid that much attention.'

The Professor shook his head. 'Well, we must certainly look for them. A pity if they were lost. A real pity.'

They followed Denk away from the temple, down into the grove of trees. Mahlia sighed with relief. The ghosts had gone again. When they were left at an empty cabin, she sat down on the bed, exhausted, whispering to the Professor, 'This whole valley is full of visions. It's packed. I can't tell the real people from the ghosts.'

'You handled it well, my dear. I wouldn't have known. Do you think it's anything helpful?'

'I don't know yet,' she fretted. 'I think he believed us about the sculptures. What do we tell him when asks? Ivory? Jade?'

'No. He'd be able to identify ivory or jade himself. We say gray stone, if asked. No intrinsic material value. Only value as history and art. And it will take an expert to recognize them. Which we are, aren't we, girl?'

They had been huddled together, not watching Badger, who stood at the door. A muffled exclamation caught their attention. He was looking up the path, a kind of frightened anticipation in his eyes. 'Carolyn,' he said. 'She's coming down!'

Mahlia couldn't stop herself. She moved to the open door, stood to one side of it where she could see and hear him. He did not move toward his wife. He waited for her at the foot of the cabin steps, only the jump-jump-jump of the tiny muscle at his jaw betraying his lack of calm.

'Badger! I didn't think you'd ever find me here!'

She was lovely; improbably lovely. Wide innocent eyes glowing under an utterly unclouded brow; lips gently parted in what could easily be happy surprise, or childlike joy, or anything else one cared to read into that face. A cloud of golden hair moved around her head as though with a life and will of its own. She was dressed in jeans and a clever, expensive jacket, hands thrust deep into its pockets, shoulders raised in mock chill. Her head tilted toward him, questioning. There was not one line of guilt or concern on that face.

'Why?' His voice was so thick Mahlia could not recognize it. 'Why, Carolyn?'

'I thought everybody would think I was dead. How did you know, Badg? Why did you come looking?'

He fumbled for a moment, drew a deep breath. 'You wouldn't have died like that, Carolyn. Other ways, maybe. Not like that. I know you too well to believe that. So, it had to be something else – like running away. Why did you run away, Carolyn? Why did you come here?'

'Why, Badger, I ran away because someone told me I was in danger. Robby, too. I wouldn't have done it otherwise.' Her voice was without guile, as though she had just told him the sun was setting. 'We'd be safe if everyone thought we were dead. It seemed best, Badger. Really.'

'Why here? I could have taken you away! To a place as remote as this, if necessary. Why, Carolyn!'

'Oh, now, Badg, don't be nasty and demanding. You know I don't like that. I've known the Shiels since I was a little girl. And Michael – well, Michael knows about this kind of danger I'm in. He's studied it.'

She turned to look back up the path. Shiel stood there, still in his fantastic robes, staring down at her. She waved to him, almost gaily. 'It was the best place to come, really.'

'Where's Robby?'

'Safe,' she said, flushing for the first time.

'Where?'

'He's safe, Badger! Come on, now. You've found me and that's one for you. Don't spoil it. I'll tell you about it later, maybe. Maybe we won't even need to talk about it. Michael thinks he has a way to get me . . . out of danger.' She pressed closely to Badger, face to face, running her fingers along his neck and jaw, around his shoulders, down his back. He shuddered, drawing away from her, and she stepped back, examining his face. What she saw did not reassure her.

'I've come thousands of miles to find you, to find my son,

and you tell me not to talk about it? For God's sake, Carolyn, what's the matter with you? Do you think I don't –'

The Professor moved ponderously onto the porch, interrupting Badger now in a firm, warning voice. 'Is this your wife? Well, how lovely she is. I'm delighted to meet you, my dear, and delighted to know that *all Badger's worries were groundless*. I'm Myron Boyce. Professor Boyce, really. You can call me My. Mr Shiel may have told you what we came about. My associate, Mahlia Waiwela. Mahlia, come meet Badger's wife.'

So summoned, she managed to walk onto the porch, to smile, to bend forward and touch fingers in a mockery of a handshake, ignoring the chill revulsion she felt when those fingers touched her own. Badger was standing to one side, fists balled, jaw so tightly clenched his lips were white.

'Listen,' Carolyn was saying. 'Michael suggests we all have dinner together tonight. There's a kind of . . . oh, a ceremony about sunset, but that's private. Just for members, you know. But after that?'

'Fine,' grated Badger, ignoring the Professor's imploring expression. 'And perhaps you and I can talk in the meantime.'

'Badg, I'd love to, really. But Michael's counting on me to make some arrangements and help. He'll have a chance to show you around before it gets dark. You won't be bored, I promise. I'll have a snack sent down, too. We all had lunch hours and hours ago. Later, Badg, okay?' And she was smiling, walking away from them, turning to wave, like someone leaving a cocktail party.

The Professor moved to stand between Badger and the retreating figure, screening him from the sight of the man at the top of the path. 'Control yourself, Ettison. Shiel's watching you. She may have acted that way because he's watching you; now take a deep breath and control yourself. You blow now and the whole thing could go down the drain and us with it.'

'Casual,' Badger muttered, so angry he could hardly speak. 'As though we'd seen each other for breakfast this morning.'

'You don't know what story she told him. None of us know what the bloody hell is going on here. We agreed, remember? No mention of Matuku. No more mention than necessary of Darinbaugh. Now you see why. We're only innocent bystanders, and you're only some poor dumb slob looking for his wife.'

'All right, all right. You can let me be a little angry. I think even Shiel would expect a dumb slob to be a little angry under the circumstances.' He looked up, saw Mahlia, flushed a deep red. 'Not exactly what I'd led you to expect, was it?'

'Don't judge yet,' she murmured. 'The Professor's right. We don't know what's going on.' Privately she thought the woman had played the part too easily to be under any kind of compulsion. No. Carolyn was doing what she wanted to do. The only question was why.

19

They barely had time to compose themselves before Shiel came down the trail, still dressed in his fantastic robes, lounging along, hands in pockets. 'I thought you might like to take a look at the temple,' he said. 'See if there's anything there like what you were looking for.'

'How long has it been there?' the Professor asked, getting to his feet with a weary sigh. He would have been quite happy not to have walked anywhere for several days. He had been longer distances over rougher terrain without feeling as tired and dispirited as he did at the moment, and the thought of dank rock chambers did not please him. Still, he slapped his thigh to summon the dogs and started out with Shiel, letting Badger and Mahlia trail along behind.

'How long has it been there?' he asked again.

'The way I get the story, it was a mining claim. Gold, I think. The miners broke through to some old rock caverns with carvings in them. Not what you're looking for, I guess. The thought at the time was the Indians made them, though it doesn't look like American Indian stuff. Well, the miners had some sickness or something, and they blamed it on the carvings. Claimed there were evil spirits in the mine, and the place was left empty. Then McCloughlin's bunch bought it back in the thirties. It was during the Depression, of course, with everybody talking about war coming. So, they moved their people up here. They're the ones who carved the front on the temple. McCloughlin wanted it to look like something he'd seen in the East. Well, after a time they died out. The last one alive was my father's sister. She had title to the place as the last survivor, I guess, and my father ended up with it. We came out here and looked it over. He wasn't interested in staying. I was a member of a small . . . philosophical group, I guess you'd call it. Back in New York. We decided to move out here.'

'A group which hasn't died out,' said the Professor loudly, covering a muffled exclamation from Badger. He had heard about the so-called philosophical group from Barry Springer.

There was a bark of laughter from Shiel, quickly stifled. 'No. No, this one hasn't died out. As a matter of fact, it's growing a little. We've built two new cabins this year, and a new storehouse.' They were passing one of the garden plots, being worked by two haggard individuals who looked, by the Professor's standards, both hungry and ill used. Male or female, he couldn't tell, until one of them raised his head and the straggling beard showed him to be a white-faced youth of about twenty-one or -two with the same unfocused eyes and dreamy smile all the other workers seemed to have, as though they didn't see or saw something that wasn't there. 'We can't raise much stuff at this altitude, of course, not in the open, but we've got greenhouses ordered.' The condition of his gardeners did not seem to distress Shiel at all.

'Still,' the Professor murmured with stony perseverance, 'it can't be self-sustaining. It must be very expensive. Fuel, for example. If you were using wood, the valley would be deforested by now.' He had seen great, eroded areas of Nepal where wood was needed as the only heat or cooking fuel, and he knew what that need did to forested slopes.

'Oh, well,' Shiel turned the blazing smile on him. 'I thought you understood. All our resident members bring a dowry when they join. Our nonresident members pay dues, of course. We live on the income from that, really. You're right, of course. Propane is expensive. And food, though our tastes are simple. One of our biggest expenses is maintenance on the choppers, two big ones to bring in freight, and the little one to taxi members from the airport.'

'And amusements?'

'Ah, well, I suppose you'd call us a philosophical foundation. The people who come here are trying to get away from amusements, as much as anything. TV, you know. And too much drinking and smoking. We want to get in touch with reality. Life up here is very real.' He smiled again, and the Professor shivered. The smile was so frankly predatory that he would not have been surprised if the man had bitten him.

They had come to the stairs leading up into the temple. 'Why is it called a temple?' the Professor asked, waiting for the others to catch up to them. 'Is it used for worship?'

'We have occasional gatherings here on the steps. There's no auditorium or large room inside. It's simply the old mine tunnels plus a warren of small rooms carved into the side of the cliff. The front is just that – a front. McCloughlin's folly. My aunt used to write that he was a real fanatic about it.' He paused to find a key from among a heavy cluster hanging at his belt. The door led to a rock-carved chamber. There were flashlights on a shelf inside the door, and he tested several before finding ones that suited him. 'It's dark in there,' he said. 'I got caught once with dead batteries. Thought I never would get out. Finally remembered all the floors slope down to go in and up to go out, but I must've crawled a mile.' He handed them each a light, then led the way into the dark corridors. 'Aunty's bunch carved all this, in the last few years before they died. Different kind of carving from the outside.'

The walls were badly carved in low relief, with figures and animals evidently intended to represent Bible stories.

165

Professor Boyce recognized Noah and the ark, though none of the animals were recognizable as to species. A lumpy snake twined around a tree full of round lumps, a figure below carrying two of the lumps. No. Those were her breasts. Eve. Breasts, apples, snake, branches, almost indistinguishable.

Some slip of an unaccustomed chisel had twisted Eve's mouth into a leering grin. It was the same in all the figures. Noah glared threateningly at his animals. Joshua led a host of bestial devils rather than avenging Israelites. There was a hopeless ineptitude to the carvings, a dogged persistence that was depressing, and the Professor turned to see Mahlia regarding them with horror. The beam of her flashlight had dropped nearly to the floor of the tunnel where words had been hacked into the stone. 'Help us. God help us.' She shivered.

'Trouble?' he whispered as Badger walked behind them, flicking the light on endless dioramas of tortured stone.

'People,' she whispered in return. 'Sad, tortured old people, caught here, trapped here by something. They were carving every religious thing they could think of. Trying to make some kind of protection for themselves.'

'Against what?'

'I don't know,' she whispered. 'Something dreadful. Something close. But it was a long time ago. I only get flickers.'

'Matuku?'

'I almost wish it were. No. Something else.'

The Professor cleared his throat, spoke loudly in the smothering dark. 'This isn't what we're looking for. All of this stuff is recent. Recent and bad.' He moved down the line, almost stumbling over Ching, Bing, and Ting who trotted silently around his feet.

'I know,' said Shiel carelessly. 'This stuff goes on for a quite a while. The older carvings are deeper inside the mountain. The old ones. The ones the Indians are supposed to have done.' He led them down the slope, deeper into the mountain. Water ran beneath their feet, and they heard it dripping somewhere.

Then they rounded a corner, and came face to face with terror.

The breasts came into the light first. Sweetly curved, perfect hemispheres, like those improbable goddesses carved in throbbing plenitude on Hindu temples, the erotic ripeness melting into a waist slender as a sapling. Badger gasped, heat flowing into his groin as though he had walked above a furnace. Mahlia flushed, tingling, aroused, and as quickly chilled. The breasts watched her like eyes. They did not offer sustenance; they were hungry mouths, pursed lips, suckers of blood.

They stepped back, widening the torchlight in which the figure stood. Hips as sweetly curved as the breasts; slender legs poised in dance, arms bent as though summoning. It smiled at them from the rock wall, and its mouth glittered with moisture like saliva, a figure in full relief, beautiful and horrible and hungry.

The dogs whined, barked sharply, ears and tails down. Lips drew back in miniature growls, and they sought the protection of the Professor's ankles.

'God,' whispered the Professor. 'What in heaven's name is that?'

She looked out at them from the wall, following them with her eyes. Fragments of paint still clung to the pale body, to the purple crown of flowers it wore, to the anklet of skulls. Beneath one foot a figure writhed, crushed. Gathered at the feet were musicians with flutes and drums, a procession of maidens also crowned in purple flowers, eyes wide and vague as though drugged.

'The musician figures are Mayan,' Mahlia whispered. 'See those long sloped foreheads and noses. So are the costumes, and the figures in the procession. But the . . . the main figure – that's Hindu, isn't it?'

The Professor nodded, moving his torch back and forth across the carving. A woman's figure which no person, man or woman, could look at without desire; a demon's face which no person could look at without terror. The mouth was half-open, a little pursed, as for some terrible kiss.

'It makes me think of Kali,' said Mahlia. 'But it isn't Kali.'

'Succubus,' murmured the Professor. 'The Terrible Night Walker. See the man beneath her foot. The succubus comes in the night and presses the breath out of people. See the little girls in the procession. Her sacrifices. She is sometimes called the Destroyer of Innocents.'

They stood in amazement, Shiel's voice coming from behind them in the dark, shockingly unimpressed. 'Is this the stuff you were talking about? McCloughlin's stuff?'

'Lord, no, man. This is carved from the wall, not brought in from somewhere else.' The Professor turned his light along the curving tunnel. The first carving was only one of a number of figures. He moved along a gallery of masterpieces: processions, individual figures, horrible scenes of blood and sacrifice, again and again the lovely, terrible woman's figure. Badger followed him, mouth open, and the dogs trailed behind, never ceasing their complaint.

Something in Shiel's disappointed stillness warned of danger, and the Professor said firmly, 'Come to think of it, McCloughlin might have incorporated the Cambodian carvings into these. And even if he didn't, there may be a treasure here. Lord, there's so much. It'd take a week just to take a good look. And what were Mayan carvers doing this far north? At this altitude?'

Badger felt the same brooding threat, sought to distract it. 'Professor Boyce would need better lights, too, Shiel. I'm no art expert, but in this torchlight, one can't see anything very well.'

The Professor assented gratefully. 'Lights. We'll need lights on stands, and some good camera equipment, and about a week or ten days. However, even if the Cambodian carvings aren't here, these may be of very great value. It's simply too early to say. I'm amazed. Who would have expected it?'

They turned and trudged out of the place, the dogs still whining, and it was not until they came into the open, out from under the ponderous mass of carved stone, that their troubled cries ceased.

'How was it,' Shiel asked casually, 'that you learned of this place?'

'Laura Beecham mentioned it,' said Badger, trying to be equally casual.

The Professor stiffened, waiting.

'Just like that? I mean, she's had almost a year to think of it.'

Badger thought frantically. Jared Shiel had seen them arrive in Baleford. Jared Shiel might well be in communication with this fantastic figure beside them. 'No, not out of thin air. Laura felt that Carolyn might have gone to Baleford, to meet a man named Darinbaugh. Up until then, we all thought Carolyn was dead.'

'Henry Darinbaugh. I hear he's dead. You know anything about that?'

'I was told he died of a heart attack,' Badger said carefully. 'While I was there looking for Carolyn.'

'Heart attack,' mused the other. 'Did you hear anything about the family curse?'

Badger started to shake his head, and the Professor interrupted in a smooth, humorous voice. 'Oh, yes, we did, my boy. That farm woman. What was her name? Frolius? Didn't she tell us about something the old man kept locked behind gates?' He laughed, the very picture of a jovial academic, reciting the superstitions of the common folk to his own enormous amusement. 'Didn't she say something about it getting away after he died, Badger? Well, Mr. Shiel, your family comes from there. Surely you would know more about it than we do.'

Shiel shrugged, an elaborate, shoulder-raising motion ending in outstretched arms. 'Did you tell Carolyn that?'

'No. I didn't mention it. It didn't seem important.' Badger said. 'Her . . . her mother told us about Darinbaugh and Baleford, and we met the Frolius couple there. They told us about the connection between Laura Beecham and your family, and that led Laura to remembering Carolyn had been here before.' He kept his face carefully blank, his voice unemotional, though he wanted to strike that smiling face before him.

169

Denk stood at the top of the path, the rifle in his hands. If one looked carefully around the valley, one could see three or four other such figures, all with rifles. It seemed wise to remain innocuous.

'She seemed to feel very threatened,' the Professor said, taking Shiel's attention away from Badger, where it had rested too long. 'Why is that, do you know?'

'Listen, I'll tell you a good one,' Shiel said, smiling a glorious smile, radiant and fell. 'My father always swore Henry Darinbaugh had a genie – you know, like in 'Aladdin's Lamp'? Oh, I don't know if it was a real genie or not, but something like that. You ever run across anything like that in your travels, Professor? Man like you should have heard of something like that.'

The old man nodded, wrinkling his face in a picture of amused concentration. 'I have, yes. I've even encountered some that I'd swear really existed, though most such things are mere pretense, of course. It's hard for a scholarly man to admit, but I've seen some very strange things.'

'You ever hear how a person catches one of those things? Let's suppose Henry Darinbaugh's genie got away. Some say it'll come looking for Carolyn because she's his daughter – if Laura told you about old Henry, I guess she must have told you that.'

'No,' Badger said honestly. 'Laura didn't mention that.'

'Well, Carolyn thinks it will come after her. That's why she came here.' He watched them narrowly, looking for any signs of disbelief. All of them bore the proper facial expressions, apparently totally absorbed in his story. He seemed satisfied with this, though Mahlia thought she might have overdone it. 'Now suppose this thing comes looking. How would somebody lock it up? Would you know about that?'

The Professor frowned. 'I could research the question, I suppose. As a matter of fact, the Frolius woman gave me a great stack of Darinbaugh's books. She didn't know what else to do with them, I guess, and felt they should be given to some bookish person before the mice got them. There might be something in them. . . .'

'Books. Where?'

'They're in the Bronco, down at the end of the trail,' said Mahlia. 'A large box of them. But surely you're not serious about this, Mr. Shiel. Did your father really believe in this so-called genie?'

The man flushed, at first angrily, then with some sudden access of humor. 'Maybe he did. I can't say. What I was thinking, though, was how frightened Carolyn is. She's sure the thing is after her. If we had some way to lock it up, then it couldn't bother her, could it?' He was still watching them closely, too closely.

Badger picked up the discussion as though he had rehearsed it. 'You mean, pretend to do it for therapeutic reasons? That's a marvelous idea. Professor Boyce, there may be something to that. It would relieve Carolyn's mind, since she's so upset. Could you do something halfway believable?'

'Oh, Carolyn's very knowledgeable about these things,' Shiel interjected, a shrillness in his voice they had not heard before. 'I wouldn't try to fool her. Whatever we do should be the real thing.'

'The *real* thing? You mean, according to the books?' asked the Professor doubtfully. 'That's what you mean by 'real thing'?'

'Well . . . yes. Right.' He gave them another radiant smile. 'Denk's taking one of the choppers to the airport pretty soon. I'll have him stop off and pick up those books for you.' And he waved, a picture of friendliness, as he turned to leave them. 'Don't worry about Carolyn, Ettison. She's a little hysterical over this whole thing, but she'll settle down. You all plan to have dinner with me tonight, about nine. We can make a list then of the equipment you need to look for those carvings. . . .'

'Carolyn?' asked Badger. 'Will she join us?'

'Sure. She should be settled down by then.'

Badger nodded, not trusting himself to speak. When Shiel was out of earshot, he muttered brokenly, 'Where the hell's Robby!'

'We'll find Robby,' the Professor said. 'The boy will be all right. We'll find him. But first we have to get out of here.'

'Get Carolyn out of here.' Badger mumbled. 'That man has her hypnotized.' He wiped his face, sheened with a gloss of angry sweat.

Mahlia, looking at him sadly, thought it was not Carolyn who had been hypnotized.

They stumbled down the hill toward the cabin.

'What's going on here?' asked Badger suddenly. 'There's something wrong with you two. What is it?'

'Well,' the Professor said, rubbing his head, rubbing his eyes, spitting to clear a nasty taste the dank tunnels had left in his mouth, 'I believe we have stumbled into a nest of devil worshippers. Succubus worshippers. Which, after our recent encounters with you-know-what, is rather more of the same thing than I'd planned on.'

'I don't think Shiel knows.' Mahlia ventured, casting a furtive glance behind her. 'I think he got the idea from the carvings, but he thinks it's just a game.'

'A tyro? An amateur? Setting off nitro in the happy belief he is putting on a fireworks display? Surely, Mahlia . . .'

'No. He doesn't know. None of them do. They're doing something here, something quite filthy. I can see edges of it. Pieces all mixed up. But they believe it's just – just something they're doing. A pretense. A game.'

'Like adolescents playing Dungeons and Dragons? He believes *he* is controlling what goes on?'

She nodded. 'Oh, yes, he thinks he's controlling it. And there's a lot of money involved. Poeple paying money to participate in – in what? That's the part that won't come clear.'

'Orgies of some kind,' the Professor mumbled. 'Or worse.'

'Worse, I think,' she replied. 'Much worse. Rape, blood sacrifice, maybe murder.'

'Is that why the dogs were whining?' asked Badger. 'They could smell the blood?'

172

'They smell the demon, boy. Demons, I should say. These are Tibetan animals, bred for centuries to guard the monasteries against assault, bred to sniff out devils.'

'When you say Shiel doesn't *know*, what do you mean?'

'We mean, Badger, that whoever carved that creature on the stone did so from life, so to speak. Whoever carved it saw a real, actual, and present creature. But this pathetic bunch of idiots playing at games don't know she is here. They have never seen her.'

'What do we do now?'

'We keep calm and remain sensible and try to think of a way to get out of here.'

'With Carolyn.'

'Oh, Lord yes, my boy. Yes. With Carolyn.' He said it with unmistakable distaste.

Badger flushed. 'I have to find out where she left Robby, and with whom. Even if that were all . . .'

'I understand. Say no more.'

They reached the cabin, and Mahlia sagged onto the porch. There were so many ghosts thronged about her that it felt like wading through fog, endless, sticky fog. Someone had left them a plate of sandwiches and a few cans of beer. Badger peered at them suspiciously, but the Professor took a large bite, mumbling something about being too hungry to worry about drugs. A large helicopter took off with a great hammering of air to fly along the trail and over the pass, disappearing beyond the rise. The little dogs looked up at the noise before sinking noses on paws once more. After a lengthy time it returned.

Moved by something a bit stronger than curiosity, Mahlia went into the forest and climbed a tree to peer between the branches at the flat meadow where the machine had landed. It disgorged an assorted group of passengers. Several fat-bellied types, complete with cigars. Two women, appearing vulpine and voracious even at this distance. Something in their walk, she thought, like the walk of a hunting shore bird. Carolyn approached the group and escorted it toward a distant grove in which a long, newly built building stood by itself.

'What do you see?' asked Badger and the Professor, below her.

'Some of those nonresident members Shiel was talking about,' she replied. 'There's a modern building over that way, beyond the meadow. Whoops.' She slid quickly down the tree. 'Denk. He's got the box of books.'

They were on the porch finishing the last of the sandwiches when the man arrived.

'Who's your pilot?' Badger asked idly. 'Must be touchy, flying at this altitude.,'

'I am,' the man replied. 'Or Shiel. And it's only touchy if you don't know what you're doing. Shiel wants you to go on inside for now. There's going to be a private ceremony pretty quick, and he'd appreciate your cooperation.'

'We won't wander around,' said Badger.

'He'd rather you went in,' the man said, hands busy with their endless tic, tic, tic upon the rifle.

They looked at one another, decided on prudence as the best policy, and went into the cabin. There was a sharp sound from outside, a bolt shot home. They were locked in.

'What the hell . . .' Badger fumed.

'Easy, boy. They're not going to risk our seeing what they're up to. Windows, Mahlia?'

'There's a metal mesh over the screens. We could pry it off, but they'd know we had.'

'Trapdoor,' Badger said, pointing upward. The outline of a square door appeared between two of the roof beams. 'See the nail holes in the logs? There used to a ladder here.'

He made a stirrup with his hands, lifting Mahlia as she heaved against the boards. 'I can't,' she said. 'It's stuck. We need to hit it with something.'

They took lengths of firewood and pounded upward, loosing a shower of dust and mouse droppings as the door shuddered upward. Mahlia heaved herself through the hole. 'Little attic,' she called down to them. 'One little window in the end wall. It's filthy. Pass me up something to wipe it with.' There was a pause. 'Oh, hell.' The men below heard breaking glass. 'I couldn't see through it,' she called. 'So I just knocked it out.'

Then she was leaning through the hole over their heads. 'I'm going to knock out the rest of it! It's a little tiny window right up against a big tree. I'll bet nobody's been up here for twenty years! They won't even be able to see the glass is gone, and I can climb the tree from here.'

'Well?' said the Professor.

'Well,' answered Badger, making a stirrup again. The old man struggled through the hole, then reached down to help Badger up. They crouched beneath the low ceiling, watching Mahlia as she broke out the glass with her shoe. When the glass was gone, the remaining crosspieces of half-rotted wood came away with one strong pull.

She went out the window.

'I'm not up to trees, my boy. Tell me what you see, if anything.'

From the window level they could see little enough, a needly expanse of forest, with glimpses of the path below. Once they had climbed a bit higher, however, there were views through the foliage in every direction. All the valley's inhabitants and visitors seemed to be assembling on the steps of the temple, deep in the shadow of the cliff. Someone brought an armload of firewood onto the stone porch and laid small piles.

'What's happening?' came a whisper – from above them.

Both of them clung to the trunk, gulping.

'What's happening?' repeated the voice. 'It's me, Molly.'

They looked up to see her seated on a branch above their heads.

'How long have you been here?' Mahlia demanded.

'Not long. I'll ask you one more time, what's happening?'

'Shiel is conducting some kind of ceremony,' Badger answered. 'He didn't want us to see it, whatever it is. He locked us in.'

'Jared Shiel's boy,' said Molly in a soft, ominous tone. 'A devil like his daddy, I've no doubt. His daddy was a devil worshipper. Tried to suck Henry Darinbaugh into that, but Henry'd have none of it. Ironic, really. Turned out Henry had the devil Jared had been searching for. Well, it's a way to get wealthy, I suppose. Offering new thrills to the bored rich.'

'The ultimate pornography?' offered Badger. 'All a nasty game?'

'It may have started that way. Michael Shiel may have taken the whole con well past pretense and into something worse.'

Mahlia described what they had seen in the tunnels, her voice cracking when she tried to find the right words.

Molly nodded. 'I'm not surprised. Devils are like crows. Very seldom only one of them. Find one, look behind it for another. That's because the people who summon them flock together, like crows. Carrion crows. Still, we won't know for sure until we see. Look, there's Shiel and some woman. Pretty. That must be –' She broke off.

'Carolyn,' said Badger dully.

'Well, Badger, it wouldn't hurt to know what they're saying to one another, would it?' He shook his head, and Molly went on. 'They're going into one of the cabins. I'll just have a listen, if you don't mind.' The branch above them was abruptly vacant.

They climbed down. The Professor had dropped back to the lower floor, where he lay on one of the sagging beds, surrounded by dogs. Mahlia and Badger sat on the other, half reclining against the headboard, both aware of their closeness, of the hinted intimacy of sharing a bed in a tension that rapidly grew unbearable. Mahlia was about to rise when the door creaked, opened, and Molly came through.

'I cleaned up the glass. Simoney's putting the trapdoor back down. You can come out and watch, if you like. . . .'

'What did you hear?' Badger demanded.

Molly flushed. 'I don't think –'

'I want to know. What did you hear?'

'Shiel – well, he's sold her a bill of goods. He isn't even sure that Darinbaugh's demon exists, but he wants it. If it does exist, he figures it will come here after Carolyn. If it does exist, he wants to possess it. So, he's telling her anything he can to keep her here. Told her the ceremony they're having tonight will bottle old Matuku. Doesn't believe it himself. Greedy bastard.'

'Does he have any idea –'

'Obviously not,' she replied impatiently. 'He's never seen it. He has no idea what it can do. Stupid amateurs, playin' with a volcano and thinkin' it's a campfire!'

'But she thinks he knows what he's doing? Well, of course she does. What should we do now?'

'Sneak up the hill and watch the ceremony if you've a mind to. Simoney and Martha and me think we should know what's going on here. It has a bad smell to it. Get yourself back here before they come lookin' for you. All innocent. Shiel won't hurt you. He figures he needs you. All three.' She turned and went out the door, partly to hide her face. She had not told Badger the first words she had overheard Carolyn say. 'Kill them, Michael. Kill them all. Before the thing trails them here. It won't come here if they're dead . . .'

They found a place behind a screening line of trees where they could look down on the temple steps. Fires had been lit and were billowing clouds of fragrant smoke up the cliffside. To one side were gathered the small group of agitated visitors, talking among themselves, shifting impatiently. The residents were gathered on the other side, and Mahlia gasped as she saw what they were doing. Dressed in straight robes and sandals, they were assembled precisely as were the carved musicians in the tunnels; drummers and flutists crouched below a line of singers, skins of spotted cats across their shoulders, plumes in their hair. They began to play, a repetitive, unmelodic chain of notes and thumps, over and over, accompanying a chant at which Simoney shook her head.

'Nonsense,' she said. 'Couldn't summon a hungry cat to dinner with that.'

The victims were brought out of the temple. There were three girls. Not more than twelve or thirteen years old, Mahlia thought, dressed in white with crowns of purple flowers in their hair. Lilac. There had been lilac bushes near several of the cabins. She thought she could smell the fragrance, even at that distance.

Carolyn. She came down the line of girls, giving each one a slender something. What was it? The question was answered when Carolyn put one to her lips and blew a shrill, wavering tone. A whistle.

'Willow,' whispered Molly. 'Damnation. Willow assents to evil. Doesn't resist. Not like rowan. Or oak.'

Carolyn was gesturing, showing the girls where they must go. Away. Away into the woods. She pointed to the whistles hanging at their necks. Blow them. Into the woods, blowing the whistles. One of the little girls said something, half weeping, plaintively, and a gust of wind brought them Carolyn's voice in answer.

'Oh, we'll let you go right after the game. All you have to do is play the part well. Keep running, and keep the whistle blowing.'

The child turned, seeking among the assembly for some familiar face, showing them her own, pale and fearful.

A buzz of avid noise rose from the nonresidents.

'Bastards,' said Molly.

The musicians broke into frenzied sound. The girls were urged away from the steps, whipped into flight. They ran toward the trees, separate, hair streaming behind them, stumbling among the roots as they disappeared.

There was a well-calculated pause before the hunters broke ranks and went streaming into the darkness after them. The nonresidents, the visitors, armed with clubs and blades, pursued the faint, tremulous plaint of the whistles.

'Molly,' Mahlia said in a broken voice. 'Molly – you can't let them . . .'

'I know, girl. Don't worry. They won't catch them.'

Molly was gone. Simoney and Martha, gone. The other three rose, sickened, and stumbled back to the cabin. Once inside, Badger looped his shoelace around the bolt and managed to pull it partly closed from inside.

'What now?'

'Now we wait. And try to convince Shiel that our only hope of bottling up the demon is if we all go back to Baleford. We're outnumbered here. Badly.'

'When will you do that? We have no idea how long the thing will be gone.'

'I know, my boy. I'll mention it when I think he's ready to hear it. When it will buy us the best deal, one that gets all of us out of here. Me to do the job. Mahlia to assist me. Carolyn as bait. I can probably make him believe the thing won't work if I'm at all upset, and if anything were to happen to you, I'd be upset.'

'And then what?'

'Then hope to God I can find something in these books to help us. Until then, play it cool, my boy. Cool. Don't seem to hurry. If you do, you'll make him suspicious.' The old man rose, stretched, went inside to the box of books, and took one of them onto the bed with him. 'If I can stay awake, maybe there's something else in here of use.'

He could not concentrate on the books, even though he felt their lives might well depend upon it. There were noises in the woods for almost an hour. Whistling, calling, three gunshots spaced widely. Then there were angry voices, not far from the cabin, moving in the direction of the meadow. After that, the sound of a chopper taking off. Badger had taken another of the the the fat books, one written in what pretended to be English, and was scanning it page by page, looking for something about demons or how to control them or Solomon's Seal. There was only one lamp in the room, an inadequate light, and both he and the Professor were struggling to make out the dim letters. Mahlia, oppressed by a swarming of visions, had drunk half the small bottle of liquor she'd brought with her and fallen asleep.

They heard no sound preliminary to the bolt being withdrawn from the door. Denk stood there, the ever-present rifle at his back.

'Shiel's found something he wants you to take a look at. Back in the tunnels. Says it may be those things you were lookin' for.'

They looked at one another, shrugging. Mahlia was still deeply asleep. 'Should we wake her?'

'Let her sleep. The tunnels aren't exactly the cleanest place in the world. Let her sleep until dinnertime. This won't take long. You'll be back before she wakes up.'

20

The door Denk took them to was not one of those on the facade of the temple, but another, lower down, half-hidden behind the enormous flight of stairs. Heavy iron brackets held an oak bar across the metal-studded door. It was fastened with a rattling chain that needed both Denk and Badger to lift it away from the padlock. That, at least, was new and shiny steel. 'What the hell's in here?' muttered Badger, sucking a finger the chain had pinched. 'The wine stores?'

'Something like that,' Denk sniggered, stepping back as the door swung open to reveal a pocket of darkness. He fumbled with a lantern hung inside the door, pumped it with a few hard strokes, lit it. The mantle burned white with a harsh, hissing glow. 'Here, you carry the lantern, Professor. Just go straight on in.' The dogs surged around their ankles as they moved through the opening. Denk closed the door behind them. His fingers began their tic-tic-tic on the rifle as he followed them. 'Shiel did think of putting a wine cellar in when we first came up here, but he decided it was too inconvenient. He's got some construction stuff in here, though. That's why all the locks.' Their light picked up a side cavern with ladders, lumber, and heavy boxes stacked inside; Badger saw dynamite, a roll of fuse. 'We have to blast sometimes to put foundations in. He doesn't want people fooling around with the stuff.'

The tunnel ran straight back into the mountain, drier and less echoing than the ones behind the temple facade. 'What is this?' the Professor asked. 'Is it a mine adit?'

'Yeah. We figure it was dug earlier than the ones up above. Shiel found it a few years ago. There's a ladder along here a little way, in real good shape, too. No rot or nothing. See there, where your light is.'

Where their light was the rocky floor fell away into nothing, a pit of darkness. At one side a wooden ladder clung tightly to the rock wall, rising into darkness above, falling into darkness below. 'Down there?' asked Badger, incredulous. 'What's Shiel doing down there?'

'Oh, he remembered something he'd seen down there, carvings, he said. He went down to take a look. Told me to come get you. This ladder doesn't go down far. Twenty feet, maybe. You'll have to leave the dogs here. . . .'

'Not bloody likely,' muttered the Professor, scooping two fluffy bundles into his jacket. The dogs' heads appeared at the jacket front, making the old man look like a kangaroo. 'Badger. Can you carry Sanbandarong?'

Grimacing, Badger scooped the remaining dog into his own jacket, where it squirmed briefly before settling down with one piercing whine. He started down the ladder after tugging at it experimentally. There was no sign of rust; the bolts that fastened it to the wall were firm and tight. After about thirty rungs, he stepped off on solid rock, holding to the ladder with one hand. Above him the light swerved and stilled. The Professor was climbing with one arm thrust through the handle of the Coleman lantern. A splash of light showed above him. Evidently Denk had a flashlight.

His voice came from above, curiously vacant. 'Look off to the right side of the ladder as you're facing it. See that tunnel? Well, Shiel's down at the end of that. Tell him I went back to get those tools he wanted.'

'Now just wait a minute . . .' Badger's voice boomed in the tunnel, momentarily drowning the sound of retreating footsteps. No answer. 'What the hell!' Bing whined again, struggling.

Badger put the little dog on the floor, waited while the Professor recovered his breath and emptied his own jacket. The three animals circled, whining, seeming confused but not alarmed.

'Right?' asked the Professor.

'If you believe what he just said, yes. *Do* you believe what he just said?'

'You think Shiel isn't down here.'

'I think it's very remotely possible and not at all likely.'

From above came the solid chunking sound of a door closing. Even through it they could hear the rattle of chains. 'No reason to relock that door if he was coming right back,' said Badger. 'What do you want to bet we're locked in?'

'Take the lantern,' said the Professor laconically. 'I didn't tell him, but I have a flash in my coat pocket. With new batteries.'

'So do I.' Badger shook the lantern gently, listening. 'This thing's almost empty. No slosh.' He went swiftly back up the ladder, returning as quickly. 'I was right. We're locked in. Which seems to be pretty much routine around here. Now what?'

'Well, Shiel wants something from us, so he wouldn't want us hurt. I have Denk tabbed as pretty much under Shiel's thumb, which would indicate he isn't likely to mean us any lasting damage. So – why?'

'To get us out of the way a while?'

'Maybe. And maybe there actually is something down here someone thought we ought to see. As long as we've got light . . .' The old man moved off along the tunnel. It ran straight back into the mountainside, extending along the same line as the higher adit. After a time they heard water running, held the lantern high to see a liquid shine upon the wall where it seeped from some height above them along the vertical surface to vanish among the stones of the floor. The

183

lantern dimmed, and Badger pumped it again, hard. There was little fuel left in it, and the plunger banged repeatedly before it could build any pressure.

'He meant us to be here in the dark.'

'Either that, or he didn't know the lantern was almost empty, or he figured once we found out Shiel wasn't here, we'd wait by the door. Which anyone sensible would do. So, onward, good sir, onward. Shall we let this opportunity pass us by in contemplation of the unworthy motives of the odious Denk?' The Professor burbled his way off down the tunnel once more, Badger half running to keep up. 'We'll use this until it goes out.'

There was a whisper from somewhere ahead of them. A sibilance, like water flowing away in a small pipe. An exhalation.

They stopped. The dogs crouched, panting, their ears high. 'Wind?' queried the Professor softly. 'Coming through some shaft somewhere?'

'Could be.' They went on, more slowly. Ahead of them the light fell into darkness again as the floor dropped away. A chasm gaped in the tunnel floor, ten feet wide, the floor on the far side sloping slightly upward and covered with gravel. Mumbling to himself, the Professor dropped a stone into the chasm. They waited. At last a fading echo reached their ears, the sound of rock striking rock – and then the other sound, the exhalation sound, repeated.

'I'm not going to try to jump that,' Badger announced. 'The way the thing's sloped, there's a better than even chance of sliding on that gravel, right into the pit.'

'Come, my boy, where's your spirit of adventure? There were ladders back in that construction stuff. I saw them myself.

'There was some lumber there, too. Would you like to build a bridge?'

'It merely occurred to me that Denk knew we would stop here. Which might mean there is something interesting farther on. Or even an egress, which, as the most sated sideshow viewer knows, is a rare and wonderful animal.'

'You really want to go over there?'

'Why not? We're here, why not there?'

Sighing, Badger turned back the way they had come. It was twenty minutes before he returned behind a bobbing light with a fourteen-foot ladder on one shoulder. 'Thanks for the help.'

'My boy, you're young and strong, while I am old and feeble. I knew you'd want me to rest.'

Badger, busy pushing the ladder across the yawning chasm, did not reply. 'I'll hold it while you go across, then you for me.' He half lay across the ladder, bracing it while the Professor loaded the dogs once more and went over the slender bridge on all fours, hands and knees, like some shambling bear. Once across, he let the dogs go and sat heavily upon the other end of the ladder. Badger was not usually a victim of vertigo, but halfway across he stopped, suddenly dizzied, listening. It was that same sound, a breathing sound, as though something sighed pleasurably in the depths. Bing was quiet in his jacket.

The lantern burned feebly behind them at the chasm side. They went on by flashlight, flicking the beams from side to side, up and down the walls, carefully on the floor to find any other holes or rifts. There were none in the floor. There were holes low in the wall to their left, however, so round they might have been drilled, large enough for a man to crawl into if he did not want to move once he was inside, with walls that looked almost polished. Badger ran his fingers on the slick stone, bringing them away coated with slime. Grimacing, he wiped his hand on his trousers and hurried to catch up with the Professor. The tunnel turned sharply, a half circle to their left, bringing them parallel to their former track, in a downward-sloping corridor little wider than their shoulders as they walked side by side. Stones on either side fell away in deep relief, light and shadow. Badger caught his breath as something moved at the corner of his vision. 'Boyce!'

'Eh?' The man turned, seeing what he had not seen as he passed. Another of the smooth walled openings in the side of the tunnel, two feet across, sloping upward toward the tunnel they had traversed on their way down. He reached the lantern toward it, lighting it. At the far end of it a pallid mass squirmed into shadow. They were not certain they had seen it. They could not believe they had not.

'What was it?'

The Professor left his flashlight in the opening, wiped his hands, his face, lifted Ching to the opening where he sniffed, whined, growled. 'Nothing diabolic, according to Padmasambhava. What could it be? Many cave-dwelling animals are pale and blind. Most of them are very small, however. Hard to tell what the size of that thing was. It could have been small. Perhaps we have a false perspective.' He did not sound convincing.

Badger thrust the light farther into the opening, peered past it up the long tube it disclosed. 'No false perspective,' he announced. 'The opening is an even diameter, all the way up. It opens into the tunnel we were just walking through. That thing was the size of a large dog.' He shuddered without reason. Again the sound came, the peculiar exhalation. Anticipatory.

For a moment they dithered, both thinking of the slender ladder and the way back as they had come. Then, with a muffled exclamation, the Professor stumped away down the tunnel once again, this time more slowly. It was he who saw the first carvings.

His hand on Badger's shoulder turned him toward the wall, where an alcove had been cut into the side rock, some seven or eight feet long, the back wall smoothed and polished. A stained altarlike stone stood before this shining surface, and into the smooth wall a picture had been engraved. Not high relief as the other carvings they had seen, these were line drawings, almost delicate, full of masterful detail.

'There's your Terrible Night Walker again,' Badger murmured. 'What's she doing?'

The glorious goddess-demon was shown in profile, bending toward a kneeling worshipper who held up one hand. With pursed lips, the goddess kissed the raised finger-tips. That same pursed-lip expression had been represented on the larger carvings they had seen in the higher tunnels.

'Odd,' mused the Profesor. 'You'd think it would be the other way around. The devotee should be kissing the goddess's hand. Let's see if there are any more.'

Twenty paces down the narrow corridor was a similiar shrine. The kneeling figure still held up its arm, but the hand dropped back from the wrist at an angle, like a glove. The demon's lips were pressed to the wrist. The worshipper's face was turned toward them, the mouth rigidly square, eyes wide in an expression which could equally have been rapture or agony.

'By the names of twenty Tonkinese devils, what is this?' The Professor hummed, hawed, mumbled to himself. 'If there are two, there may be more.' He drifted off down the tunnel, still mumbling, Badger and the dogs close behind. There were more of the two-foot holes low on the tunnel walls. He thrust his light inside several of them, peering up the sloping length to the place it ended in open space. Badger justifiably prided himself on a sense of direction, and he knew it for one of the same holes he had seen on the way down. The mountain was as full of holes as a cheese, and the various curves of the twisting tunnel they walked were connected by a network of them.

The third carving, twenty paces away, was poised above an altar stone on which small hillocks of wax still bulged from some ancient votive light. The Professor held his flash high, moving it from side to side to bring out the detail. The devotee still knelt, the goddess's hand around the upper arm, raising the elbow to those ever-pursed lips. From the elbow the lower arm depended slackly at an impossible angle. Once more Badger thought of a glove, hanging limp.

'What's the old phrase?' he asked. 'Something about turning one's bones to water?'

'What do you mean?'

'Well, the demon kisses the fingers and the hand goes all limp. Then the demon kisses the wrist and the lower arm

187

goes limp. The next carving, if there is a next one, will have the whole arm flopping.'

'Ah.' The old man leaned nearer, bringing the light almost to touch the carved face of the kneeling figure. This time there was no mistaking the agony in that face. The eyes were closed, the mouth sagged open in something far past despair.

They went on, Badger flicking his light on both walls at the round holes near the tunnel floor. The next carving was a repeat of the first. 'Not quite,' commented the Professor. 'The first one was kissing the right hand. This is the left.'

'And the right arm?'

'I can't see it, It's behind the figure.'

'There's another little detail. This time there's someone holding the victim.'

It was true. A masked priest in feathered regalia held the victim braced against his legs. As they stood regarding this, both made somehow aware of their own bodies, of their solid skeletons within, the sound came again. Nearer. The dogs whined sharply, ears down.

'Do we go on?' Badger, fatalistically.

'Not far, I think. Still, I'd like to see more of this series. Perhaps just a few more. . . .'

They went four more. Numbers five and six were the same as two and three, wrist and elbow, with the masked priest holding the victim. In carving number seven, the victim was laid flat upon an altar stone and the succubus leaned forward to kiss the toes of the right foot. From the incised drawing it was impossible to tell anything about the arms, only one of which was shown, lying flat upon the altar.

'Have you seen enough!' Badger, whispering, skin prickling as though in a chill wind. 'Toe, ankle, then knee. Right leg, then left.'

'And each time, the part which has been kissed goes limp, you think?'

'Look, Professor, these aren't exactly illustrations out of a pathology text. All I said was that it looks like that. Kind of boneless.'

188

'I'm trying to remember if there's any disease which actually dissolves the bone.'

'I can't recall having heard of anything like that.'

'That doesn't mean such a disease might not exist in some out-of-the-way corner of the world. Perhaps a disease which used to exist but doesn't any longer. Very ancient, maybe. These things were drawn as an explanation, do you think?'

'Oh, see, Aunt Xilopetl's bones are all jelly because the demon kissed them?'

'Either that or the pictures illustrate a legend. A myth. Like the mutilation of Osiris or the flaying of Xintecacoatl.'

'I don't know. All I know is it's damned dark down here. We've been in here . . . almost two hours. These batteries were new, but they won't last forever. The dogs don't like the smell of the place, and I don't like the filthy pictures. I'll take right leg, left leg on trust without seeing the carvings.'

'You don't want to go on?'

'Frankly, Professor,' he hissed, 'every nerve I've got tells me to get out of here.'

'Very well, my boy. But I want to come back here when all this is over. These carvings are quite unique. More so, in their way, than the ones we saw above. Fruit for a dozen years' research here. The graduate students will fight each other for –'

They both heard it at the same moment. That anticipatory exhalation, abruptly sounding in the tunnel behind them. Ting, Ching, and Bing growled deep in their throats, making the sound of much larger dogs. Both of the men recognized the sound as the same one they had heard several times since entering the tunnel. At a distance it had resembled a breath, a sigh. Closer, they knew it for what it was: something heavy, moving on gravel. A sliding, crunching sound. Uphill. Between them and the way they had come in.

'Down, or up?' the Professor whispered.

'The way out is up.'

'There's something there.'

'There's something down, too. I've heard it repeatedly.'

'Up, then.' They began to move cautiously back the way they had come, covering the floor and walls with circles of light as they went, the dogs close at their heels, still growling. Their own feet crunched on the gravel. They found themselves tiptoeing, trying to walk silently, breathing shallowly.

Badger's light caught something near the floor on the right. Light-colored. Shapeless. It moved into the wall with astonishing speed, leaving behind a shiny slickness which the light skidded across, glistening.

'What in God's name . . .?'

Badger had already lengthened his stride, knelt by the hole, and lighted it. The hole was blocked by something, something pale that moved up the sloping tube and away.

'Where's it going?'

'Ahead of us, Professor. The other end of this tube is this same tunnel, a little higher up.'

'We'll have to get past it, then.'

'Unless it keeps moving away from us. Come on. I hear more of whatever they are behind us.'

They trudged up the sloping way. It had not seemed this steep on the way down. The dogs stayed tight at their ankles, unwilling to move ahead or trail behind. Badger turned once to flick his light behind them. Pallid movement, uncertain in the bad light, but following them. He thought of the speed with which the creature had moved into its hole, and he shuddered. It had been large. The size of a large dog, or a bulky, deformed human being.

They stopped once to breathe, to listen. The grating seemed to come from every direction, ahead of them, behind them. Joined with this was a new sound, a soft kind of singing that made them catch their breaths to listen. One wanted to hear more of that, much more of that, but the adrenalin pumping through their bodies did not allow pause. Badger found himself knowing this, being glad of this. He thought of Ulysses and the Sirens and wished frantically for something to stop his ears with. Except if he did, he could not hear the scraping sounds behind him.

190

They had come to the turn in the tunnel, moved rapidly around to their right. There was movement in the tunnel before them, everywhere, crunching sounds, a flickering movement as of things withdrawn. Badger thought of slugs in the garden, disappearing under the mold when leaves were moved aside to let in the light. When they flashed the light again, there was nothing there, only the hint of paleness in a dozen disks at the side of the tunnel, disks that vanished as they watched, appalled. The hole dwellers were retreating. Like slugs, they did not like the light.

'Let's get the hell out of here,' Badger muttered, searching the darkness ahead for a sign of the lantern they had left burning. No light there. There had been very little fuel left. 'Careful. It wasn't far to that chasm where we left the ladder.'

They trotted, lighting the holes in the tunnel wall as they went, seeing the movement there, far back, far down, slow, reluctant movement. They knew that whatever moved away did not move far and returned when they passed. Abruptly they were at the chasm, frantically searching for the ladder.

Which was not there. There were large flattened places in the gravel, a hint of glistening slime, two deep scars where the ladder end had rested. And nothing else. Ten feet away the other side of the chasm shone in their torchlight.

'Come on, Professor. That's no jump. The other side is downhill, so we'll make it easily.'

'I can't. Sorry, my boy, but this artificial hip of mine won't take that. I can scramble about like a monkey so long as there's something to hold to, but a jump like that – I know it's no distance for a young man. You go ahead.'

'Go ahead and what?' grated Badger. 'Leave you here?'

'I'm no martyr, Badger. If my eyes didn't play me false, there were several ladders in that storeroom up above. I had rather thought you might bring one back.'

'There were more than one. I grabbed the first one I saw. It'll take time. Those things will be back.'

'Those things don't like light. It's possible they have

191

intelligence. The displacement of our bridge may not have been accidental. It is possible they are intelligent enough to know our light will eventually burn out. The longer we dither here, the more likely that is. There can't be much juice left in either of these lights. Will you go and try, or shall we talk ourselves into darkness?'

Stung, Badger handed the old man his own flash-light and backed down the tunnel. It was not much of a jump for a young man, if he could keep his footing on the gravel. Then he was pushing off from the chasm edge, reaching out – and the siren song caught him from the depths. He fell heavily on the far side, unable to move, hearing only that song.

'Badger! Badger!' His name, and he didn't care. Someone was singing to him. He wanted to go to the someone who sang. He found himself turning, crawling back the way he had come. Back to the edge of the chasm, hanging his head over, his shoulders, his arms. Something went by him, tossed from the far side. Snarling drowned out the song, and something bit him, hard!

'What?' He sat up, Ting was snarling at him, biting his leg, nipping him. Across the chasm the Professor shouted at him, at the dog. 'Get him, Thisrongdetsan. Bite him. That's it. Nip him good. For God's sake, Badger, get moving, will you? Look there!'

He turned a flash back the way they had come. Pale forms there, shapeless, amorphous, at the very edge of the light, edging away. 'Will you get a move on! Put something in your ears, boy. Move.'

Badger struggled to his feet. The song was still there, but he could resist it. He turned away from the chasm, into the dark. Behind him he saw one of the lights go off. The Professor was conserving the batteries. Putting his hand on the right wall of the tunnel, he moved as quickly as possible, counting his steps. They had not come far from the ladder to the chasm. A few hundred yards at most. He counted a hundred paces, began to panic, then realized his steps were not as long in the darkness as they had been in the lantern light, soothed himself with this thought, and banged his head against the ladder. As he started up it, Ting whined, and he stopped long enough to thrust the dog inside his jacket. Then he was up the ladder and feeling his way down the wider way. The storeroom would be on his left. He put his hand on the left-hand wall. He had a book of matches in one pocket. There were four matches left in it, as he remembered. He would need those in the storeroom. The way seemed to go on and on. Farther than he remembered. Could he have mistaken which side the room was on?

Cursing, he stopped, dropped Ting out of his jacket, searched for the matches. Jacket pockets. None. Pants pockets. None. He knew he had them. Had to have them. Couldn't find the damned ladder without them. Wanted to scream, wanted to curse, kick something. Found them in shirt pocket. Why shirt pocket? Damn. First one wouldn't light.

Badger took himself sternly in hand, took a deep breath, and lighted a match. In the feeble glow, he saw the curved entrance to the storeroom at his left hand. He went in, kicked an empty box into splinters, lit a handful of these. In the dance of firelight he saw the other ladder. A ten-foot ladder. Remembering his leap across the chasm, Badger doubted it would reach. There were some two-by-fours, fourteen-footers. There was another lantern, sloshing almost full. He lit it. Dynamite. Detonators. Fuse. He grabbed half a dozen sticks, filled his pockets, picked up two of the two-by-fours, hung the lantern on a free thumb, and struggled back out the door, Ting whining at his heels.

'You're going to have to walk, dog,' he muttered. 'Walk, and wait. I can't manage you and all this stuff on the ladder.'

He left the lantern at the top of the ladder, shining out into empty space, and dropped the two-by-fours by their ends. Ting whined above him as he plunged down the ladder, collected the two-by-fours, and ran into the darkness, trying to hold the lumber straight so that it didn't catch him up against the tunnel walls. There was a feeble, very feeble glow ahead.

'Professor!' he yelled. 'I'm here.'

The Professor stood very near the gulf, his back to it,

shining one flashlight into the tunnel before him. At the edge of the light the pallid forms were assembled in their bulky dozens. Badger saw eyes gleaming in the light, circular mouths, nostrils, an almost human assemblage of features. They crept slowly forward. At the Professor's feet Ching and Bing circled and growled.

'I hope you brought a ladder, my boy. Or a bo'sun's chair. Or something. I have this very strong idea that these creatures want to eat me.'

'Two-by-fours, Professor. The ladder wasn't long enough. I'm edging them over now.'

'You'll need light to keep them at bay while I cross. Otherwise they'll tip me in.'

'I've got something better. Move a little to your left. Okay. Do you want me to come over there and get the dogs?'

'Actually, they can make it quite well on their own. Go, Padmasambhava. Go, Sanbandarong.' Tails waving jauntily, the two dogs trotted over the two-by-fours like circus performers, laughing at Badger with their tongues, then turned to growl once more at the things on the other side. The Professor set the flashlight down facing the creatures and turned to sprawl onto the narrow slats. They sagged beneath his weight, creaking, then slipped on the far side, sliding toward Badger. Only a few inches of their length remained on the far bank. Cursing, Badger braced the ends against his feet, straining to hold them while he fumbled with a detonator and short length of fuse. He had two matches left.

He lit one of them.

'No,' said a voice from the far side of the chasm, a breathy voice. 'Woke up. Hungry.'

Surprised, he lifted the fragile light. One of the pallid bulks heaved itself forward into the light. A slug. A vast, pinky-gray slug, one end of it lifted toward the light. Two blue eyes, a gray, circular mouth, two holes where a nose might be, two convoluted flaps where ears might be. No teeth. No jaw. And yet it breathed language at him out of a totally inhuman mouth. 'Hungry.'

The flame reached his fingers and he juggled it, cursing.

The creature was edging forward, almost at the ends of the two-by-fours. 'Hungry,' it said again. The Professor was two-thirds of the way across, pulling himself along on the sagging boards. 'Hungry.' It moved closer, thrusting its hideous bulk against the boards. Behind it, the other creatures came closer, one of them pushing its awful head end against the flashlight, pushing it to the edge.

He had one match left.

He lit it, applying it to the fuse, which caught, sparkling like some Fourth of July firework, sputtering and shedding sparks. He held it, seeing the weird assemblage on the far side by its light, their mouths open, like babies.

'They have no bones,' he said aloud. 'No bones.'

At his feet the boards quivered. The Professor crawled past him. Across the way the nearest bulk heaved itself onto the boards to follow. With calm deliberation, the Professor turned, pulled the boards toward him, then let them go. They dropped into the chasm in slow motion, the pinky-gray bulk falling with them, a long, soundless drop with no echo at the end of it.

'If you're going to throw that, my boy, I'd do it now!' The sparks had almost reached his hand. With a muffled curse, Badger heaved the explosive into the tunnel across the chasm as the flashlight was pushed into the pit. He watched it, fascinated, as it fell, a dimming light, into a squirming worms' nest of fetid flesh far below.

Then the tunnel fell in behind them. They ran, not listening to the cacophony of screams, hisses, thrashing noises, and over all these the siren singing. Badger thrust his fingers into his ears. Ahead of them the lantern at the top of the ladder glowed like a star. They and the dogs were up it in less time than it had taken to come down it, were moving toward the chain-locked entrance once more. On the lower level behind them they heard scraping sounds.

'I'm going to blow that gate,' muttered Badger. 'For God's sake, don't let that lantern go out. It's all the light we have.'

'There's something behind us.'

'At the bottom of the ladder, yes. I don't think they can climb it. There aren't any of those wormholes up here. At least none I've seen. Let's not hang around to find out.'

'I hope that explosion didn't destroy the carvings.'

'Were you planning on going back?'

'Well, when one encounters a new life form . . .'

'Not new, Professor. Not new at all.'

'I don't understand.'

'Think it out.' Badger was busy with fuse and detonator once more. 'Let's try this once with two sticks at the bottom of the door. If that doesn't blow a hole in it, we'll have to try it with stones piled on the dynamite. This'll be safer for us, if it works.'

He lit the fuse from the lantern, dragged the Professor back into the storeroom, and crouched against the wall, dogs gathered close. The explosion could blow a hole in the door. It could also bring the tunnel down on their heads. Or it might do nothing much, and the slugs might find a way to this level. He had only a moment to consider this possibility before the fuse burned down to nothing.

21

Mahlia was still sleeping when Carolyn came, and she woke reluctantly as the woman shook her.

'Wha?' she mumbled, trying to focus, expecting somehow that the double vision of dream would be there still, as soon as she was awake.

'Badger wants you,' Carolyn said, standing away from her, near the door. 'He's found something he wants you to see.'

'Where's the Professor?' Mahlia sat up, dizzy. The liquor had let her sleep, but it had done nothing to give her a clear head.

'With him,' said Carolyn, shaking her long blond hair out of her eyes impatiently, tapping her finger against the doorjamb, eyes swiveling back and forth inside the room. 'Come on. They said to hurry.'

Mahlia stumbled to her feet. Something. Something just beyond her reach she should be thinking of. She ran fingers through her hair, shook her head. Not able to think. She put on her jacket and followed Carolyn out onto the path.

'Where?' she asked. The sun had dropped below the

mountain. Shadows were filling the valley. 'Where are they?'

'Down in the cabin by the lake. They found some – what you call 'em. Carvings. They said to hurry.' And Carolyn was hurrying, striding off down the path toward the distant cabin. It stood alone, half-hidden behind an outcropping of rock, shadowed by three gigantic spruces. There was a lilac bush in bud at the corner of the building. Smoke rose from the chimney, comfortingly ordinary. Mahlia shook her head once more and followed.

Carolyn opened the door and stook back for Mahlia to enter first.

Then Carolyn shut the door behind her from outside and bolted it.

Mahlia stood in an empty room, stupefied, staring at the small fire on the hearth. She spun as the woman spoke to her through the window, a window covered on the outside with heavy wire mesh. 'This is the place we keep our . . . participants. I thought you'd like to see it. Mahlia. That's your name, isn't it?'

The face outside the window became several faces, Carolyn faces, Carolyn faces with heavy gates superimposed, Carolyn faces weaving lilac crowns. 'Where are Badger and the Professor?' Mahlia asked, keeping her voice calm. 'Why have you brought me here?'

'You know why, sweetie. Shiel says you may be a grown-up virgin, is that true? Never had a man?'

Mahlia refused to answer. There could be no answer, neither truth nor lie would serve. Shiel might have said that for some reason of his own. Or he might have said nothing of the kind. Certainly the victims she kept seeing in ghostly shadows were virgins – if girls eleven and twelve might be supposed to be so. 'Do you have some particular interest in virgins, Carolyn? I'm considerably older than your usual victims, aren't I? Is that how you got brought up here originally, Carolyn? Did Michael Shiel intend you as one of his virgin sacrifices?' It wasn't a guess. As she said it, she knew it was true, without question. There was not even horror left to feel at the fact.

Carolyn giggled, a high-pitched, obscene little twitch of sound. 'Well, he thought I was, you know. Except by the time I got here, he knew differently.'

'How old were you?'

'Who remembers? Fourteen. Fifteen. Not too young to be a hunter, Michael said. I got to be a hunter then. Until Daddy Miles dragged me back home. Michael made me go. To save trouble. Michael didn't want legal trouble. Didn't want the fuzz.' She giggled. 'He told me I could come back if I wanted to. Any time.'

'Anyhow, I wasn't too young, and he says you're not too old. You'll do. Some of the hunters like them a little older, a little bigger. They run farther.' Again that obscene giggle. 'I guess it's like fishing. They like a good fighter before they finish them off.'

'That's the agenda, is it? A few phony spells and stinks. A little chanting, just for effect. Then some drugged little girl is hunted to death by a bunch of cult-crazy rapists?'

'It's not phony!' Carolyn screamed at her. 'It's real. If we do it right, it will trap that thing. Michael says so. We were all set to trap it tonight, but the ceremony went wrong. The shits got away. They never get away, but they did. Gone. The hunters were mad, but Michael calmed them down. Not me. I'm not calmed down. I've got to do it over. Do it right!' Shrill, raving, she was screaming into Mahlia's face. 'It'll go back in the tunnels with the other one, Michael says. It'll forget all about me!'

'You think Badger will take you back when he finds out?' Mahlia asked, thinking that he probably would.

'What makes you think he's going to find out? He's down in the mines looking for treasure. Your Professor friend is down in the mines with him, him and his dogs. When Shiel left in the chopper, Denk told them they'd found something. He put them in the old tunnel. Maybe they won't get out at all. They're locked in. How're they going to find out what happened to you, pretty face? Telepathy?' She slammed a second bolt home on the outside of the door and stalked away into the falling dark.

The room held no light but that from the coals of the fire. If they find out, Mahlia thought despairingly, someone will have to tell them. Molly, where are you when I need you?

'Here,' came a whisper.

She stared into the shadowy corners. No one. 'Where?'

'Here.' The voice came from near the ceiling. Mahlia peered upward, seeing only a spider's web with a fat spider centered upon it – a fat spider. Wearing a kerchief and a dark coat over a print housedress. 'Hi,' said the spider.

'Molly? Is that you?'

'Only in a manner of speaking, Mahlia. Don't worry about it. A little imaging; a little transmission. Enough reception to have heard that woman. Not very nice, is she?'

'Badger thinks she's been hypnotized,' Mahlia answered dully. 'He's in love with her. He thinks she's perfect.'

'Ah,' whispered the spider. 'Do you really think he does?'

Of course she thought so. She had just said so. No. No, she didn't think so. 'Perhaps . . . he is struggling.'

'Perhaps he is, Mahlia. All our lives long we are changing, and each time it is a struggle. What are you going to do now?'

'Do! I'm locked up. If this charade follows the ghost patterns I've been watching all day, I'm due to be sacrificed at moonrise. What do you suggest?' She felt slow, weak tears sliding down her cheeks and made no move to wipe them away.

'There are those who might wish to be sacrificed at moonrise. I am told that the virgins who went to their deaths in the wells of Dzibilchaltun and Chichen went willingly.'

'That's crazy. They may have. I don't.'

'Well then, girl, wipe your face. You're acting like a victim.'

'Damn it, spider, I *am* a victim.'

'Not yet,' whispered the spider. 'Not yet. Now, dear, Simoney wants to compose a spell-song. It must be a spell to include the whole valley, all within it. A song which will take their silly game and make it real. A song to awaken what is here, for there is something here. Something even old Matuku will find difficult to handle. Help us.'

'I don't know how.'

'Of course you do. You have *seen* things in this valley. Tell Simoney all about it.'

'What did you see?' Simoney asked, a whisper from the shadows. 'What vision did you have about this sacrifice?'

Mahlia pressed hands against her aching temples, forced herself to concentrate. She had seen so much. 'I saw a child, a girl, perhaps eleven or twelve years old. Prepubescent. Crowned with lilac. Aaaah. Lilac . . .'

'What is it about the lilac?'

'There's a lilac bush growing at the corner of this house, another one up the hill. Near the old house, all fallen in. A woman planted it there. I saw her. It must have been fifty years ago. Her husband said the world would end soon. He believed it. He and all the rest. She didn't believe it. If she contradicted him, he beat her. So she planted the lilac, her way of saying, "The earth will go on." She lay on her bed in that old house, thinking of the empty cabins, of those who had died, smelling the lilac, listening. . . .'

'Did you hear anything?'

'Drums. And the child was blowing a whistle. A shrill keening. Pitiful. Sorrowful. And there was a harsh, shrieking birdcall in answer. I looked up to see it, gray against the evening sky, white bands upon its wings.'

'A nighthawk. What else?'

'A wall of willow around the streamside where she ran, shadow over the reality. Tall, magenta thistles, their faces turned to the east.'

'Musk thistle. And the chase?'

'I didn't see all of it. Only the child, running, blood on her forehead, near the end. She'd been raped, I think. She was holding herself. But they'd let her go, to run some more. I knew what they were going to do.'

'So,' sang Simoney in her spider whisper. 'By the lonely lilac. . .'

'By the tall musk thistle,' sang Molly.

'Through the wall of willow . . .' Martha's voice, from far away.

'By the lonely lilac
And the tall musk thistle
Through the wall of willow
Comes the shrieking cry
Of the nighthawk's mate
Over where you lie
On your pillow,
Late.
In the sullen hours,
Among empty rooms
Wishing night on by
As the lilac blooms
And a running child
Crowned with purple flowers
Breathes a nightbird cry
On a willow whistle
By the lonely lilac
And the tall musk thistle.'

The words caught her like a net, held her, contained her within the vision and the time. She was lost in the chanting. The air in the cabin began that same curious curdling she had felt at the Professor's apartment, thickening and thinning, stretching the fabric of time and place and person. A spell, she thought. And they have caught me in it.

'Not just you,' whispered Molly. 'Everyone.'

'Among empty rooms
Wishing night on by
From our sleepless bed
As the nighthawks cry
In the waiting wild
Plotting endless dooms
On pursuers' heads
While the running child

Serenades the thistle
And the lonely lilac
On a willow whistle.'

'Shhh,' whispered the spider-Molly. 'They'll be here in a moment for you, but you won't be here for them. Lie against the wall, back in the corner. They won't even see you. . . .'

'Plotting endless doom
On pursuers' heads
And our spell is spun
As we bring the bloom
From the lilac bud
And the hunters run
To the sound of drums
To the scent of blood
And the demon comes.'

The scent of lilac was suddenly overpowering. Though she had been told to lie down, Mahlia risked a quick look out the heavily screened window. The bush at the corner of the house was in full bloom, filling the air with a fragrance so heavy as to be almost stupefying. A drumbeat came from the hill, pulsing like a heart, and torchlight glowed there, flowing down toward the cabin. She stumbled away from the window and lay down as directed, still hearing the three voices. . . .

'On the shadow loom
Weave a semblance child
And our spell is spun
As we bring the bloom
From the lilac bud
In the waiting wild
Where the hunters run
To the sound of drums
To the scent of blood
And the demon comes.'

In the center of the room a Mahlia-semblance stood, white, pale, a shadow girl. The door burst open to a ragged platoon of wild-eyed residents and guards, Denk in their midst, Carolyn leading the pack. Through slitted eyelids, Mahlia watched as they took the shadow semblance out of the place, a white dressed Mahlia, yet not a Mahlia, a child, yet not a child, crowning her with the lilac blooms, placing the whistle on its thong around her neck. And yet . . . and yet, it was not the semblance who wore the lilac. Each of them reached out to crown that semblance, and each of them ended with a crown upon their own heads, men and women both, crowned with lilac and unaware.

Carolyn's voice came clearly through the noise of the throng. 'Bring her out. Give her the drink. Bring her out now. The moon's rising. Quick. Quick.'

So the semblance was brought into the night, fed the draught that each of them drank, believing another drank it. Carolyn drank it. And it was Carolyn who ended with the whistle around her neck.

Carolyn.

'Don't,' Mahlia whispered to the spider singers. 'Badger won't forgive you. He won't forgive me. He'll think I did it. Don't. Please.'

'Silly girl,' sang Martha. 'We're not doing it. She's doing it. You can get up now.'

She reached the window in time to watch the semblance dart away into the night, in time to hear the piping of the whistle. The mob waited impatiently for the moon to show above the edge of the mountain as the drums rattled, like snakes about to strike.

She heard the chopper coming, a wham, wham, wham of air thrusting down at the trees around her. Shiel had returned. From the face of the cliff where the temple stood came an explosion of sound and a flash of orange flame. Something had blown up. Torchlight bloomed there, and figures moved within it like dancing shadows. Badger and Professor Boyce had found their way out of the tunnels. Mahlia recognized Badger's black silhouette as he stiffened,

204

listened, then moved slowly toward the drum sounds. The Professor came after him, dogs leaping at his ankles.

'Shiel didn't know she was doing this?' Mahlia whispered.

'Of course not. Shiel thinks Matuku is the source of power and wealth. He wants Matuku saved for himself, not frittered away on one of their hunts. This ritual is something he's created for his "hunters," but he told her it would work to capture Matuku, just to keep her from leaving. It did a good deal more than that. Carolyn thinks the demon will respond to this ritual. She's got the wrong ritual, I'm afraid. Or the wrong demon.' Molly's voice faded, vanished.

The moon rose, a silver edge upon the rockfall, and the mob before the cabin burst into motion, dispersing, each in its own direction, each crowned with lilac, each pursuing something it alone could see, something it alone could hear. Carolyn fled among them, her voice a nighthawk screech. 'Follow her. Find her. Hold her for the demon.' And she paused to skip madly widdershins around the lilac bush, calling as though to some household pet, 'Come, demon. Come, demon. We have a tasty thing for you. Come, demon.'

'Carolyn! Carolyn! What are you doing!' Badger's voice from the top of the path.

She heard it, looked up for one brief instant, then darted away into the dark, laughing. 'Too late, Badger. We took her, your girlfriend. Your pretty virgin, Badger. We took her. Old demon will like this one.'

She was lost in the surrounding darkness, but the sound of the willow whistle came back pleadingly.

'Carolyn's blowing it?' Mahlia whispered. She couldn't believe the woman wouldn't realize what she was doing.

'She doesn't know she is. She thinks you are. They tell the victims that blowing the whistle will keep them safe, a kind of protection. It isn't, of course. It only leads the hungry hunters to the prey.'

Badger came running down the hill. When he saw Mahlia standing beside the cabin, he gave a glad cry and plunged forward to pull her roughly against him, arms tight around her. 'Mahlia. She said . . . she said . . .' He stepped away from her, holding her at arm's length. 'She said those bastards had you. . . .' He could not have said how he felt at that instant, the combination of joy and anger defeated him. He drew her close to him again.

Before she could answer, Shiel shouted at them from the path, 'What's going on here?'

'I don't know,' Mahlia said, half releasing herself. 'Carolyn tricked me into coming here, then she locked me in. Later she brought a whole mob of people here, all dressed in lilac crowns with drums and whistles. They've run off into the dark.'

'Without you!' He was incredulous, angry. 'They brought you here and then went off without you?'

'They were chasing someone. I think you'd better find Carolyn before she hurts herself,' Mahlia said. 'She was acting very strangely.'

The man ran wildly back up the hill toward the temple. They heard the sound of a door slamming, then he emerged into the moonlight of the temple stairs, carrying a rifle.

As though aware for the first time that he was holding Mahlia in tight, possessive hands, Badger let her go. 'Do you know which way she went?' he grated. 'What does she think she's doing?'

'She thinks she's using me for a virgin sacrifice to the demon.' The words were flat, unequivocal. Mahlia wanted him to know. It would hurt him, but he must know. 'She thinks she is killing me, Badger, to save herself. She's killed people before, when she was here as a child and since she's been here this time. She doesn't mind. She thinks it's rather fun.' She stopped as she saw the expression of anguish on his face.

'Oh, Mahlia, God, you've got to be wrong! It's Shiel. He must have drugged her with something.'

'Really?' the Professor drawled, bringing Badger's eyes away from Mahlia. 'Really? I think not, my boy. Shiel wants the genie for himself. He wants it safely locked up. And Carolyn is the bait. Why would he risk losing the bait in one of these obscene rituals? Look at him. He's trying to head her off. No. He didn't put her up to it. Carolyn thought of this one all by herself. Or there may have been some influence from below. . . .' He gestured back toward the tunnels they had recently left. 'There's something there. It's awake now.'

Mahlia nodded, half sobbing. 'Molly wakened it. She said so.'

Badger held himself rigid, staring in the direction Shiel had gone, carefully not looking at Mahlia. He didn't trust himself to look at her. 'I won't let myself believe that about Carolyn,' he said at last, choking on the words. 'I won't. I believe you believe it, Boyce, but I must not. For the love of God, she's my *wife*. Maybe she's been drugged. Misused. God, maybe he's hypnotized her. Maybe she's insane. But I've got to . . . got to give her a chance.' Now he did turn to Mahlia, begging her to understand, all the time wanting only to hold her and keep her safe. 'I have to.' His jaws were clenched so tightly that the cords of his neck stood out like ropes, and he trembled with his own frustrated longing for her.

'I understand,' said Mahlia in a broken voice. 'We'll help you if we can, Badger.'

'Then let's find her. Let's get her out of this.'

'Shiel won't hurt her,' murmured the Professor, shaking his head. 'He needs her.'

Badger didn't hear him. He was already running up the path, following Shiel into the forest.

'What do we do now?' whispered Mahlia into the empty room.

'Silly man!' came Martha's voice in a spider whisper. 'We'll do what we can, girl. Go along with them. We'll sort it out later.'

The two went after Badger, slowly, feeling no need to hurry. There was nothing they could do to move or change whatever was happening. The moon rose higher. From here and there on the forested slopes came drum taps, heartbeats of sound with the lonely whistle shrilling among them, piping like a lost soul. Badger turned off to the left, into the heavy woods that stretched from the side of the temple around the curve of the cirque and halfway up the slope. Above that line the rocky cliffs grew too steep for trees to grow, looming above the valley like an imprisoning wall, sheer cliffs of moon-silvered stone frowning down at them. Badger could not go far. Again they heard the whistle sound and Badger's voice, at some distance from it, shouting, 'Carolyn!'

'I was supposed to be blowing that whistle,' said Mahlia. 'They intended me to be piping away like a little bird.'

'You saw it? In advance?'

'I've been seeing it or things like it ever since we came into this valley. Little girls, mostly. Some older ones. None of them very old. Drugged. Told it was a game and that blowing the whistle would keep them safe. Then hunted down and raped, killed. By men and women both. Thrill seekers. Bloodthirsty devils. Sacrifice, they called it.'

'To what entity, Mahlia? Was there actually some . . . some supernatural presence?'

She sighed, terribly weary of all this. 'Molly says there's something here, something very old and terrible. But it's been asleep. Up until now it's all been pretense, a game, an excuse for doing what they wanted to do anyhow. Shiel hasn't collected the world's best citizens here.'

'Do you think Molly's right?'

'Yes, I know she is. There is something monstrous. Not Matuku. Something that was here when Shiel took over the place, something that dreamed, something that dragged people into its dreams. Whatever it was is certainly here now. Something ancient and horribly female.'

The Professor nodded. He did not mention the carvings they had seen deep inside the mountain or the threat they had escaped. If they had escaped. He was not sure he believed all of that himself and did not think he wanted to mention it to anyone, ever. Art or no art. 'I presume you escaped through the intervention of –'

'Yes. They're here. Somewhere. And they're angry at Badger.'

'Angry? Or unsympathetic?'

'They think he's a twit. Let's face it, Professor. I think he's a twit. My God, what does it take to make him see what she is!' And she was suddenly sobbing on the old man's broad chest, the tears opening a long-shut floodgate.

'A twit. Yes, child, he is that. Not as pragmatic as you or I. But then, he's a very faithful twit, give him credit. Faithful unto death, that's our Badger. Come now. Cry and be done with it. We must keep our wits about us.'

Though for a time they could find very little to apply their wits to. They followed the sounds of the hunt, at first up into the forest, then down again, actually following the dogs, who seemed to seek out the drums, which were at first widely dispersed but began gradually to congregate in the woods at either side of the temple. More and more of the drumbeats came from there, more and more of the shouts and cries. Mahlia and the Professor found a small clearing up the slope from the temple and stopped.

'No closer, I think, my dear. Something seems to be congregating down there, and I don't want us to find ourselves in the midst of a mob.' They sat in the moonlight beside the dogs, who had thrown themselves flat upon the blanket of pine needles. From a grove just beneath them on the flat floor of the valley, the whistle sounded. Above them on the slope they heard Badger's voice calling Carolyn's name once more.

Mahlia caught her breath, tugging the Professor's arm to turn him toward the temple. Light flowed from the cliff face, from the carvings, the pillars, the stupas, particularly from that doorway they had blown open beside the stairs. Pale, pustulant light, lurid and deadly, it flowed onto the wide flight of stone stairs and began to coalesce, rising, wavering, a pillar of gellid substance, glowing like a beacon, more and more brightly.

'That's not the thing they were chasing!' Mahlia whispered. 'That's not the thing Molly had them following!'

It was not. It began to shape itself, curving, roiling, arms stretching from it, and legs. Breasts forming from it, and hips. It was more seductive than the semblance that had run from the cabin, more voluptuous, more fatal. It raised a long, silver-white thing to its curved lips, played upon it, a bone whistle calling sirenlike into the darkness.

Mahlia tugged the Professor, crawling with him into the shadow of the trees. 'Don't let it see you,' she whispered frantically. 'Don't let it see you!' The call of the bone whistle tugged at her groin, her breasts. She saw sweat start out on the Professor's forehead, saw him gritting his teeth, murmuring some polysyllabic thing she could not understand. A chant. Some kind of protection. The dogs were utterly silent, tails and ears down, creeping almost on their bellies into the shadow of the trees. Above them on the slope, Badger turned, listened, plunged downward toward the siren song he had heard in the tunnel. From where they lay, Mahlia and the Professor could hear him crashing through the woods toward them, brittle branches snapping like shots, stones rolling beneath his feet.

On the opposite slope, Shiel also heard the song and began moving toward the sound.

The pale form turned on the temple steps, whirled, seeming to move toward itself from all directions simultaneously. A dozen men and women broke from the forest's edge, their little drums tap tapping, encouraging themselves with hoarse, lascivious cries which built to a frenzy as they caught sight of the creature on the steps. Even as it seemed to run from them, it seemed to be there awaiting them. One, quicker than the rest, cried out with fervid bloodlust and plunged toward it, throwing the drum to one side.

'That's Denk,' Mahlia said. 'He thinks it's me.'

He may have thought it was Mahlia. He did think it was something that could be violated, for he stopped to fumble with his trousers before approaching the thing, warily, arms wide, as though to catch some cowering creature. To those watching, there was only the piping silver figure, calm as stone, smiling a close-lipped smile that did not open until he came within reach of its arms. . . .

And then the lips opened to reveal what lay behind.

A taloned hand of pale fire took Denk by one shoulder and pressed him down, inexorably down into a kneeling position. Another fiery hand took Denk's right hand and raised his fingers to those smiling, pursed lips, to the fang-rimmed circlet that lay behind them.

The demon smiled, and sucked.

One finger, another, another, the thumb. His hand flapped bonelessly as he turned his head toward them, eyes wide in realization of ultimate horror. The thing bent toward his wrist, sucked. The bones came out in one long piece, crunching between the thing's teeth, the arm bones, then the elbow and the bone from the upper arm. The demon turned, whirled, fled, even as it quietly sucked upon the last bone, sucked it into itself like some monstrous candy stick. On the steps at its feet Denk lay, making a shrill keening sound of agony.

Those observing from the clearing could hear it. The others who were approaching seemed oblivious. The thing made a little moue of satisfaction as she bent down and pressed her lips to the top of Denk's skull. . . .

Mahlia saw. The Professor saw. Badger and Shiel, still high upon the hill among the trees, heard Denk's voice raised in a final agony. The hunters saw nothing, heard nothing. They came on, hunger unallayed, to participate in the hunt. On the steps of the temple a boneless creature writhed and flapped as it made moist, indescribable sounds of pain. Above it the succubus stood smiling, munching, waiting.

'Did you ever see anything like that before?' asked Martha of Molly where they stood suddenly beside Mahlia and the Professor. Her voice trembled.

'Succubus,' said Molly breathlessly. 'A very big one. Big enough, at any rate. I knew there was something here. I even worried if it would be big enough. We may have done something incredibly stupid. . . .'

'You think the other one will come?' whispered Simoney.

'With us having opened a channel and Carolyn dancing all over the mountainside calling it as though it were a pet dog? Of course it'll come.'

'We've seen this one before,' the Professor said, moistening his lips with a tongue almost too dry to speak. 'Badger and I. Carved in the tunnels inside that mountain. Old carvings. A lot longer ago than fifty years. And something more than that? You've summoned something more than that? You mean Matuku?'

'Watch and learn,' Molly said, her voice hard. 'Right now he's our best hope. If we haven't made some terrible miscalculations. Watch and learn.'

The succubus still twirled upon the steps; people hurled themselves forward into her embrace. Those already embraced, fat pallid slugs, lay thrashing upon the steps, hideous lumps of flesh, still alive. From the clearing in front of the temple the willow whistle sounded a last time, plaintive. Carolyn came from the grove clutching her whistle and the lilac crown, staggering drunkenly. From the temple stairs the succubus bent toward her with a rising effulgence, the siren song swelling.

Carolyn stumbled toward the stairs.

From just behind them, Badger cried her name and plunged downward, tripping over the Professor and the dogs to fall sprawling.

On the opposite side of the steps, Shiel emerged from the forest and started toward her also, at first not seeing what hummed and glowed upon the steps of the temple.

And out of those woods at that instant came the Wendigo, Matuku-pago-pago, Kachang-inda-cham-gunga, Star-Eater, Demon of the Pit, in a howling fury that tossed trees to either side even as they exploded in cold.

'MY CAROLYN,' boomed the great voice.

Carolyn, crowned with lilac, crept unheeding toward the steps of the temple.

'MINE,' called the figure on the temple steps, growing visibly larger, wider. The woman shape began to swell into something else, something greater. The siren song stilled in the face of this threat. Carolyn stumbled and fell, lay on the rocky ground as though dazed.

Simoney's voice whispered in the forest, a tiny song among the silences:

'And the hunters run
To the tapping drum,
To the scent of blood
And the demons come.'

Below the watchers, Carolyn turned on her belly and crawled as though in slow motion, a ponderous swimming across the earth, without progress, in place.

'MY CAROLYN,' boomed Matuku, a tree exploding in flying, deadly spears, one burying itself not an inch from Ching. With a muffled yelp, all three of the dogs tried to burrow under the old man's body.

Badger rose, stumbling across Ting as he tried to go down toward Carolyn, and Molly tripped him. 'Stay out of it,' she hissed at him, pushing him down. 'She may get lost in the shuffle down there, but not if you call attention to her.' For a moment it seemed Badger had not heard her, but then he subsided, heaving great panting breaths as he watched.

'MINE,' shrilled the succubus. 'CROWNED IN LILAC. MINE!'

The white form spun itself outward into a towering cloud which stamped with iron feet upon the step, once, twice. A wide, deep crack opened, running down the staircase from top to bottom. More white vapor poured out of the crack into the spinning form, strengthening it as it moved away from the steps and toward the mountainside. Two forces, one visible, the other invisible, became a maelstrom, a hurricane of flight and pursuit.

'I'll give you three to five on Matuku,' whispered Martha, trying desperately to keep her voice steady.

'Shush,' hissed Molly. 'I think we're already in over our heads.'

They might have spoken after that, but no one could have

heard. The storm broke over them as though the world's
end had come.

Trees exploded up the opposite slope, ranks of them,
ascending the mountain like an upside-down avalanche,
receding toward the summit in a tumult of sound. Up this
flattened trail the whirling succubus pursued, a tornado of
white fire following the path Matuku had laid. A growl like
thunder came from the mountaintop, then the mountain
itself exploded in fire, a putrescent yellow fire without heat
but with all the stench of death and destruction. 'MINE,'
cried some great voice away upon the mountain ridge, far
away, coming closer, the sound riding over them like some
locomotive behemoth, clanging and hissing as it passed,
dopplering away up the other hill. 'MINE.'

White fumes continued to pour from the crack in the
temple steps, the crack itself widening, gaping, beginning to
growl monstrously. The steps began to tilt toward the
center, rising at the outside edges, the struggling, boneless
creatures slipping, flopping, dropping into an abyss that
suddenly opened where the crack had been. The vast stones
of the stairs slid downward inexorably into that same
chasm. The two sides of the chasm snarled, ground together
like millstones, heaving the temple steps into gravel, into
blowing dust. The abyss closed, chewed with heaving,
gigantic jaws, then gaped again, hungrily.

The temple facade crumbled, pillar by pillar, tumbling
outward from the mountain in slow motion to reveal an ant
warren of tunnels behind the facade, a hundred dark tunnel
mouths in which fat white things the size of children struggled away from the light with sickening slowness. The
wreckage fell forward into the gaping chasm. Ash spewed
from the hole; wind rose; with an ear-shattering roar, the
jaws of the mountain closed once more to leave a jagged pit
of destruction.

As if in response to this roar, a hurricane shriek came
down the mountain from behind them.

Several of the lilac-crowned hunters remained huddled
on the valley floor. Unwisely, they tried to run from the

pandemonium that hurtled upon them. Matuku spun them up in his passage, arms and legs whirled outward, screams unheard in the violence of sound, their spinning marking where Matuku went in pursuit of the succubus, visible in their blood for one long instant as the demon confronted its adversary. The succubus did not stand to fight. It fled laughing upward, like the fiery spew from some hellish volcano, teasingly. Matuku pursued it, bellowing toward the stars.

For a moment there was silence.

Carolyn lay at the edge of the pit, teetering upon its brink. Like a crippled insect, she turned to crawl away from the fury, up the hill toward them, scrambling crabwise, moving more and more quickly, looking up as she reached the edge of the trees to see Badger's eyes locked upon her own.

She whined into the silence, a narrow knife-edge of sound. 'Badger. The people I left Robby with are named Cartwright. Brian and Genevieve Cartwright. In Denver. You find him and bring him here. If you give Robby to it, it'll let me alone. It will, won't it? You bring Robby here.' She collapsed at his feet.

'Go,' Molly said. Though little more than a whisper, it sounded loud in the silence. 'Go, Simoney, Martha. You know where to take him. Quick, now.'

There was a receding sound, a *whoosh* of air.

There was time for nothing else. In that instant the succubus returned from the zenith, ricocheting off the opposite wall of the cirque in sheets of molten rock which flowed toward the lake to send up curtains of explosive steam. Part of the mountain wall collapsed in an earthshaking avalanche, stones as large as houses bounding into the valley. The remaining trees began to explode, one after another, an endless string of leviathan firecrackers, javelins of splintered wood screaming over their heads. They clung to the ground, witless under the sound.

The remaining cabins began to smoke, then burst into flame.

215

In a momentary lull, they looked up to see the succubus standing where the lake had been, wreathed in steam. Matuku faced her from what had been the shoreline, a nightmare figure outlined in the same steamy mists. The succubus reached out with voluptuous woman's arms which turned into tentacles of fire. Heat and cold joined in an intimate embrace and exploded in a white-hot, blue-cold blast which vanished outward in a direction they could not follow. Dust and rock fell around them in an endless, deadly rain.

They could not hear, could not see. They clung to the mold, half-buried in detritus, unsure they were alive. Gradually their ears stopped ringing. Gradually the dust began to clear. Badger turned as in a dream to find Molly, only Molly, leaning over Mahlia's limp form, pressing her folded kerchief on a bleeding gash there. She looked up to meet his eyes and smiled, grimly. 'Well, boy. You wanted to find your wife and you've found her. She's all yours. Pick her up.' She pointed to where Carolyn lay, staring stupidly at the sky, then went back to reviving Mahlia, not seeming to care whether Badger brought Carolyn or not.

The Professor turned over, lay where he was, feeling himself all over, each bone, one by one. Then he fished the dogs from their half burrows under his body and felt them all over as well. Finding himself and them whole, he heaved upright and swayed there for a time. 'Well, madam, that's using an atom bomb to kill a garter snake. I suppose you'll tell me that's not the end of –'

Molly shook her head at him impatiently, wrapping the kerchief around Mahlia's head. 'Lord, no, scholar-man. Old Matuku's a bit more than a garter snake, wouldn't you agree? I'm not sure the succubus was any larger than needed. It doesn't matter. We used her, and lucky we didn't get killed doing it. I didn't know the creature from under the mountain was that strong. Hubris! Wicked pride. Sometimes we think we're so good at what we do. But it's no end. It's only a sidetrack is all. Buying a little time.' She gasped, pressed her hand to her side. 'One of those rocks got me,

I'm afraid. Nothing one can protect against, really.'

'But it's not the end of them?' Badger asked, disbelieving. 'How could anything have survived that last explosion?'

'Those creatures aren't mortal, not the way we think of it. They blend and meld and change and flow apart and together. The succubus will return here. It's tied to this place. *It* won't follow us, and if we get out of here quickly, we've bought ourselves a little time against the other one. All we're doing is buying time while we wait for you to find an answer, Professor. Dodging and hiding and waiting.' She rose, pulling Mahlia to her feet.

'Where the hell do you think you're going?' It was Shiel miraculously unhurt, leaning against a tree with the shaking rifle pointed in their direction. The man trembled so that it seemed impossible for him to go on standing, 'Put her down!' This last was addressed to Badger, who had just heaved Carolyn's limp form over his shoulder.

'Don't be more of a fool than you can help, Shiel,' the Professor said, wiping dust and pine needles from his face and arms. 'You think you can control that?' He gestured at the valley around them, broken like a plate. 'You want to try? You want to be standing there when it comes back for her? Or for you?'

'You're going to tell me a way to control it! You said you could find a way!' he screamed, the rifle weaving.

'Well, that was mostly bluff, Shiel, and I haven't found anything. Besides, there are two of them, and both could be back any minute. You've been summoning the thing from under the mountain long enough, and it's finally heard you. I'd suggest if you know a quick way out of here, you take it and take us with you so that nobody's left here to mention your name, just in case.'

'I can leave you here dead,' the man snarled, slamming the bolt of the rifle home. 'And you won't mention anything.'

Molly laughed, and went on laughing even harder when the rifle swung in her direction. 'Michael Shiel, you were born a greedy fool to a greedy fool of a father, and you've not betrayed your heritage one bit. You think that creature – either of those creatures – can't suck anything they want out of our dead minds? Buy yourself a little time. Fly us out. Matuku may be pretty unhappy with you by now. And if he isn't, I have friends who are. How'd you like to find yourself crowned with purple. Michael? You'd make pretty bait for that hunter. Let it suck your bones.'

'I'm no virgin!' he snarled.

'Oh, Michael, Michael. That was *your* ritual. The succubus doesn't care. Weren't you watching? Did you see how Denk died? How many virgins were there among those it nibbled at?'

He began to shake. Molly motioned with her hands. The rifle fell from his grasp, and he turned away toward the flat meadow beside the lake. 'The biggest of the helicopters,' Molly said conversationally as she directed them to follow him. 'It wasn't damaged.'

'The books!' cried the Professor. 'I've got to get the books!' He gathered the dogs into his arms.

She gestured toward the mountain wall where the temple had been, toward the blazing ruins of the cabins. 'Not likely, Professor. Time for books is done. You'll have to think of something else. And I hope you think of it quickly. We're running out of tricks, the girls and I.'

22

The helicopter dropped them at the Denver airport, and when they left it, it took off to move back the way they had come. Mahlia wondered at Molly's leaving Shiel free and moving about, but she had no time to worry about it. Badger was determined to go into the city to search for the Cartwrights. Mahlia said no.

'Robby isn't there, Badger.'

'Carolyn said –'

'It doesn't matter what Carolyn said. The minute they knew where Robby was, Simoney and Martha went after him. They have him by now.'

'Where? In God's name, where?'

'He's safe, isn't that enough? Do you want to know? Do you want Carolyn to know?' She hated herself for asking this question, for his face turned bleak and hard.

'No,' he responded. 'I don't want her to know. I wanted you to know. Well then. Where do we go now?'

'To Baleford,' said the Professor. 'If there's any hope of locking the creature up, my boy, we'll find it in that maze, just as Darinbaugh did.'

'I should think it would have learned to be shy of the maze by now.'

'It may not learn, or think in the way we do. I doubt it even knows "where" in the sense we do. It will follow us as it has thus far, and whether we go to new places or the same old place may be all one to it. The one thing it probably wouldn't fall for again is that chicken blood trick of Molly's, though I can't even swear to that.'

'To Baleford, then,' said Badger dully as he went to make arrangements. Mahlia stared after him, unsurprised, sorrowful, sympathetic, thinking how tired and old he looked. If asked, she would have said she had given up wanting him for herself. She would have believed she told the truth, and only someone like Molly would have known it for the lie it was. She ached for him and could do nothing to assuage that ache.

For his part, he had steeled himself to bear Carolyn's presence, as he would bear the presence of a poisonous snake or a caged scorpion which might, by some unbelievably rare chance, be something benign in disguise. He no longer believed any of his own fictions about her, and yet he clung to that one-in-a-million chance that he could – they all could – be wrong. Until he knew. Until he was sure. Thinking it to himself, all the time afraid he was already sure.

She sat with them, for the most part silent, though from time to time she would ask in an obscene whisper if they were on their way to get Robby so the demon could have him instead. Mahlia and the Professor ignored her as best they could.

When Badger returned, he was shaved and combed. 'We've got over an hour,' he explained. 'I thought perhaps if I looked a bit more normal, I'd feel a bit more normal. I remembered that car, too. Sitting there on the side of the mountain. I called the rental place in Colorado Springs and told them where it was. Told them I'd arrange to have it picked up or pay for them to do it. They didn't even sound surprised.' He looked out the window, went to get a copy of

the *New York Times*, looked at his watch, carefully not looking at Carolyn.

She, however, kept following him with her eyes,
snakelike. 'Badger,' she whispered time after time, 'are you
going to get Robby?'

She was asking it still when they drove into the Frolius
farmyard and confronted a surprised Ron Frolius.

'Well! So you did find her! Won't Molly be surprised to
hear that. She just got home a few hours ago. Been visiting
her mother, down in Orlando. Old lady's been real sick
lately. Come on in. Molly! That young fellow found his
missus.' He led them inside. Mahlia sank into a saggy old
chair with a feeling of gratitude. The place felt safe.
Carolyn, on the other hand, stalked around the kitchen as
though it were a cage. 'Badger,' she whispered, 'we have to
go find Robby.'

When Molly entered the room, briskly wiping her hands
on her apron, it was to confront Badger's pleading gaze.
'You got trouble, boy?'

'Please, Mol . . . Mrs. Frolius. Carolyn seems very
upset. Is there anything you could . . .' He couldn't finish.

'Well, well. So this is your wife. Pretty thing. Seems a bit
distraught, doesn't she? I think some herb tea, just for a bit
of calm.'

Mahlia and the Professor heaved simultaneous sighs of
relief. If they had heard that vicious whisper one more time,
they felt they could not have controlled themselves. How
Badger managed it, Mahlia didn't know. She watched with
a good deal of detached interest as Molly brewed tea out of
an old stoneware canister taken from the back of a cup-
board, gave it to the stalking, whispering woman, and
insisted she drink it, sip by sip. And then Carolyn became
quiet.

'Nobody's slept in a long time, have they? I thought not.
Well, we had five children in this house, so it's got bed-
rooms and to spare. I suggest each one of you find a bed and
lie down on it. We'll put Carolyn in the spare room down
here. By suppertime, you'll feel a bit more rested.' She fixed

221

Badger with a firm, unyielding eye, and he acquiesced, almost without argument.

He did linger long enough to ask Molly if she had heard from her friends. Molly nodded.

'Everyone's in good health, thank you. Nothing to worry about, Badger. Get some rest.'

Mahlia refused to leave the chair. 'I'd like to stay here,' she said, knowing Molly would know why. There were no visions in this room. No troubling dreams. There was only the warmth of the kitchen stove and the slow, ruminative talk of the two Froliuses, quiet and calm as cows. She half dozed, listening to them. When Ron went out to feed the chickens, she went on half dozing.

'You know he's only being faithful to a vow, don't you?' asked Molly conversationally. 'He knows what she is. He saw it up there on the mountain.'

'I know,' she murmured. 'But he'll go on being faithful to the vow forever.'

'That's as may be,' said Molly. 'That's as may be.'

'You know,' said Mahlia, half dreaming, 'the one thing I couldn't understand was why you used chicken blood on that old picture of Roger Bacon.'

'Why not?' said Molly. 'They were both fryers.'

Mahlia might have imagined that, or dreamed it.

When she woke, supper was on the table. Carolyn was still asleep, but the rest of them ate together. Badger was distant, abstracted, plotting something that required his complete attention. He ate, chewed, swallowed, all without seeming to see the rest of them at all. When they had finished and Ron Frolius had gone out to see to the cow, he said, 'We can't go on like this, you know. We have to bring it to an end, somehow.'

'I gather you've thought of something,' said Molly, clearing the last of the dishes away.

'I've thought how Matuku followed blood,' he said. 'Followed it back in time, when it wasn't even really the right blood, not what the creature was seeking. So, it seemed to me that Matuku would probably follow real blood into

Darinbaugh's bottle, if the bottle had the right real blood in it.'

'Likely enough,' said Molly. 'Into it, and right out of it again once the blood was eaten.'

'Not if it got stoppered while the thing was in there.'

'How did you plan to do that? Hold the bottle in your hand?' She peered at him over her glasses. 'A split second or two? Pretty risky, Badger.'

'I know. So, I thought about that maze of Henry Darinbaugh's. You know, when the children came out – the banker's kids – they came the long way. Matuku was using them to get him out, and they came the long way. He couldn't come across the lines. Isn't that right? It's the only thing that makes sense. Otherwise, what good would the gates have been? They didn't block anything physical. It was purely a – oh, topographical barrier. The demon can't cross the lines, and it can't find its own way out. And then I looked at the bottle and realized that the design was the same. Which, I suppose, is what makes Solomon's Seal work.' He ran hands through his hair, smiling tiredly at Mahlia. 'I should have thought of this a long time ago.'

'So should I,' said the Professor soberly. 'Lord, it should have been obvious.' He looked at the younger man in amazement, shocked at how easily he had begun to disregard him and how foolish it was to have done so.

'Well, it seemed to me what we needed to do was leave a blood trail. Real blood, and fresh. The Professor thinks it may not fall for chicken blood again. So, it should be the blood it's looking for. Darinbaugh blood. Carolyn's, of course. Not enough to hurt her. Some in the bottle. And a trail of blood through the maze with the bottle at the center, with me across one of the lines with the stopper in my hand. It can't cross the line to get at me. If I can get the stopper on while it's still in there.'

'The amount of blood that bottle would hold wouldn't occupy it for long,' objected Mahlia. 'Hardly an instant.'

'Can you think of anything else?'

She shook her head. No. She could think of nothing else.

'Not just the blood,' said Molly. 'She can actually walk it. Leave a trail. Footsteps. Body smell. It may work. I can't think why it wouldn't.'

'I'll tell Carolyn,' Badger said, heaving himself out of his chair. 'Once this is all over, she'll forget it. Become herself again.' He said it, not as though he believed it, but as though it were a line of dialogue he had written for himself that had to be said. They watched him as he left the room, each one wondering what Carolyn's response would be, each one thinking she would not consent.

The door banged open and Badger stood there. 'The window is open in her room. She's gone.'

'Bathroom,' said Mahlia. 'She may have gone to the –'

'I looked. Not there. Where would she have gone, Molly?'

'I don't know. She shouldn't have been able to think of anything like that for hours.'

Badger left the room again, the Professor following. Molly was calling to Ron, and he to her. They heard Ron's voice. 'Jared Shiel was hanging around here when I came out to feed the chickens. I chased him off, but he might 've come back. . . .'

There was a confusion of shouts, people running. Then they heard Ron calling from outside. 'Footprints under the window. A man's footprints!'

The dogs were barking, racing away toward the drive, only to return, panting. There were oil stains and fresh tire tracks along the drive.

'Shiel?' asked Badger. 'Was this Shiel?'

'Not Michael Shiel,' said Molly. 'I set a geas on him before we left. He went back to Lhamballa to wait for *her*. His friend from the tunnels under the mountain.'

'Jared Shiel?'

'Ron says he was here. Old fool. Meddling with what he'll never understand. Pure greed. He thinks there's wealth to be had, and he wants it.'

'Well, you can show me where he lives. We can start looking there.' Then he noticed her face, withdrawn, concentrating. She was looking at the little dogs, who were coming toward her across the yard, whining, ears and tails down.

Badger made a dismayed sound. 'I've seen them do that before. They do that whenever the thing . . . whenever Matuku is around.'

'No time to find Carolyn,' agreed Molly. 'You'll have to get the blood somewhere else.'

'We can try that,' Badger said. 'If the thing hasn't caught on. . . .'

'Real Darinbaugh blood,' said Molly. 'Robby's.'

'He's *here*!'

'Next door at Martha's. Come on in while I phone. You got the bottle where you can lay hands on it?'

'I can't do that!' He stared openmouthed after the woman. 'Mahlia. I can't bleed my own son for bait!'

'You can do it if you have to, Badger. If you think it's the only way to get the thing trapped.'

'Not Robby! I was ready to do it with Carolyn, because she . . . she's an adult. She'd made some choices of her own. But Robby . . . Lord, Mahlia, he's my son! What if it fails?'

'There isn't time for this, Badger,' said the Professor. 'you either will or you won't. No time for dithering. Make up your mind. She's phoning now. Martha will be here as soon as you can breathe twice. You want me to do it, boy? I'm not as fast on my feet as I was once, but . . .'

'Oh, no. No! I'll do it.'

The dogs were circling again, sniffing the air, tails up, then down, then up again, alternately growling and whining. 'The thing is casting about for us,' said Mahlia with sudden conviction. 'Like a searchlight, peering into time or space. The dogs sense it going past, getting closer.'

Molly came out of the house. 'Well, got yourself up for it? If you can't, don't diddle about with it.'

'I'll do it!' he grated, furious. 'It was my idea!'

'Thinkin' it is one thing,' she said obscurely, walking past them to the gate. They heard a car start, over the rise,

225

and its lights soon crested the hill. 'He may not remember you,' said Molly conversationally. 'It's been a year, Badger. He's only a baby.'

'I know,' he said. 'God, you think I don't know?'

They went to meet the car, Martha edging herself out of it with a sleepy burden. 'Is this home?' asked the child's voice. 'Is that Daddy? Did he come to get me?'

'It's Daddy, Robby. Right here.' Mahlia had never heard a voice with so much emotion of so many kinds: joy, fear, anger, hate, love all mixed into a burning intensity. 'Come to Daddy.' He pulled the child almost roughly into his arms.

One little arm reached out. The other held a masked, fuzzy creature much the worse for loving. 'That's Robber,' said Mahlia. 'He's still got Robber.'

They began to walk toward the maze field, cutting around the hill, Badger stopping suddenly. 'Where's the bottle? I forgot to get it!'

'It's all right, Badger,' the Professor said. 'I've got it. I'll give it to you when you go into the maze.'

'I'll need . . . God, I'll need a knife. Something.'

'I've got that,' said Molly. 'My little boning knife from the kitchen. I held it in the lamp flame to clean it. I've got a little sip of something for the boy, he'll never feel it. Stop a minute. Here, Robby. Have a little drink of this. Nice, isn't it. Got honey in it.' The boy murmured sleepily and drank again.

'Where – where do you think?' asked Badger.

'Oh, forehead, I think. Scalp cuts bleed like crazy, but they don't do much damage. The Professor'n me'll cut across the lines and wait for you. You'll need somebody to take the boy.'

'Me,' said Mahlia, surprising herself. 'I'll hold him.'

The last glow had faded from the edge of the hill, but a swollen half moon had begun to throw silver and shadows where they walked. Below them the flat of the maze field glowed, the dark lines seeming to shine of their own darkness, a polished black. The gates swung open, creaking, so finely balanced that the slight wind moved them despite their weight.

Ting growled and crouched. The other dogs whined quickly, then silenced, crouching as well, as though some great, horrid scythe passed over them. Then they growled once more, began to run.

'Quickly,' the Professor panted along, pushing Badger before him. 'It's getting closer.'

It took them a moment to find the maze entrance. Grass had grown up around the outer edge. Molly cursed herself silently. She should have had Ron mow it, just in case. Then they found it near a lone tree. Badger's hand trembled so with the knife that Molly took it from him and made a quick, hard pass at the little boy's head. Blood welled from the cut, but he didn't seem to feel it as he smiled up at the moon. The Professor held the bottle beneath the flow, wiping the outside carefully so that all the blood would be inside. 'Go, boy,' he said. 'Fast. It's almost a mile. Let the blood from Robby's head fall onto the path. Watch your feet.'

Badger entered the maze, Mahlia behind him. She had some sense that he might fall, or drop Robby, or need directions. She didn't know why she was there, but she was there, racing just behind him. They turned, passed the Professor, turned, passed him again. Blood dripped from Robby's head upon the turf. Molly was walking across the maze, the bottle in her hand; she waited to let them pass, then pass again. Around, around, a wide circle, a narrow wedge, a circle again, out to the edge and back inside, then out to the edge once more. How could they know they had not missed a line, stepped out of the path? Only the moonlight, only their own concentration. The dogs growled, whined, whined again. 'Hurry,' cried the Professor. 'Hurry!'

They heard it then, upon the ridge of hills, trees exploding like dynamite in the cold of its passage. And they heard something else as well.

A man's voice, harsh as a crow. 'They're tryin' to get it for themselves!'

A woman's voice. 'Robby. I have to give Robby to it myself!' It was Carolyn.

As they turned in their mad flight, they saw two figures leave the cover of the trees and hurry toward them. One tall, cadaverous, black-cloaked like a crow. Jared Shiel, Badger thought. Coming to do what, for the love of God? Interfere? Now?

'Get him, Padmasambhava,' cried the Professor. 'Sic 'em, Thisrongdetsan. Bite his feet, Sanbandarong.' The little dogs needed no urging. They fled toward the black figure like tiny cloud shadows, black on the earth, snarling and nipping at his ankles.

'Get 'em off me,' the black figure cried, kicking madly. 'Get 'em off me.'

'Go back, Jared Shiel,' cried Molly in a Cassandra's voice. 'There's nothing here for you but danger and death.'

'That's Darinbaugh's Demon coming,' he cried 'I want that bottle, Molly. Henry promised it to me!'

'Henry promised you nothing, now go back!'

Carolyn was not bothered by the dogs, was not deterred by Molly's voice. She came across the maze field like a demon herself, hair flying, her face fixed in an expression that was more like that of the carved succubus than anything human. 'Give him to me,' she growled. 'And I'll give him to the thing. It'll be grateful. It'll be my friend, then. Give him to me!'

She launched herself at Badger, avoiding Molly's attempt to trip her, but not escaping Mahlia, who met her in midair. They fell to the field, Mahlia trying desperately to hold the woman away from Badger, who threw one despairing glance behind him as he fled, turning, turning. Matuku was coming with the sound of storm, the thunder of avalanche; Badger's arms were cold as ice; Robby shivered in his grasp, the blood congealing. And there was a ways yet before they reached the center.

Outside the maze the grass of the pasture crisped, turning black, floating upward like ash. The smell of death was like filth in their throats, choking them. Jared Shiel backed away, pulling his cloak over his face, and the Professor called the dogs urgently, stepping over the line onto the maze and gathering all three of them into his arms.

The lone tree near the maze blew up. Jared screamed, staring in horror at the long ragged spear that penetrated his chest. He stumbled away – too late. The trail of black grass that marked Matuku's passage halted and turned, attracted by the smell of fresh blood. It moved toward Jared Shiel as he, with frantic, crabwise steps, tried to avoid it. 'Get it away from me!' he howled. 'Get it off me!' They danced in the moonlight, Jared and the blackened grass, moving this way and that, as though Matuku sniffed at him. Then the demon moved, all at once, catching the end of the spear that impaled the man and spinning it like a top. In the instant it was all around him. blood flowing into it in a cloud, illumined by that cloud and completely visible. It had grown since Laura's death. It loomed monstrous at the edge of the maze.

It whirled there only long enough to drink what had been Jared Shiel, then dropped the dried husk and moved purposefully toward the entrance to the maze, seeming to sniff, to bend, to draw in breath as it moved onto the blood-marked path.

The Professor stepped over the line, out of the maze, watched with horrified attention as the red-flushed monster went by, faster than anything human could have moved. 'Watch out, Molly,' he cried, voice rasping in the cold. 'It'll have to pass you!'

'I know,' she cried. 'I know.' All her attention was on Badger and the boy, moving too slowly, too slowly, and on the struggling women. In a moment the demon would come upon them. 'Mahlia!' she screamed. 'Move!'

Mahlia was locked in a frantic embrace with Carolyn, trying to keep from being choked by the woman's furious hands, trying to keep her from escaping to pursue Badger. She heard Molly's voice as from a great distance, understanding the urgency at some visceral level and feeling the strength that came to her from Molly like the helping blow of a great hand. She heaved desperately to one side, pulling Carolyn with her so that both of them rolled over. Carolyn scrabbled at the ground with one hand, trying to anchor herself. The thing went by, a cold so intense it froze the air in their lungs. Carolyn screamed and held up her hand, blue as ice. The thing had touched it. She glared at Mahlia for an instant, broke free with superhuman strength, and turned toward the center of the maze. Badger was there, Robby in his arms. Molly was setting the bottle down. Badger was there, waiting, waiting. Carolyn began to run toward him, Mahlia after her.

Molly stepped across a line. The demon passed and she stepped back again. 'Now, Badger,' she said. 'Now.'

He seemed stupefied. She reached across to the center and pulled him gently. 'Now.' As she took Robby from him, he shook himself, fighting down the cramped roiling of his bowels, his sick fear of the demon.

'Yes,' he told himself. 'Oh, for God's sake, Badger, yes. Now.' He could not fail in this, and yet at that moment he had no hope of succeeding. It was too large, too powerful, too hideous an enemy for a mortal. Molly laid a hand on his shoulder and he caught his breath.

He stepped back across one line, one hand-wide line, separated from the bottle only by that and a few feet of empty air, eyes on the bottle; beyond that the disturbance of bloody air that was Matuku; beyond Matuku the hurtling figure that was Carolyn. He should call to her. He should try to stop her, his wife, Carolyn. But beyond her was . . .

'Stop, Mahlia,' he bawled. 'Stop!'

Mahlia heard him, threw herself to one side in a tumbled fall, arms and legs flailing. Carolyn did not stop. She seemed not to see the demon, but only one little boy being carried slowly away in Molly's arms. The whirling bloody air was above the bottle now, spinning, a screaming maelstrom, its head dipping to scent the contents of the bottle, which rocked and tipped in the fury of its approach. 'MY ROBBY,' it said, lifting itself like a great beast readying to pounce, beginning to spin downward, down into the bottle that old Darinbaugh had kept, that Friar Bacon had found, that Solomon himself had created. 'MY ROBBY,' a maelstrom of blood and wind and terrible noise.

Carolyn did not see it. As she entered the maelstrom, her eyes were still fixed on Robby where Molly carried him away.

Matuku did not pause. 'MY CAROLYN,' it howled, drawing her into itself as it went. She whirled, shrank, screamed, reached out for Badger, one hand coming free of that whirling force to grasp his arm. She was pulling him, tugging him across the line. . . .

Then her grasp broke. He fell back, as though burned, watching as she became part of the spiraling tornado, which shrieked its way down into the bottle marked with Solomon's Seal, to vanish with one shrill echo as from unimaginable distance.

Badger was shaking with cold, so frozen he could barely fall upon his knees to fumble with the stopper. Too cold. Too quick. He couldn't get it in his fingers. He was sobbing. His hands were covered with frozen blood. The shrieking began to return, a wisp of turbulent air rising from the bottle. . . .

From behind him Mahlia gripped his shoulders, whispered his name, and the stopper slipped home.

It was the Professor who came across the maze to pick the bottle up and place it carefully in his pocket after wrapping the top with tape which went several times around the container. The dogs trotted after him, sniffing. They circled the field, pausing to growl briefly at what had been Jared Shiel.

Mahlia did not hear them. She was holding Badger, warming him with her own body grown suddenly fiery for his sake, and she had no intention of letting him go. No intention at all.

23

Badger never returned to the apartment he had lived in with
Carolyn. Vivian went there for him, packing his clothes and
Robby's, arranging at the same time for the sale of everything in the place and a sublease. She took the clothes and a
box of toys back to her own building, where she knocked on
the door of Greenleaves two.

Mahlia answered the door.

'Vivian! Oh, I am glad to see you. Robby's been
demanding his train, and a new one just wouldn't
do.'

'I'm surprised he remembered.' Vivian was not quite
sure that she understood what had happened to Robby. He
had been rescued from the boat, she had heard. And taken
away by some nice people who just hadn't bothered trying
to find his family. Carolyn was dead. Drowned, after all.
When Vivian had heard that Robby was alive, she had had
one instant of terrible fear that Carolyn might be still alive.
She was ashamed of it afterward. It just went to show how
deep prejudices went sometimes.

'I don't quite understand this apartment business. I'd

think Badger would want to take Robby back to familiar surroundings.'

'Too painful,' said Mahlia. 'Simply too painful for him. You understand.' She knew that Vivian did not, but that Vivian would convince herself she did.

'Well, there have certainly been a number of shocks lately. Poor Miles. Though he is a lot better than he was.'

'Badger's over at the hospital visiting him now. He made arrangements to take Robby too. The doctor thought that might do Miles a lot of good.'

'The way he adored Laura, it came close to killing him. What a terrible accident.'

'Did they ever find out what caused it?' Mahlia asked innocently. 'Badger thought perhaps lightning?'

'No one knows.' Vivian shook her head. 'Well, Briggs is bringing up the rest of the things from the garage. Don't forget we expect you all at dinner tonight. We'll eat early for Robby's sake, and then he can go to sleep whenever he likes. I hope Badger is better. Something's eating at him, you know. He's acting just as he used to when he was a little boy. Not sulky, exactly. More as though he had a pain he couldn't tell you about. How long do you think Badger will stay here?'

Mahlia commiserated, tut-tutted, shook her head as Vivian went back to her own apartment. She knew what Badger was eating himself up over. And she didn't know how long Badger would stay. She did know the Professor had suggested he stay an indefinite time. The place was large enough, and safe, and Badger slept reasonably well here, when he slept at all. Perhaps it was the knowledge that the dogs were there, on guard. Or the mandalas on the wall. Or the heavy, locked case in the Professor's bedroom which held the strange bottle with the curvilinear design. Or perhaps it was the Professor himself. Badger seemed to have grown fond of him.

If anyone moves out, it really should be me, she thought with only a twinge of guilt. She had no intention of doing so, of course. She checked her watch, frowning. Molly had better hurry. Badger and Robby would be home within the hour.

Thisrongdetsan barked sharply. 'Shush, Ting,' she said, looking up as he disregarded her and barked again. Molly was on the terrace with Simoney. She knew they could open the door themselves if they liked, but it was a courtesy to open it for them.

'Sister,' murmured Molly, coming in and shaking herself. Her coat was wet from the light rain.

'Sister,' murmured Simoney in a similar tone. 'It's wet out there. Cold, too.'

'I thought you weren't coming, it's so late.'

'Caught in a little headwind,' said Molly. 'Not much. How're you getting along?'

'Well, I've got the first five chapters memorized, and –'

'Twit,' said Molly fondly. 'I didn't mean with your studies. I meant with him. Badger.'

'He hasn't said anything yet. He's too worried.'

'Get him drunk.'

'He doesn't drink much anymore.'

'Use your head, girl. Chapter six. Transubstantiation of qualities, Subparagraph nine (a), Vintner's delights. Oh, well, you'll get to it in time. No hurry, I shouldn't imagine. Would you think so, Simoney?'

'Well, if she doesn't hurry, I might,' said Simoney, surprisingly. 'He's a very good looking man. Sexy, too.'

'Simoney!'

'Well, you asked.'

'Where are you headed?' Mahlia asked, flushing, a touch annoyed and eager to change the subject.

'Orlando. Mother's better and she wants to have a family conference. It makes a good opportunity to take care of – you know. Next time, perhaps you'll be ready to come along?'

'Next time,' Mahlia promised. 'I'll be ready. Molly, I've been meaning to ask you for days what happened to the little girls. The ones on the mountain.'

'A little amnesia,' she said roughly. 'Poor little idiots.

Half the girls in America want to be models. All someone has to do is promise to take their picture, and they'll follow any rapist along like a pet dog. Well. They're home now. God knows if they'll stay. I don't.' She shook her head. 'You got the stuff?'

'I have it.' She gave them the little bundle. Nail clippings. Hair. The bandage from the cut on his head. They had not thought about this while they were in Baleford. Only later . . . later. And since then, Badger had been eating his heart out.

'I'll call you,' said Molly, giving her a sympathetic look. 'Okay?'

They left the way they had come. Mahlia shook the tears from her eyes and went to her bedroom to burrow out the book Molly had lent her. Chapter six.

While they were dressing for dinner, Mahlia knocked softly on Badger's door. 'Badger? Can I come in a minute?'

He greeted her in shirt-sleeves, with that half-shy look he had used with her ever since that night on the maze. Half-shy. Half-longing. Committing itself to nothing.

'Badger. Would you do me a very great favor tonight?'

'If I can.'

'Whatever wine George serves us, would you drink some of it?'

'My God, woman. You want the moon.'

'Please. It would mean so much to Vivian. She's feeling very left out. We need to make her feel like – family. You know.'

He frowned. 'All right. I'll guarantee to drink one glass of whatever he serves, even if it poisons me.' He turned, looking for his tie. 'What's that smell, Mahlia? Like smoke?'

'Smoke,' she said innocently. 'I haven't any idea.'

Back in her room, she put out the brazier, tucked the herbs and resins back in her lingerie drawer, and closed the book. One quick spray of cologne. A smile at herself in the mirror. And she went to the door to wait for the menfolk.

'I venture to say no one in New York knows about this wine,' said George, working diligently at the cork. 'It's an obscure little California winery almost on the Oregon state line. I heard about it from a cousin of the owner. It took me weeks even to get a few bottles shipped. There.' The cork came free with a muted plop, and a fragrance filled the room, fruity, flowery, like a breath of orchards under a warm spring sun. 'Here, Badger. Try this.'

Badger sipped. Sipped again. Drank. 'How much of this do you have, George?'

The older man looked at him narrowly, as though afraid of being teased. 'Several bottles. Is it good?'

Mahlia tried it. Nectar.

'C'n I have some?' whispered Robby. 'Please?'

'Sure, honey.' All the children drank wine in France, watered or unwatered, and Mahlia thought it made them less likely to be show-off drinkers later on. 'Sip.'

The little boy sipped and sighed. 'Oooh, that's good. Except it burns a little.'

'Well, wine does that.' She saw Badger's face across the table, looking at Robby with such longing, such fear.

Totally unaware, Vivian smiled at him, at Badger, at Mahlia. The wine *was* good. How wonderful. George had at last found one decent wine. What a pity there were only a few bottles. She sighed and began to fill their plates from the buffet.

Badger drank several glasses. George, expansive under the unaccustomed praise, gave him a bottle to bring home, and he opened it while Mahlia put Robby to bed. The Professor wandered in, ruffling his white hair and whistling at the dogs, smelled the wine, and insisted on a glass for himself. 'Lord.' He sighed. 'What a marvelous vintage. Absolute witchery.'

He wandered out again, not seeing the look Badger fastened on his back. 'Yes, it is,' he murmured. 'Absolute witchery.'

She returned to the living room, pausing to flick a bit of dust off a rotund Buddha, who went on smiling at her in thanks.

'Mahlia.'

'Mmm?'

'Did you do something to George's wine?'

'Ah . . . not really.'

'What does 'not really' mean?'

'It means I didn't do anything to it, really. Except to let it be as good as he wanted it to be. That's all.'

'That's all.'

'Well, he knows, you see. George does. He knows what people really think about his wines, and his restaurants. George knows he's a bore. He keeps trying, so hard, to find something other people won't know about. It's because he wants so badly to please someone. He is an awful bore about it, but he simply can't help it.'

Badger nodded slowly. He had had most of a bottle by himself. 'No other reason?'

'No. What other reason could there be?'

'Molly showed you how, I suppose?'

'No. No. I just learned.'

He sighed. 'I don't care, I guess. It's a wonderful wine. It makes me feel relaxed and happy.'

'That's what Robby said. He said it made him feel all warm inside.'

'I haven't felt warm inside for a while.' He said nothing more. She waited patiently. Finally, 'Mahlia . . .'

'Yes, Badger.'

'I invented her, you know.'

'Carolyn?'

'Yes. I made her up. She was beautiful, diabolically beautiful. I wanted her. I'd never had girlfriends. I wore size twelve boys' clothes until I was almost nineteen. I'd never had a lover. I invented her. My fairy princess.'

'I understand that, Badger.'

'I remember that conversation we had with the Carvers at Vivian's party. Whether it was easier to believe someone you loved was faulty or possessed. I laughed at it all. You asked how someone would know, and Myrtle Carver said it was easy. If it was really a demon, the spells would work.'

238

He was silent, sad. 'And they did work. So we know she never really existed.'

'No,' Mahlia agreed. 'She was Matuku's child from the beginning. Laura knew that, though not in so many words. There was never any affection between them. Laura herself wasn't the kind of woman who . . . well.'

'Miles invented Laura, too.'

'To some extent. But he need never be disillusioned about that. He can remember her fondly. Her and Carolyn both. In time he will forget. Really. Darinbaugh's Demon is locked up now. When the Professor gets tired of gloating over it, he'll wrap it in lead and drop it in the ocean, somewhere very deep, just as Henry Darinbaugh planned.'

'And Robby's safe,' he said, leaning back with his eyes shut. There was a question there. He wanted her to answer.

She didn't answer. Slow tears welled at the corners of his eyes. The wine. He shouldn't have had so much wine.

The phone rang. Mahlia answered it. It was Molly.

'Mahlia. We've been over the stuff very carefully. Mother says she finds nothing at all. No sign. Verity says the same. I don't know how the child escaped, but evidently he has. Maybe you can find out how that happened. Mother would love to know.'

'Molly. Thanks. I'm glad.' She wiped tears from her own eyes, glad tears, aware for the first time how frightened she had been.

'Lord, girl, aren't we all. Simoney was frantic when we first thought of it. Well. I didn't want to tell you until now, but we found the key to old Henry's gates. I had Ron mow the maze field, and there it was. I thought you'd like to have it. For Robby. He'll be heir, won't he?'

'Well, I'll keep the key for him anyhow. I'm so glad. Good night.'

Mahlia hung up the phone, turning to Badger with a smile. 'That was Molly.'

He stiffened, made a gesture as though to repulse some hideous presence.

'You know why she called, Badger. You'd thought of it, hadn't you?'

He shook his head in denial, throat tight.

'You know you had. It's all right. He's all right.'

'How does she know?' he whispered. 'How does she know that devil didn't get into him while Carolyn was pregnant with him?'

'Because he's clean of it. There's no demon in him. That's why. They know.'

'I thought . . . I thought you said pregnant women were vulnerable.'

'Yes, And men who have killed. And unnamed children.'

He sat up, a little muzzy, the wine still blurring the edges of things. 'Robby was never unnamed,' he said. 'Before he was ever conceived, I'd named him.' And then he took her in his arms and cried.

And when he had finished crying, he began to make love to her.

And when he had made love with her, he lay half-asleep in the tumbled bed and told her that he loved her.

And then he fell asleep, saying as he did so, 'I think we'll name it Sean if it's a boy. Elaine if it's a girl.'

Mahlia was busy making some small, almost microscopic adjustments within herself. She pulled his arm more closely around her and nestled her breasts against him. 'Elaine', she agreed drowsily.

They already had a son. It would be a girl.

THE END